A Cowboy WINS

COWBOYS
of Crested Butte

BOOK FIVE

USA TODAY BESTSELLING AUTHOR

HEATHER SLADE

MORE FROM AUTHOR HEATHER SLADE

BUTLER RANCH
Kade's Worth
Brodie's Promise
Maddox's Truce
Naughton's Secret
Mercer's Vow
Kade's Return
Butler Ranch Christmas

WICKED WINEMAKERS
FIRST LABEL
Brix's Bid
Ridge's Release
Press' Passion
Zin's Sins
Tryst's Temptation

WICKED WINEMAKERS
SECOND LABEL
Beau's Beloved
Coming Soon:
Cru's Crush
Bones' Bliss
Snapper's Seduction
Kick's Kiss

ROARING FORK RANCH
Coming Soon:
Roaring Fork Wrangler
Roaring Fork Roughstock
Roaring Fork Rockstar
Roaring Fork Rooker
Roaring Fork Bridger

THE ROYAL AGENTS
OF MI6
Make Me Shiver
Drive Me Wilder
Feel My Pinch
Chase My Shadow
Find My Angel

K19 SECURITY
SOLUTIONS TEAM ONE
Razor's Edge
Gunner's Redemption
Mistletoe's Magic
Mantis' Desire
Dutch's Salvation

K19 SECURITY
SOLUTIONS TEAM TWO
Striker's Choice
Monk's Fire
Halo's Oath
Tackle's Honor
Onyx's Awakening

K19 SHADOW OPERATIONS
TEAM ONE
Code Name: Ranger
Code Name: Diesel
Code Name: Wasp
Code Name: Cowboy
Code Name: Mayhem

K19 ALLIED INTELLIGENCE
TEAM ONE
Code Name: Ares
Code Name: Cayman
Code Name: Poseidon
Code Name: Zeppelin
Code Name: Magnet

K19 ALLIED INTELLIGENCE
TEAM TWO
Coming Soon:
Code Name: Puck
Code Name: Michelangelo
Code Name: Typhon
Code Name: Hornet
Code Name: Reaper

PROTECTORS
UNDERCOVER
Undercover Agent
Undercover Emissary
Coming Soon:
Undercover Savior
Undercover Infidel
Undercover Assassin

THE INVINCIBLES
TEAM ONE
Decked
Edged
Grinded
Riled
Smoked

THE INVINCIBLES
TEAM TWO
Bucked
Irished
Sainted
Hammered
Ripped

THE UNSTOPPABLES
TEAM ONE
Furied
Merried

COWBOYS OF
CRESTED BUTTE
A Cowboy Falls
A Cowboy's Dance
A Cowboy's Kiss
A Cowboy Stays
A Cowboy Wins

TABLE OF CONTENTS

1

The bull he'd gotten on the night before wasn't just a rank bucker, he was mean as all get out. There wasn't anywhere on his body that Bullet didn't hurt.

His ribs still ached from getting under one a few months ago, and if the weather was cold, it hurt to breathe. His twenty-five-year-old body felt more as though it was forty, or sixty.

It didn't help that he was back in Oklahoma, or that he'd gotten drunk the night before simply because he didn't want to face the *shitstorm* his life was becoming. Maybe that's why his body hurt so badly, because it was being pulled in so many directions.

He wasn't supposed to be here. He was supposed to be in Colorado, living his dream. Instead, he'd gotten another call from his mother-in-law, telling him to get "home" because his baby needed him. It wasn't the first time he'd heard the same message from her, and each time, he felt worse than the time before, because it wasn't supposed to be this way.

They were supposed to be a family. Every few weeks, he and his wife would try to work things out between them. Each time, it ended worse than the previous.

The last one had been so bad he knew there wouldn't be a next time. As he held his baby boy in his arms, the child's mother had attacked him. And she'd done it in front of her entire family.

She was sick—bipolar disorder. If she'd just take her medicine, none of this would happen. But she refused. The slightest thing could set her off, and he never knew what, or when, it would be.

Last night, when he heard the local stock contractor was bucking bulls, he knew he had to get on one. Had to. Riding bulls was in his blood. He thought about it all the time, even dreamed about it.

His sister called it "adrenaline addiction," but it wasn't criticism. She was the only one in his family who understood. Even though Lyric had never tried to ride a bull, or a bronc, or even barrel-raced, no one understood rodeo better.

She was the founder of RodeoChat, a social-media-based outlet for rodeo news. Lyric managed to keep her finger on the pulse of rodeo around the world. She knew the schedules, statistics, and habits of the cowboys and cowgirls who competed across the field in every event. Since its founding, Lyric had interviewed hundreds of them for her weekly Twitterviews and YouTube videos.

That's why she understood. When he'd tried to explain how he felt to their parents, Lyric had backed him up. In fact, she'd compared it to their dad's life.

"You know how it feels," she'd told him, "to be on stage, in front of thousands of people. It's the same thing for Bullet, just a different thing drivin' it."

As the lead singer of Satin, one of the most successful international heavy-metal rock bands, Nate Simmons was no stranger to adrenaline addiction.

"Thousands of people aren't threatening to kill me when I'm on stage, that's the difference," his dad had countered Lyric's argument.

His father wasn't wrong. Every time Bullet got on the back of a bull, he knew he could die. It was that simple. Eight seconds. That's what it took. If he could stay on the back of the bull for eight seconds, he'd conquer both the beast and himself.

His mother shook her head, that day, and looked between him and his father. "Neither of you will ever grow up."

"It's why you love me so much, isn't it, Guinevere?"

Bullet envied his parents' relationship. It was as if they were still dating, even though they'd been married for over thirty years, a rarity in the music industry.

It hurt to roll over, but he needed to charge his phone and see how many messages his soon-to-be-ex-wife left him. It was early; maybe there wouldn't be any yet this morning.

Oh, Jesus, it was worse than he thought. There were ten calls from his mother-in-law. What the hell? The woman was becoming a pain in his ass.

He checked his texts without listening to her voice messages, and saw there were at least twice as many of those. He rubbed his eyes and tried to focus enough to read, but his head was pounding like a damn jackhammer. How much had he had to drink last night?

He didn't read through all of them; it wasn't necessary. The last one she'd sent was the only one that mattered.

Callie in ICU at Mount Mercy GET HERE.

Bullet listened to the messages from his mother-in-law, but it was hard to get anything more out of them other than Callie was in the hospital, and he needed to get there right away.

It took him less than five minutes to throw his gear in a bag and get on the road. It was an hour's drive to get to the hospital, which wasn't far from where Callie's parents lived.

But right now, all he could think about was where his son was. Callie's mother didn't mention Grey in her messages. He called his grandmother, the woman who raised him and his sister while their parents were on the road, with the band. She didn't live far from Callie's parents. Maybe she'd know.

"Hey, Gram—"

"Oh, Bullet, I'm so glad you called. Callie's parents have been tryin' to get in touch with you. Something awful's happened—"

"I know. I'm on my way to the hospital right now."

"Oh, thank goodness, Callie—"

"I'm sorry to keep interruptin' you, but do you know if they have Grey with them?"

"They didn't tell you? Grey is here, with me."

"Is he okay?"

"He's fine. It's Callie who's in rough shape. You better get to the hospital quick, Bullet."

"I'll come by once I've seen her. Tell Grey his daddy loves him."

"I will, Bullet, and I'm so sorry."

Before she said anything else, Bullet said goodbye and hung up. Whatever was going on with Callie wasn't something he wanted to hear over the phone.

He pulled the truck over and looked up at the sky. "Lord, thank you for keepin' my boy safe, and please, lay your healing hands on his mother."

He rested his head against the steering wheel. His life had been one *clusterfuck* after another since the day he met Callie.

The night he met her, she was drunk, underage, and about to get in a shit-ton of trouble. Against his better judgment, he'd agreed to get her out of the bar they were in, and take her home. That, actually, wasn't what she'd asked him to do, but until she was sober enough for him to determine whether she was at least over eighteen, there was no way he'd take her up on what she'd offered.

He had to stop twice on the drive to her house, that night, so she could throw up alongside the road. At least she gave him enough notice that he had time to pull over. If she'd gotten sick in his truck, he might've been tempted to let her walk home.

Two years later, it had never gotten better. Drama was her middle name, and if it didn't happen on its own, Callie created it. He wasn't sure, now, if he would've married her if she hadn't gotten pregnant. Sometimes he thought he probably would have. Other times he hoped he was smarter than that.

When he found out they were having a boy, he told Callie he wanted to name him Henry Greyson, after his granddad on his mother's side. She liked the name, so she didn't give him a hard time about it.

It hadn't been that simple three years ago, when his first child was born. The baby's mama fought him on the little girl's name every step of the way. It wasn't the only thing she fought him on. In fact, there was little she didn't fight with him about. He knew that was because he'd refused to marry her, and he'd wanted a DNA test to prove he was the father.

When the tests came back positive, they settled on Hannah Pearl. He'd wanted his little girl named Pearl. He didn't know why; he just loved the sound of it. He called her his perfect Pearl, never Hannah. It drove the girl's mama crazy, but he didn't care.

His daughter lived in Texas with her mama full-time. She moved there to be closer to her family, which meant a twelve-hour drive each way in order to see Hannah Pearl. He didn't get to see his daughter very often, and they were long overdue for a visit.

When he got into town a couple of days ago, Callie was on a bender. He'd finally found her in a town or two over, drunk as shit, but with her cousin, thankfully. He'd picked her up, carried her ass to his truck, and drove her home. She railed at him the whole way, but he'd learned to tune her out.

She'd seemed better yesterday, although she wasn't very talkative. She usually had a laundry list of everything he'd done to piss her off. Not this time.

When he left her parents' house last night, Callie was sound asleep. Grey was too, in the crib in her room. Her mom and dad weren't home, but he'd figured they would be soon.

Bullet drove past the hospital and pulled into the bar he saw across the road. He needed a drink before he faced whatever trouble Callie got herself into this time.

He downed three shots, one right after another, not missing the looks the pretty bartender was giving him. Any other day, he'd stick around and see what else she'd give him, but today he couldn't.

He threw a twenty on the bar and stood to put on his jacket.

"Where you goin', cowboy?" she pouted.

"My wife's in the hospital—" He was thinking about offering to come back, but as soon as he said the word wife, the bartender glared at him and walked away.

"Can I help you?" asked the woman behind the desk in the lobby.

"Uh, yeah. Let's see, my wife is in the ICU. I think that's what the message said. Lemme look." He pulled out his phone. "Yep, the ICU."

"Name?"

"Bullet Simmons."

The woman waved her hand in front of her face and glared at him. "Her name is Bullet?"

"No, ma'am. That's my name. My wife's name is Callie."

"Take the elevator to the fourth floor and turn right. You'll need to show your identification when you get up there."

He turned the corner and waited for the elevator.

"Drunkard comin' to see his poor wife who's in intensive care. Wonder what put her there?" he overheard the woman say to the next person in line. He was damn sick and tired of people thinking Callie's problems were because of him. Damn sick and tired of it.

Right after they married, his in-laws had sat him down and told him about Callie's illness. Might have been nice if they'd told him a little earlier. Maybe they thought he wouldn't have married her if they had.

While she was pregnant, she'd been good about taking her meds. After the baby was born, not so much. She was afraid they'd affect her breast milk, and she was determined to breastfeed. Grey wasn't ten days old when she had her first fit. That's what Bullet started calling them—fits. He had no idea what started it, but suddenly she was screaming at him. Then she pummeled him with her fists. It took him a minute to react, that first time, and when he did, it'd been to hold her at arm's length. When she couldn't reach him to hit him, she'd turned her head and bit his arm.

He'd almost backhanded her that day, out of instinct, but stopped himself. Before it could get worse, he left. He was less than a mile away when he turned the truck around. What was he thinking? He couldn't leave their baby alone with her.

When he got back to the house, she was on the bed, sobbing into a pillow. The baby was in the bassinet next to the bed, also sobbing. Screaming was more like it. He called her name, but she didn't appear to hear him. Was this what it was like when she was home alone with Grey? Did she just leave him in his bassinet, screaming?

He picked the baby up, that day, and drove to his in-laws' house. Later that night, he moved Callie, the baby, and himself in with them. He hadn't wanted to, but he didn't see he had any choice. They'd agreed it wasn't a good idea to leave her alone with the baby.

Callie's dad stood when Bullet got off the elevator and approached the ICU waiting area.

"Hello, son," his voice broke, and he turned away from Bullet.

"What's goin' on?"

"It's Callie."

"Is she…oh, God," he couldn't continue.

"No, but she's unresponsive." When he saw tears ran down his father-in-law's cheeks, Bullet felt as though he might cry, too.

The door opened, and Callie's mom joined them in the waiting room.

"*Where…in…the…hell…have…you…been?*" she spat at him.

"Now, Mama," his father-in-law began. "This isn't Bullet's fault."

"Isn't his fault? Did I hear you right? Did you just say this isn't his fault?" She turned and jabbed Bullet in the chest with her finger. "Why did you leave last night? Why? Answer me. What was so damn important that you left our little girl all alone?"

Bullet backed away from her, but she kept coming at him. Callie's father put his arms around his wife's waist and stopped her. When he did, she broke down in tears.

"She tried to kill herself last night, Bullet," she sobbed. "And where were you? Where were you?"

Bullet felt the air leave his lungs. She'd been asleep. He doubted she or Grey would wake up before her parents got back, which he figured would be any minute. They never stayed out past seven-thirty or eight. He hadn't left much before then. What the hell had happened?

The intensive-care nurse led Bullet to Callie's room. "You'll have fifteen minutes."

Nothing could have prepared him for the way she looked. There were tubes going into a mask that covered half her face. There was another smaller tube that went directly into her nose. There were wires everywhere, and an IV in her arm.

He fell into the chair next to her bed, and reached out to touch her. Her skin felt cold, and clammy. And it looked gray. Soft tears fell down Bullet's cheeks as he took Callie's hand in his.

"What have you done, sweet girl?" He lowered his head and let himself cry.

Someone rested her hand on his shoulder. He hadn't heard anyone come in. He looked over his shoulder at his mother-in-law, tears rolling down her cheeks too.

"They need us to make a decision."

Bullet stood and moved away from her. "What kind of decision?"

"Look at her," she sobbed. "She's on life support, Bullet."

He knocked the chair over on his way out the door. He couldn't deal with this right now.

When Bullet came back the next day, the ICU nurse tried to stop him from taking Grey to see Callie, but he pushed right passed her. If what his mother-in-law told him was true, and they needed to make a decision about taking Callie off life support, he wanted Grey to see his mother one more time to say goodbye.

He had to hold the boy tight to keep him from scrambling out of his arms to crawl on the bed. It near broke Bullet's heart to see how much the boy wanted to go to her. He looked toward the door and saw the same nurse who tried to stop him, with tears rolling down her cheeks. Bullet couldn't stop himself from crying either.

This was the hardest decision he'd had to make in his life so far, but Callie was gone. The doctors said so. She'd never wake up again. She'd never hold their child again.

He carefully lowered Grey onto the bed and showed him where he could put his arms around his mama. Grey rested his head on her tummy, and started humming the same lullaby Bullet knew Callie sang to him.

He picked Grey up and went in search of his in-laws. He'd made his decision; they'd be taking Callie off the machines that were keeping her alive.

"I can't believe you're taking him away from us," said his mother-in-law.

"It isn't like that. I'm not taking him away. You knew I was trying to build a life for us in Colorado. The plan was always to move Callie and Grey there as soon as I got my footing."

Bullet took Grey out of his mother-in-law's arms, shook his father-in-law's hand, and told them he'd be in touch.

They'd buried Callie the day before, and there wasn't any reason for him to stay here a day longer. He was anxious to get him and Grey back to where he knew they belonged. It was a thirteen-hour drive, and he'd heard the weather wasn't so good. He'd get as far as he could today, sleep, and then make the rest of the drive in the morning.

He didn't know yet where they were going to live, or how he was going to take care of Grey and work at the same time, but Billy and Jace assured him they expected him to come back, and they'd figure it out.

He wasn't the only one with a baby, they'd told him. That was true. However, he was the only one without a baby mama. That had to make a difference.

Since they'd hired him a few months ago to help with their new rough stock contracting business, he'd never felt as though he was just another hand. They asked his opinion about things. There were even a few ideas he'd had that changed the direction of the new business. The job was important to him because it allowed him to stay in the rodeo business. Someday soon he planned to be on the bull riding side of the business rather than the rough stock side.

"It's you and me, partner," he said as he buckled Grey into his buddy seat. "Wish you could ride up front with me, and keep me company, but you're still too young for that. You're safer back here."

Bullet opened the bag of toys and books his mother-in-law packed for them and tried to put them within Grey's reach.

"We got a long-ass drive ahead of us. You be sure to let me know when you need somethin', okay, buddy?"

Grey looked at him, and then picked up one of his toy trucks. "Voom, voom," he said, and plowed the truck into Bullet's abdomen.

"Ouch," he squealed, which made Grey laugh. If this was how it was all the time, Bullet could handle it. But he knew better. About an hour in, Grey would get fussy. It would probably take them twice as long to get to Colorado than he was planning. He figured he'd be stopping a lot more often than he wanted to.

"This is our life now buddy," he kissed Grey's cheek, and climbed in the front seat. "Here we go."

"Voom, voom," answered Grey.

"I stopped earlier than I planned to," Bullet told his sister. "It'll probably take me three days to get to Crested Butte, but I didn't have a choice. Grey's fussy, and I can't keep him trapped in the back seat of the truck for hours on end."

"I'm headed to Crested Butte now." Lyric told him. "Dad is on tour, but they're trying to get there too."

"They don't have to leave the tour. Grey and I will be okay." Bullet felt his eyes fill up with tears. What the hell was wrong with him lately?

"It's more than just leaving the tour. They're planning to buy a house in Colorado."

"When did they decide to do that?" Bullet shook his head. He never imagined his dad would agree to leave Los Angeles. His mom had been ready to leave years ago.

"They've been thinkin' about it for a while."

"Where're they gonna live?"

"I don't think they've decided yet. Maybe Aspen. Mom wants a place there, but said it might be out of Dad's 'comfort zone,' whatever that means."

Bullet knew what it *didn't* mean. His parents could afford to live anywhere in the world they wanted to, so it wasn't about money.

He wanted to suggest they look near Colorado Springs, or Crested Butte, since that was where he and Grey would be most often, but that was being selfish. Just that they'd be in the same state made him feel better.

"How was Gram?" Lyric asked.

"Same as always. Says she misses us, but that she wants us to live our own lives."

Their grandmother was the single consistent force in his life when he was growing up, and still to this day. She believed in her son-in-law's career enough to encourage her daughter to travel the world with him, while she took care of their twin babies. Now that he was older, with kids of his own, he understood how much Gram sacrificed for them. It was one of the reasons he wanted to name his son after his grandfather, her husband. To honor her, and in some small way, thank her for all she'd done for him and his sister.

"She ask you about getting on bulls?"

"You know she did." Gram was the reason Bullet and Lyric got into rodeo in the first place. She'd been a world-class barrel racer back in the day. That was how she met Gramps, a bull rider himself.

Their mom, Guinevere, was the only child Gram and Gramps had. She'd never been interested in rodeo, only rock music. When Guinevere and Nate got married, and he was starting out in the music business, Gram helped manage his band. She'd get Satin booked at fairs and festivals where she was also booking rodeo events. Soon other acts asked Gram to manage them. She was in her eighties now, and still managed a handful of bands.

"She never let raisin' a couple babies stop her."

His sister was right. Gram still did more in a single day than most people accomplished in a week. This coming summer she was being inducted into the ProRodeo Hall of Fame for her decades-long support of the industry. The ceremony would take place at the organization's headquarters in Colorado Springs. He and Lyric, along with their parents, would be there to celebrate with her.

"Listen I gotta go. Grey's wakin' up from his nap."

"Wait. Bullet? You still there?"

"Yeah, I'm here."

"Callie wasn't my favorite person, you know that. But I'm still sorry she's gone. I can't imagine how hard this must be for you. I'm sorry I wasn't at the funeral."

"It's okay. Gram was there." After the service at the graveside, she asked him to take her home rather than to his in-laws' house. When he dropped her off, she invited him inside.

"It wasn't your fault," she'd said to him. "People like Callie need professional help. They need medical help. If they choose not to accept the help they're offered, there's little the rest of us can do about it."

Gram had told him their grandfather had struggled with the illness too. "They didn't call it being bi-polar in those days. They called it manic depression. Your grandfather would go for weeks being the happiest guy on earth. Suddenly he'd change, and sink into terrible depression."

Gram had never told Bullet this before. He wondered if Lyric knew. Gramps hadn't tried to kill himself as far as Bullet knew, and Gram hadn't said anything to make him think he had. What she did say, more than once, was there wasn't anything Bullet could've done. "It was the illness," she'd said. "Not you."

"I'm glad Gram was at the funeral with you."

"Thanks, Lyric." Bullet hung up before he started crying again. He hoped he could get Grey to bed early tonight. He badly needed the sleep himself.

When he finally did fall asleep, he was plagued by dreams of Callie trying to tell him something. Just as she was about to, he'd wake up. When he fell back to sleep, there she'd be again.

When he woke the next morning, he couldn't shake the feeling that his life was about to change. He hoped it was for the better.

* * *

1961

Bill kicked at the dry dirt under his feet as he walked down the driveway. He turned, when he reached the road, and looked back at the house. He'd probably never see it again. When he came home, his mama and baby sister wouldn't be living in it anymore. It no longer belonged to them.

It'd been a long three years since his daddy first got sick. Bill was only eight when it started. Life was good back then. In the summer, folks would come to their ranch for a week or two at a time. In the fall, the dude ranch part of their business shut down, and hunters would come.

That's how his daddy got sick. They still couldn't say what it was, but his mama remembered seeing a bite after he spent a day guiding hunters. He wasn't the same after that.

At first he got real weak. Bill had to pick up more of the chores when that happened. As his daddy's health got worse, they had to cancel the rest of the hunting trips, and then in the spring, he didn't have enough strength to get the dude ranch operational again.

His mama started selling off cattle to pay the bills. Next went the bulls, and finally, the horses.

When his daddy died, last week, his mama told him two things. The first was they had to sell the land and their house to pay off the medical bills. The second thing she told him was that, as the man of the house, even though they wouldn't have an actual house for a while, it was his responsibility to find work and help support the family.

His eyes filled with tears he quickly brushed away with the back of his hand. Flynn men didn't cry. That's what his daddy told him. And since he was a man now, he was done with crying.

All that mattered, at this point was finding work. There were three other dude ranches within a hundred mile radius; one of them had to be hiring. He might be young, and he might be little, but there wasn't a harder working cowboy in the State of Colorado. He'd prove himself so.

2

"Hey, Daddy. I'm calling to let you know I landed safely and I'm checked into the hotel. You can call back if you want, or we can talk tomorrow."

Her father insisted Tristan call when she traveled, especially when it was on behalf of their family business. It didn't matter that she was turning twenty-seven in less than a month. She was still his little girl, he'd tell her, and it was his duty to make sure she was safe.

Duty was an oft-used word in her father's vocabulary, as were honesty, integrity, faith, and family. They built their business on those words.

Tristan's father and grandfather started Lost Cowboy Company a few years ago, wanting to offer American-made apparel that was inspired by the ideals the nation was built on. Their ads, social media posts, the clothing they offered, even how it was made, represented a strong adherence to the principles her family lived by.

Tomorrow morning she was meeting with the guys from Flying R Rough Stock. They'd spoken a few times since their first meeting at the National Finals Rodeo last December. They were close to finalizing a deal in which Lost Cowboy would team up with them to sponsor competitors on the rodeo circuit.

Billy Patterson, a former Saddle Bronc National Champion, was one of the primary partners in the rough stock contracting business. His involvement gave Flying R a foot in the door to every rodeo circuit in existence. It would take Tristan months to lay the groundwork she would be handed by teaming up with them.

Jace Rice had also been at most of their initial meetings. She liked Jace as much as she liked Billy. They were the kind of men that embodied the principles of the Lost Cowboy brand.

Their other partners, Ben Rice and his brothers, Matt and Will, were Jace's cousins. Ben attended their initial meetings, but she didn't know him as well as she knew Billy and Jace. Ben was the lead singer of the band CB Rice, but had his own stake in the rodeo industry through his wife, who'd placed fourth at NFR a few years previously.

The meeting tomorrow was at their headquarters, the Flying R Ranch in Crested Butte, Colorado. Tonight she was staying in Gunnison, near the airport. When she said she'd rent a car, Ben's wife, Liv, insisted either she or one of the guys would come get her and bring her to the ranch.

"You should stay with us," Liv told her. "We have more room than we know what to do with. It would be silly for you to stay anywhere else."

Tristan spent enough time traveling and staying in hotels that she accepted the invitation without hesitation. If they were able to nail down the details of the partnership on this trip, she'd be spending a lot more time with the Flying R team. She might as well get to know the people she'd be working with.

"It's nice of you to come and get me," Tristan said to Liv the next day when she picked her up.

"It was my pleasure. I had to come into town anyway."

Tristan smiled at the little girl in Liv's arms. "Who's this?"

"I'd like you to meet Caden. Caden, can you be a lady and shake hands?"

Tristan held out her hand and Caden shook it. "How old is she?" she asked Liv.

"Almost two handfuls," Liv grinned.

Tristan remembered hearing Liv retired from barrel racing when she had a baby. There was also something about another daughter, who was married to Billy Patterson. That didn't seem possible. Liv didn't appear old enough to have an adult daughter. Tristan must've gotten the story mixed up.

"I have a couple of stops to make. I hope you don't mind that I picked you up first. I thought you might like to see some of the town."

"I'm glad you did, and yes, I'd like to. I might be spending a lot of time here." Tristan looked up and down Main Street, but there wasn't much to see.

"You may fly in and out of Gunnison, but you'll spend more time in Crested Butte than you will here."

"I'm relieved to hear it," Tristan laughed.

"The market offers more, so when I have a lot of shopping to do I come to Gunnison. Otherwise, CB has everything we need."

"CB Rice, Mama," Caden shouted from the back seat.

"Okay, sweet girl, we can listen to your daddy sing on our drive back." Liv pushed a button on the console and music started playing.

"She doesn't like to listen to much other than her father's band," Liv explained. "I guess it's better than her asking me to play Disney music over and over again."

"This is good," said Tristan after a few minutes. "I haven't heard their music before."

Liv smiled and turned the music up.

They stopped at the market, and when they were almost to Crested Butte, Liv asked if she was hungry.

"I am, but I should probably check with Billy and Jace about when we're meeting," Tristan answered.

"All set?" Liv asked when Tristan hung up.

"Yes, we're not meeting until three, so I have plenty of time." As anxious as she was to do what she came here to do, and finalize their partnership, Tristan found herself relieved that she'd have more time to spend with Liv and Caden.

They went to lunch at a place called the Sunflower, which the sign said was a "communal kitchen," and where everyone who came in seemed to know Liv.

Tristan couldn't remember the names of half of the people she was introduced to. Liv told each person Tristan met that her company, Lost Cowboy, was partnering with Flying R Rough Stock, as though it was a done deal.

"Everyone is so friendly."

"Speaking of friendly, there was more than one cowboy chattin' you up. What's your story? Is there a special young man at home waiting for you?"

No, there wasn't. Not even close. She'd been too busy helping run the business, and when she wasn't working, there wasn't anyone at home who interested her. Most of the people her age had grown up there, like she had. They'd all known each other for years. Dating any of them would've felt as though she were dating a cousin, or a brother.

There'd been one special young man. At the time Tristan believed he was "the one." She'd met him halfway through college, while she was still barrel racing. He was a hot, young, promising bull rider who took her heart, and her virginity.

He'd promised they'd see each other when she went off to design school in New York City, and they did every few weeks. It was a three-year long distance relationship that ended when Tristan discovered she wasn't the only woman in his life. There were barrel racers and buckle bunnies criss-crossing the country that "won the heart" of the cowboy she'd believed was hers.

She was still propositioned when she was on the road, but having a one-night-stand with a cowboy she'd never see again would hardly be in line with the principles of the brand she represented. If word got back to her father, her travel days would be over before their business really took off. Not to mention she'd learned her lesson about getting involved with cowboys a long time ago. It wasn't something she'd ever do again.

"Hello? Tristan?" Liv waved her hand in front of Tristan's face.

"Oh, sorry. I don't remember the last time I was on a date. Not much time for that these days."

"We'll have to see about that, now won't we?"

Tristan felt the color rise on her cheeks. "We'll see is right."

"Here's your Happy Hippie," the waitress said as she set the plate in front of Tristan. She couldn't resist ordering it when she read the name. The wrap was made with olive tapenade, sun-dried tomatoes, caramelized onions, artichokes, banana peppers, and mozzarella. "I could eat this every day," she told Liv after she'd taken a few bites.

"Wait until you have dinner here," Liv murmured in between bites of her own food. Tristan hoped she'd have occasion to.

* * *

1961

It was dark and cold. The sky had clouded over and hid the light of the moon. Maybe he should stop for the night. Try to find a tree to lean up against until dawn. Bill turned to see lights of a truck coming down the road. It had been more than two hours since another one had. He started walking backwards, and stuck out his thumb.

The truck slowed, and the driver rolled down the window. "Who's that? Is that you, Billy Flynn? Whatcha' doin' out on the road this late at night? Your mama know where you are, boy?"

"Yes, Mr. Patterson. She knows." He hoped for a ride, not a hide-tanning. He slunk away from the truck and kept walking down the road.

"Where ya goin', son? Come on now. Get in the truck."

Bill opened the door and climbed in. "Thanks. I 'preciate this."

Mr. Patterson turned in the seat to look at him. Bill wished he'd just put the truck in gear and keep on down the road.

"I don't know if you know this, but your pa and I were friends from way, way back. Since we were younger than you are now. I was sure sorry to hear about his passing, Billy."

"Thank you, sir. And I'm Bill now." He'd never be Billy again. Billy was the name of a child, and he wasn't a child any longer. He was a man, with the responsibilities of one.

"That right? Well, where you headed, Bill?"

"Sundance Trail, sir."

"What's at Sundance Trail that you need to get there in the middle of the night?"

"Lookin' for a job," he mumbled in the direction of the window. He turned back around. "You know if they're hiring?"

"Doubt it, but I know somebody who might be."

Bill sat up straighter and waited for Mr. Patterson to continue. When he didn't, he asked who it was.

"You ever hear of P-Bar Ranch?"

Bill shook his head. He hadn't.

"It's over the pass, in McCoy."

He hadn't heard of McCoy either, but if they were hiring, he didn't care where it was.

"You can stay at the house tonight, I'll take you up to the ranch tomorrow. I was headed there anyway."

"You were?" Bill asked. "Why?"

"It's my brother's place, and it's gotten big enough that he needs a partner. I figure if he needs a partner, he probably needs a few more cowboys, too."

Bill wished they could go straight there tonight, but sleeping in a warm bed sounded mighty good right then.

"Thank you, Mr. Patterson." Bill held out his hand to shake.

"Call me Clancy. And you're welcome, Bill."

"This place is incredible," Tristan said when they drove through the gates of the Flying R Ranch. It was nestled in a valley between two sets of mountains; more predominantly, to the east was Mount Crested Butte, which she could've guess based on its formation.

Tristan pointed to a stream that followed the road and appeared to be frozen over. "What's that?"

"Cement Creek. It divides the entire ranch in half. In the past, Ben's family raised cattle on one side of the creek, and horses on the other. It's gotten more complicated now that they're heavier into rough stock."

"How long has the ranch been in his family?"

"Four generations. Ben's great-grandparents were the first generation in Colorado. They bought this land. Their son, Ben's grandfather, bought another ranch, closer to the butte, and developed the ski area, but this was his home." Liv pointed as they drove past a sprawling ranch house.

"Ben's parents, Bud and Ginny, live here now. Our place is over there," she pointed north. "Ben's brother Matt's place is that way," Liv pointed south. "And we passed the turnoff to Will's place on our way in. His house is set a little further back, so you can't see it from the road."

"It's heavenly."

"The first time Ben brought me here I had a similar reaction. I always thought my place over in Black Forest was the most beautiful ranch I'd ever seen."

"You had a ranch?"

"I inherited it from my parents. It's where I raised my daughter Renie after my first husband died. Renie's husband, Billy, bought it from me before they were married. You've met Billy, haven't you?"

"Yes, I have. You know I heard something about your daughter being married to him, but I thought I'd gotten the story mixed up."

"Why's that?"

"Because you don't look old enough to have an adult daughter."

Liv beamed at Tristan. "Thank you. You're good for this old girl's ego."

Tristan shook her head. "Old," was the last word she would've used to describe Liv.

"You've met Lyric, haven't you?" Liv asked when they walked into the house, and saw a woman sitting at the kitchen counter.

"Of course I have." Tristan walked over to shake Lyric's hand. "Nice to see you again."

Instead of taking Tristan's extended hand, Lyric stood and hugged her. "I need a hug bad, and you're closest."

Lyric hung on longer than Tristan expected. She felt Liv's hand on her shoulder. "My turn."

When Liv hugged her, Lyric started to cry.

"What's wrong, sweetheart?"

"Bullet's wife killed herself."

"Oh, honey, I'm so sorry," Liv gasped. "How's Bullet?"

"On his way here. With Grey."

Tristan wished a hole would open up in the wall so she could disappear. "I'm sorry to intrude. Is there somewhere else I can wait for my meeting?"

Lyric wiped at her tears. "Intrude? If you're gonna be part of things around here, you better get used to drama. There's been nothin' but since I met this family. Today it's my turn to bring it."

"The other thing you'll have to get used to is Lyric telling you exactly what she thinks the minute she thinks it." A woman whom Tristan hadn't met walked into the kitchen.

"Hi," she said. "I'm Bree. Jace's wife."

"I'm Tristan, um, with Lost Cowboy."

"It's nice to meet you. Jace asked me to tell you they'll be a few more minutes. The guys are tending to a heifer that had twin calves. I've never seen anything like it, although Jace said it isn't that unusual."

"It's more common with dairy cattle than it is with beef cattle, but from what Billy said, there've been five sets of twins born so far this year."

"Lyric, how do you know this? Even I knew nothing about any twins being born?" asked Liv.

"Just gotta pay attention is all. Sometimes I think I'm the only one who does around here."

Bree laughed. "See how she is? You'll get used to it."

Jace and Billy came in the front door a few minutes later. Tristan wondered if it didn't bother Liv, all the people who walked into her house as though they owned the place.

"Sorry we're late," Billy said to her.

"I heard you had some excitement."

"Yeah, we did. Uh…can you wait for another minute?"

"Of course," she answered, although he didn't appear to be listening to her.

Billy walked straight over to Lyric and wrapped her in a hug. "You okay?" she heard him whisper. Lyric started to cry again, and buried her face in his shoulder.

Billy had a reputation out on the circuit for being self-involved. Guys complained that he kept to himself, and didn't form relationships with anyone. What she was witnessing was the antithesis of what she'd heard about him.

"I guess you talked to Bullet already. So you know what happened."

Billy nodded his head.

"He's worried. You need to reassure him that he'll have help when he gets here. Got it?"

Billy smiled. "Got it."

"Don't you worry, Lyric," Jace added. "Bullet is one of us. He's part of the family, just like you are. We'll help him the same way we'd help one another."

"What's goin' on in here?" asked Ben Rice as he walked in the front door followed by two other men Tristan didn't recognize.

"Come here and give me a kiss," he said to Liv, and then looked over at Tristan. "Don't we have a meeting?"

When Liv tugged on his sleeve and pointed to Lyric, Ben did the same thing Billy and Jace had done, going straight to Lyric to offer his condolences.

Tristan wished her dad was here with her. She'd already convinced him that partnering with Flying R was the right thing to do, but if he had any doubts about the kind of men they'd have as partners, this would've eliminated them.

In less than two hours they'd be in Crested Butte, and instead of three days it had taken them four. He had to hand it to Grey, though, he was hanging in pretty good. Bullet made sure to stop at the first sign he was getting antsy and give him time to run around and play.

Every hundred miles or so he'd stop at a store and let Grey pick out a new toy. Other times he'd try to find a park where he could play. It wasn't as easy once they got to Colorado, where snow covered most of the play-grounds. Grey loved it though. He didn't need a slide or a swing, he loved rolling around in the fluffy, white powder. That was another thing he had to get on one of his stops, snow clothes. The boy didn't have any to speak of. He hadn't needed any in Oklahoma.

He didn't miss the girls checking him out when they stopped at a store, or to get something to eat. He fig-ured having Grey with him would cramp his style, not that he was looking for any company right now. Instead, Grey seemed to attract more attention.

Women would sit right down at the table without being invited and ask about his baby. When they asked where his baby's mama was, Bullet answered simply. "She ain't in the picture anymore."

They'd express disappointment when they heard he was just passing through. One or two offered to let him and Grey stay the night. Bullet declined though. It didn't feel right so soon after Callie's passing. Plus, he needed to stay focused, and get them to Colorado.

"Almost there, baby boy," he said to Grey, who was just about to doze off. If Bullet was lucky, Grey would sleep the rest of the way.

"Our new life is about to begin." Bullet hoped he was doing the right thing, not just for himself, but for Grey too.

There were still a few things to nail down, but for all intents and purposes, the partnership between Lost Cowboy and Flying R Rough Stock was a go.

Liv helped Tristan get settled in a guest room on the lowest level of the three-story ranch house.

"There's a hot tub off this room that you're welcome to use." Liv pointed to the door off the family room. "You'll have complete privacy. There's one on every level," Liv giggled. "Ben really likes hot tubs."

Staying here was better than any hotel she'd ever stayed in. In addition to the hot tubs, there was a sauna too. And dinner tonight had been fabulous. Ben grilled steaks, just like her father did. It made her miss him even more, and that much happier when she saw his name pop up on the screen when her phone rang.

"How's my baby girl?"

"I'm good, Daddy. I miss you."

"You do?" The surprise she heard in his voice made her feel terrible.

"How's Gramps?"

"He's sittin' right here. You wanna talk to him before we hang up?"

"I'd like that."

She went over the questions the Flying R team asked during the meeting. Her father was as anxious to finalize this deal as she was, and said he'd get back to her with the answers the next morning.

Tristan didn't feel sleepy when she hung up after talking to her grandfather. The hot tub sounded like a nice way to relax and wind down, and since Liv said she'd have privacy, she decided to go in, even though she hadn't brought a bathing suit with her.

Grey was asleep in the crib that was still set up in Caden's room. Liv assured Bullet that her little girl could sleep through a train wreck, and even if Grey woke in the middle of the night, he wouldn't bother her. She handed him the extra baby monitor, and told him he could sleep downstairs in one of Ben's son's rooms. The boys were at their mother's house this week.

"Oh, and Tristan McCullough from Lost Cowboy is staying in the guest room down the hall."

The name sounded familiar. Was she the same woman from Lost Cowboy he met in Las Vegas? He sure wouldn't mind running into her in the hallway in the middle of the night.

He took a shower, and then remembered there was a hot tub on the patio.

* * *

1961

Once they turned off the main road, Bill kept thinking the ranch would be around the next bend of the dirt road. It felt as though they'd been driving for hours since they could only go ten miles an hour on the washboard-ridden road. He was beginning to feel sick to his stomach.

"You look green over there, boy. You want me to pull over for a bit?"

Bill wouldn't be making a good first impression on Clancy's brother if he got sick to his stomach riding in a damn truck. He waved his hand. "Nah, I'm good. You can keep goin'."

"It ain't much further," Clancy laughed. "We'll get some pop in ya when we get there. That'll make you feel better."

"I said I was fine," Bill snapped.

Clancy grinned at him, and rolled down his window. "It'll be a might dusty, but the fresh air that comes with it will do you good. Hey, look there. We're here."

Bill looked up and saw the main gate of the ranch. It was closed, so Clancy stopped the truck and jumped out to open it. Maybe Bill should've done that for him.

"I'll get it," he said after they pulled through. He didn't want Clancy to think he was lazy, so he jumped out and closed the gate behind them.

Getting out of the truck for just that short amount of time settled his stomach. He looked off in the distance, and thought about telling Clancy he'd walk the rest of the way in, but from where he stood, he couldn't see any buildings. Who knew how much further it might be? Could be miles.

As he studied the view, he understood why the ranch was set as far back as it was. From where he stood, he could see all the way to Utah. Hills layered on rolling hills in shades of golden brown. Soon it would turn a thousand shades of green as the earth warmed and the plant-life came out of dormancy. He breathed in deeply. Horses. It was a smell not all found pleasant, but to him, it took him back to happier times. Day after day he and his father had ridden their land on the backs of horses. He'd give anything to go back to the time before his daddy got sick.

"You gettin' back in the truck or not?" Clancy shouted at him.

Bill climbed in. "Quite a place your brother's got here."

"Ain't just his anymore. I'll be a full partner soon as he deposits the bank draft. So I'll say thanks for the both of us."

He didn't ask how much land the ranch encompassed, that would be rude. Plus, if things went the way he hoped they would, he'd be out riding that land and could figure it out for himself.

"Uh, so…if you're a partner, who makes the decision about hiring somebody lookin' for a job?"

"Guess I forgot to tell you that part. It was a stipulation of my partnerin' up. We're a package deal, young Flynn. I don't have any doubt you'll work hard for us, son. Just like your daddy taught you."

Bill looked out the passenger window and hoped the tears that filled his eyes went away before they rolled down his cheeks. "Thank you, sir. I won't disappoint you."

4

Tristan opened her eyes, and turned to look when she heard the patio door open.

"Uh, hi, ma'am. Sorry, I didn't know anyone was out here."

"Hi. Um...I was just about to get out. If you wouldn't mind turning around, I'll grab my towel."

"You can stay, I'm happy to share," he smiled.

"I've been in too long as it is. Now if you'll turn around—"

"You know, you look familiar. Have we met somewhere before? Maybe another hot tub?"

"Very funny. No, we haven't."

"I think you're wrong, we have met. I'm sure of it."

"Listen, I'm a bit embarrassed by this, but I'm not wearing a swimsuit. So again, if you'd please turn around, I'll leave."

"Now what fun would that be?" he chuckled. "I don't mind, I'm not wearing one either." The man rested his hands on the edge of the hot tub, and when he did, his towel fell to the ground. "I'm Bullet," he said. "And if I'm not mistaken, you're Tristan."

"You aren't going to turn around, are you?"

"Nope, I'm sure not."

She shook her head and waited to see if Bullet was joking. When he didn't make a move, she stood, and climbed out around him. "Hell with it," she muttered, walking in the house, leaving both her towel and Bullet behind her.

Bullet climbed into the warm water, and couldn't stop chuckling. That was a mighty fine looking ass he watched walk away from him. He couldn't wait to see the rest of the feisty Miss McCullough.

He leaned back and looked up at the sky. It felt good to be back in Colorado; even if it was damn cold, the welcome was warm.

Lyric and everyone else assured him before he left Oklahoma that the Flying R partners would help him and his baby get settled, but he'd been skeptical. It was one thing for the partners to work their schedules around their wives and children. They were mostly family.

He wasn't a partner, though, he was a hand, and he hated relying on other people to make his life work. He needed to figure out how to do this on his own before they got tired of making exceptions and fired him.

He wished he'd grabbed a beer; he sure could use one right now. No matter what Gram told him, he still felt guilty about Callie killing herself, especially since he kept dreaming about her. He closed his eyes again and wished leaving her memory behind him was as easy as it had been to leave Oklahoma.

He jumped when he heard the sliding door open. He must've drifted off, which was not too smart in a hot tub.

"You left this inside."

As Tristan brought the baby monitor closer, he heard Grey crying.

"*Shit*. Sorry." Bullet got up.

Tristan turned her head away, and held out a towel for him.

"You can look. I don't mind."

She didn't turn around. "Just go take care of your baby."

"Your eyes still closed?"

"Yeah. Why?"

"Just wanted to make sure you weren't tryin' to steal a peek at me goin' inside, like I did of you."

"Just go."

"Thanks, darlin'."

"Not your darlin'."

"Not yet anyway." He closed the sliding door behind him.

Underneath the robe Tristan found in the closet, she wore her usual sleeping attire—sweatpants and a camisole. She'd also thrown a sweatshirt on before she took the baby monitor out to the man in the hot tub. May have been overkill in hindsight.

She'd gotten two glimpses of his nakedness, and every time she closed her eyes, there he was. *Of course* she looked when he went inside. True to the arrogant bastard form he'd shown thus far, he'd slung the towel over his shoulder instead of wrapping it around his waist.

The curve of his ass alone was enough to make her drool. He was lean, and over six feet tall. How much over, she wasn't sure, but every bit of him was cut. Wide shoulders and strong pecs covered with dark chestnut hair that trailed past his flat six-pack abs...and those arms...how would it feel to be wrapped up in them?

Bullet's piercing blue eyes were surprisingly warm, and his smile could easily have convinced her to shed her three layers of protection, and climb right back in the hot tub with him.

When he rested his hands on the edge of the hot tub, Tristan couldn't help but notice their strength. Hands of a boxer, her mother had called them.

Her mom had been gone a long time, since Tristan was fifteen, but she still remembered her words. "Marry a man with strong hands, so when he takes yours in his, and tells you everything will be okay, you believe it will be." Her father had strong hands, and she never doubted everything would be okay when he had her hands in his.

The next morning, Tristan pulled the pillow back over her head, hoping for a few more minutes sleep, but it wasn't enough to drown out the ruckus above her.

In a house full of ranchers, rough stockers, and toddlers, Tristan guessed everyone had been up for hours. Maybe she would've been better off staying at a hotel. That way when she slept in, she wouldn't feel as guilty.

She pulled out her phone to check the time. Seven? She was feeling guilty about sleeping until seven? She rolled back over and groaned. She'd go for a run, but Liv warned her yesterday that she should give herself time to adjust to the altitude.

"We're at ten thousand feet," Liv told her. "Don't be surprised if you get winded walking up the stairs."

Someone upstairs was making breakfast, and it smelled really good. And coffee. Tristan pulled her sweatshirt over head, and went in search of the heavenly scents.

Bullet knew he should go out and help with the morning chores. Lyric had offered to keep an eye on Grey a couple of times. When she pinched his shoulder and whispered that he should consider earning his keep, he relented, knowing he couldn't put it off any longer.

"You know how long that Tristan lady is staying?" he whispered back.

"Oh, no. No way. You aren't goin' down that road. She is strictly hands off to you, bro."

"Why's that?" And since when did Lyric tell him what to do, or in this case what not to do?

"She's gonna be partnerin' with Flying R and we don't need any of your drama landin' on her."

Bullet had several responses for his sister, backed by a temper fueled by the buttons she was pushing, but he kept his mouth shut.

When he got a glimpse of Tristan coming up the stairs, he closed the door he'd just opened and walked back into the kitchen.

"Good morning, everyone," she muttered. The sound of sleep that lingered in her voice filled him with lust. He folded his arms, leaned against the wall, and watched her. She was tall, almost as tall as he was, with long, dark blonde hair, and eyes that sometimes looked blue, but right now, looked green. She was thin, but curvy—womanly. Her movements were graceful as she reached up to open the cupboard Liv pointed to, slowly took the cup from it, and then turned to fill it with coffee.

Bullet closed his eyes and imagined wrapping his arm around her waist as she did, sweeping her hair to the side, and nibbling on the nape of her neck. He'd trail kisses from her hairline to her shoulder—

"Dude, weren't you headed outside?" Lyric barked louder than necessary.

"Yeah, yeah. But I don't want to be rude and leave without saying good mornin' to Miss Tristan." Bullet walked over to where she stood with her knee bent just slightly, and one bare foot resting on top of the other. Her perfectly-manicured toes were painted a reddish-orange that made him want to lick them, one by one.

"I hope you slept well after your visit to the hot tub," he whispered causing her cheeks to pinken just slightly. He leaned in closer. "Good morning, sweetness. *Ouch!*" he gasped when someone slapped the back of his head.

When he turned around, Bree was standing behind him. Her arms were folded in front of her, but she was smiling.

"He tried to charm the pants off me the first time I met him too."

Bullet smiled. "And when was that?"

"The morning you were sleeping naked on my sofa."

Tristan smirked. "Ah. Evidently naked shenanigans are part of your regular repertoire."

Bullet put his arm around Bree's shoulders. "You're givin' me a bad name with the lady. Now tell her the truth. You ain't never seen me naked."

"He's right. I haven't actually seen him naked." Bree looked from Bullet to Tristan. "Wait. Have you?"

Tristan took a sip of coffee, weighing her words. "Yes, a couple of times." She added a shoulder shrug to suggest it wasn't any big deal, and then set her coffee on the kitchen counter. She opened the refrigerator door, hoping Bullet didn't notice how her hands shook.

"Did I hear your sister say you were headed outside?" Tristan turned back around and looked into the blue eyes focused directly on hers. He didn't just stare, his eyes were penetrating, as though he could read her mind through them.

"What's the plan for today, Tristan?" interrupted Liv.

"I'm waiting to hear from my father. Besides that, I'm compiling a list of competitors we've targeted in the past, but didn't have enough capital behind us to interest them."

"I can help with that," Lyric offered.

"I was hoping you would. Maybe you and I can put our heads together and see if there's anyone you can suggest that we haven't taken a look at yet."

"I can add someone to your list," Bullet interjected. Tristan had almost forgotten he was there. That's how she got when she started thinking about business. It consumed her.

"Who's that?" nudged Lyric. "As if I don't know."

"I'm a perfect fit," he smiled directly at Tristan.

"A perfect fit for what?" He wasn't seriously suggesting Lost Cowboy sponsor him, was he?

"Come on. Look at me." He waved his hands up and down his body. "Just think how good your gear will look on me."

Tristan almost laughed out loud. Yeah, he'd look great in it. All of it. But there was so much more they took into consideration before they asked anyone to wear their brand. She didn't know much about Bullet, but from what she'd seen so far, he was exactly the kind of cowboy they wouldn't sponsor.

Bull riders had a bad rap to begin with. Many who competed in other events on the rodeo circuit thought they were arrogant assholes. And for the most part, they were right. Their arrogance was part of what drove them. If they didn't have their heads one hundred and fifty percent into bull riding, if they weren't the same percentage confident in their ability to cover their bull, they didn't have a prayer. It was as much man against himself as it was man against beast. If a rider had an inkling of doubt in the few minutes before he got on the back of a bull, he might as well walk away before the chute opened.

Tristan understood how much Bullet had on his plate. His wife just died and he was responsible for raising his child, who Tristan doubted was much more than a year old. What kind of man got on the back of a bull when they were a single parent? One who didn't embody the principles of Lost Cowboy, that's the kind.

Even setting that aside, there was so much more. What happened last night told Tristan everything she needed to know to scratch Bullet off her list, not that he was on it in the first place.

"Players need not apply" should be stamped on her forehead. Not just for her brand, but for her too. While he tempted her on a physical level, Tristan knew she'd never actually succumb to him. Never.

"How old are you?"

"Twenty-five, ma'am."

He tipped his hat when he said it, the one her father would never have worn in the house.

Too old on one level, too young on another. In the world of bull-riding, he was middle-age. If he hadn't made his mark as a bull rider by now, chances were good he wouldn't. Her guess was he didn't have enough time to get to practice pens. He'd never make any of the cuts without practice.

And for her on a personal level? He was a year younger than she was, and ten years less mature. He was a baby. A baby with a baby.

When she poured the cream into her coffee, her hands no longer shook. Bullet lost his charm, on a number of levels.

"Sorry, cowboy. I wish you the best of luck out there." Tristan looked at Lyric. "Give me a half hour to check in with the office, and get my notes together?"

"Sounds perfect."

Tristan went downstairs without looking back.

"I'd say you've been dismissed." Lyric whispered.

Yeah, he sure had, and it stung. He could read the thoughts as they ran through her mind. Not good enough. That's what it boiled down to. He wasn't a good enough bull rider for her brand, and he wasn't a good enough man for her. He saw the light turn off. It was that quick.

Bullet went outside without another word. What had he been thinking anyway? The last thing he had time for was a woman. Even on a temporary basis. He kicked at the dirt, furious with himself for not being able to keep his head on straight.

It was way past time for him to grow up. He had a child, and not just one.

Bullet walked into the barn and started mucking out a stall. If all else failed, a stall always needed mucked.

***

1961

Instead of staying in the bunkhouse with the rest of the cowboys, Clancy told Bill he'd have a room in the main house with him and his brother. Clancy was building a second house, and when it was finished, he'd move in there. Clive was getting married and soon his wife would be living on the ranch full-time as well.

Bill figured that was the main reason Clancy's brother had been looking for a partner in the dude ranch. There were times during the year that he and his mama and sister rarely saw his daddy. Running a ranch was hard work, even if you could afford a lot of help.

As far as he knew, Clancy hadn't married yet either. "You got kids?" he asked one night, thinking that might be easier to ask than if he had a wife.

"Nope. Not that I know of anyway." Clancy winked at him.

"So no wife either?"

"Nope. No wife either." Clancy stood and poked at the fire. "Here's the thing. Women like the idea of a cowboy. They want to catch 'em, kind of like a wild horse. Soon as they got 'em caught, they wanna tame 'em. Soon as they got 'em tamed, they don't want 'em anymore, so they go off in search of another cowboy."

Bill didn't think his mama ever tamed his daddy, but he couldn't say for sure. Clancy reminded him a lot of his father. They were close in age, and had a similar build—tall, with broad shoulders that came from working a ranch every day.

Clancy got a lot of attention from the women who vacationed at the dude ranch. Even the married ones, especially when they heard he was single. They were fascinated by his bright blue eyes, and wanted to run their hands through his ginger-colored hair. There were times Bill felt embarrassed for him, but it didn't seem to bother Clancy.

"Anyway, I let 'em think they got me caught and soon as I see any sign of them trying to tame me, I end it. We both stay happier that way."

Clancy sat back down. "Gotta say the one thing that bothers me about it all is that I don't have any youngens." He studied Bill. "I figure since your pa passed away, you don't have a daddy, either. We're a pair, ain't we?"

Bill nodded his head. The last few weeks at the ranch Clancy had looked out for him. He gave him free rein, but never enough that he could get out of hand. Bill worked hard, like he promised to. At the end of a long day, he liked to go back to the house, where he had his own room. Some nights he fell asleep before he finished the letter he tried to write his mama every day. If he did, he'd finish it the next night. They didn't go to the post office in town that often, but he mailed every one of them in a separate envelope.

Since Clancy was in charge of sending Bill's pay to his mama, they'd get a money order at the bank in town for half of Bill's earnings. The other half he deposited in an account his Bill's name. He would've sent it all, but Clancy told him that was the way his mama wanted it.

5

"Hey, Daddy."

"Hey, sweetheart. I got your info."

"Can you email it to me?"

"Of course. Now tell me what's goin' on."

"Nothin'."

"Try again, and tell me the truth this time."

Her father always knew when Tristan was lying, not that she did it very often, and almost never to him. This wasn't really a lie as much as she didn't know how to answer him. She really liked being around the Rice and Patterson families. They had so much *fun*. And there was no shortage of love either.

She'd grown up an only child, like her father was. She didn't know much about her mama's family. They weren't spoken of often, even when her mama was still alive.

After her mama's funeral, she never saw them again. It bothered her, but since she hadn't known them before her mama passed away, it wasn't as though she missed them. She missed her mama though, every day. Still did. Every single day.

Tristan never felt a lack of love from her father or her grandfather. There were neighbor ladies who were close to her mama that made she sure she had someone to take her shopping for her prom dress, and stuff like that. And there were always lots of friends. Her father knew everybody, and everybody knew him. She was popular in school too, and had friends from rodeo. But they weren't family. Not like the Rices and Pattersons.

"I just miss you," she said finally.

"You can come home whenever you want to. We don't have to finalize this deal in person. You can get on a plane tomorrow and be sittin' at the dinner table with us by nightfall."

"I know. It isn't that bad. It isn't bad at all really. It's more that I wish you and Gramps were here too. They're all so nice. I know you already know they are, but being here with them, it's just...I can't explain it."

"Well if you figure it out, you know how to reach me. In the meantime, let's talk a little business. That okay with you?"

"More than okay." Talking business would be just the thing to get her out of her funk.

Grey loved going for rides in the truck. "Voom, voom," he'd say, and off they'd go. Bullet was worried that after being stuck in his buddy seat for hours on the drive from Oklahoma to Colorado, that Grey would pitch a fit about getting back in it. But he didn't.

"Let's go to the Secret Stash," Lyric suggested. That was fine with him. He was already feeling as though he'd worn out his welcome staying in Ben and Liv's house, and he'd only been there a day. He didn't know how Lyric did it. She didn't seem to have any trouble hanging out with them, eating their food, or staying in their house. Bullet felt as though he and Grey were an imposition. But then Lyric didn't work for them. He did.

"They don't think of you that way."

"How'd you know what I was thinkin'?"

Lyric raised her eyebrow. Sometimes he felt as though he knew how his twin sister was feeling, and sometimes he didn't. She got him more often than he got her. She used to say it was because he didn't try.

"I should find a place for us to live, but I wouldn't know where to start. I mean, should I look here, or near Monument?"

"I have a few ideas 'bout that. We can talk about it over dinner. Okay?"

Yeah, that sounded good. Sometimes he felt as though Lyric was a decade older than him. She had her shit together in a way he doubted he ever would.

"I got the place in Palmer Lake to myself with Bree and Jace married. And payin' the rent isn't an issue for me. In fact, I'm thinkin' of askin' Paige and Mark if they'd consider sellin' it to me."

Paige and Mark were Bree's parents, and Lyric had been renting the house near the lake from them for a couple of years. Originally she and Blythe were going to live there together. Blythe was Bree's sister, who was now married to Tucker, Jace's twin brother. Just thinking about how many overlaps there were in the Rice family made Bullet's head hurt.

"If you get a place here in Crested Butte, I could stay with you. Then when you're in Monument, you could stay with me."

"Havin' me and Grey livin' with you won't cramp your style?"

"What style? Come on, Bullet. All I got time for right now is chasin' my dreams. Gotta stay focused to shine bright, ya know."

He did know, and he wasn't very good at it. Not like she was.

"Your problem is you think too much with the wrong part of your anatomy." She fisted her hand and knocked the side of his head. "You got a good brain in here, bud. You're smart as I am, maybe smarter. But instead, you're too busy chasin' skirts and breedin' babies."

His sister was right, but he wished she hadn't put it that way. He was already feeling bad enough about himself after his run-in with Tristan that morning.

"It'll be all right," Lyric said, and hugged him. "You're in a good place now, with good people. All you gotta do is put a plan together, and then stick to it. Don't let yourself get sidetracked with stuff that don't matter."

"Like chasin' skirts?"

"Exactly. Now tell me, what's your dream, Bullet?"

"You know what it is."

"Maybe I do. Maybe I don't. Tell me your dream. Say it out loud. And then tell me how much you want it. From there we'll figure out how to start makin' it happen."

Bullet loved his sister's positive attitude. She was a lot like their parents that way. They focused on what was in front of them, and rarely looked back.

"Okay, here it is. My dream is to be a world champion bull rider."

"See? That wasn't so hard. What do you have to do to make it happen?"

"Get on bulls."

"Simple right?"

Bullet looked at Grey sitting in the high chair next to him. "Not simple at all."

"Lots of bull riders have kids."

"I don't know of any whose kids don't have a mama."

"Maybe not, but how many of 'em have a twin sister?"

Bullet didn't think that was really the same thing, but it made him smile anyway.

"So how much do you want it?"

"More than anything."

"Anything?"

"Anything."

"Well all right then."

He and Lyric talked until Grey looked as though he was about to fall asleep in the high chair.

"We better get back."

"Yep, we should. You feelin' better?"

He smiled. "You already know the answer, don't ya?"

She hugged him and smiled. "Yeah, I do."

Liv invited Tristan to join her out on the porch after dinner.

"He's not so bad you know."

"What's that?"

"Bullet. He's a good kid. He just needs guidance. A mentor maybe."

"Maybe. I don't think it matters. I don't see him making it as a bull rider."

"You don't? That intrigues me. Why not?"

"His son, for starters. I can't imagine he'll be getting on many bulls this year. And if he does, he should be ashamed of himself. His first priority should be that little boy."

"Are the two mutually exclusive?"

"Come on, Liv. You're not new to rodeo. You had a pretty good scare yourself barrel racing. And I'm not saying barrel racing isn't dangerous. I had a few bad spills when I was still competing. But it certainly isn't as dangerous as bull riding."

Liv had an accident her first year as a serious competitor. Talk was she was paralyzed, but she was able to come back from it, and compete again.

"Not to mention his age. He's not a kid anymore."

"My goodness, Tristan, he's twenty-five. I was forty when I started competing."

"Again, no offense, Liv, but it's different."

"You don't think he has a chance?"

"No, I don't. And more importantly, I think it would be irresponsible of him to even try."

"You're entitled to your opinion Miss Lost Cowboy, but I'm here to tell you, you're wrong."

"Bullet—"

Before she could say another word, he carried Grey inside and kicked the door closed behind him. He didn't care what she said, or what she thought. She didn't know him, or what he was capable of. He'd show her, but more importantly, he'd show himself.

He got Grey settled in a clean diaper and pajamas, set him in the crib, and hooked the baby monitor to his back pocket. She thought he was irresponsible? What the hell did she know?

"I didn't see him there."

Liv looked up at the stars. Tristan wasn't sure she heard her.

"Liv?"

"Never doubt the human spirit, Tristan. Even when situations seem impossible, or people seem incapable."

"That's something my daddy would say."

"I haven't met your father yet, but my guess is he's a smart man."

"The smartest."

"I'm sure the apple didn't fall too far from the tree. I bet he's compassionate too."

Tristan's cheeks heated with the dressing down Liv gave her, but she didn't argue. She was quicker to judge than she should be. She knew that.

"Neither of you are wrong," said Lyric, walking up the porch steps. "He's gonna have to work damn hard if he wants to catch his dreams. He knows it, and he's prepared to do it. No matter how the odds are stacked against him."

"I should've kept my mouth shut. I hardly know him. I had no right—"

"You always have a right to express your opinion. In fact, overhearing what you said is only gonna make him try harder."

"I doubt my opinion matters to him."

Even as dark as it was on the porch, Tristan caught the smile that passed between Liv and Lyric.

"Someone's lookin' for her mama." Ben came out on the porch carrying Caden. Liv reached out for her, and the little girl snuggled in on her lap.

"Hello, my darling child. Do you want mama to read you a bedtime story?"

Caden shook her head from side to side. "No book. Tell a story, Mama."

Tristan stood and went inside. Lyric followed her. "It might make a good story," Lyric said.

"Caden's bedtime story?"

"No, my brother's."

"Oh. Well—"

"Maybe he's the 'Lost Cowboy,' who finds his way back. Maybe his story is exactly what your brand needs."

"And what if he doesn't find his way back?"

"Don't let him know. Don't let anyone know. Follow him yourself. See how he does."

Tristan shrugged her shoulders. "Maybe."

"Worth considerin' is all I'm sayin'."

She found the idea as intriguing as she found the man. Lyric might be on to something. The Lost Cowboy brand really was about *bringing back* the ideals her father and grandfather believed in. But was Bullet up for the challenge? Especially given he'd know nothing about it. If the story was going to be authentic, he couldn't know. No one could. Not even Lyric. Bullet needed to turn his life around for himself, not so Lost Cowboy would sponsor him. That's the only way it would work.

* * *

1963

The cowboys who worked as ranch hands were headed to Glenwood Springs for a bull-bucking. Bill wanted to go along, but he wasn't sure they'd let him, and he couldn't bring himself to ask.

When he finished his afternoon chores, he thought about taking one of the horses out for a trail ride. Nobody minded if he did, but they didn't like him to go alone. He'd have to see if there was anyone staying behind who'd go along.

He was walking past the dining hall when Sadie, the ranch cook, called out to him. "Where you off to, Billy boy?"

It drove him crazy that she called him Billy. He'd politely asked her to call him Bill, but she didn't pay any attention to him.

"I was thinkin' on goin' for a ride, ma'am."

She motioned him over. "You want some company out on the trail?"

Did she want to go for a ride? Bill sure hoped not. He doubted she could even mount up without a block. And what horse would she ride? The woman had to weigh at least three hundred pounds.

"My nieces are visiting this week. I'm sure they'd like to go with you."

Oh jeez. Nieces? That meant there was more than one of them. This was turning into work. "They know how to ride, ma'am?"

"Sure do. In fact, they can both outride you."

Bill doubted it, but if they thought they could outride him, they could certainly saddle up their own horses.

"This is Misty," Sadie told him. He recognized her from the day before. She'd been sitting on the fence, trying to get the cowboys' attention. She looked like trouble to him.

"And this here is Dorothea," Sadie continued.

"Aunt Sadie, I told you nobody calls me Dorothea." The little girl turned and looked at Bill. "Hi," she said, holding out her hand. "I'm Dottie." She had blonde, curly hair that looked almost white, big blue eyes, and a smile that lit up her face.

He'd introduce himself to her if he could remember his name. The prettiest girl he'd ever seen his life was waiting for him to answer, and he couldn't speak.

6

"Signed and sealed," Billy smiled and shook Tristan's hand. "Welcome aboard."

"I could say the same to you, but your outfit is quite a bit bigger than ours."

"There ain't nothin' stoppin' you from growin'. Soon instead of Wrangler National Finals Rodeo, we'll all be goin' to Vegas for the Lost Cowboy NFR."

"Right," she grinned. "Well, since our deal has been made, it's time for me to head home." She'd miss being at the Flying R. She'd gotten used to the noisy, fun-loving cowboys, and the chaos of toddlers under foot all the time.

Liv put her arm around Tristan's shoulders. "I hope not for long. Billy, can't you figure out a reason for Tristan to work out of Flying R headquarters, at least part-time?"

"As a matter of fact..."

Wait. What? Was Billy serious? Was there a reason she'd have to work from here instead of home? If he could come up with one legitimate enough, she'd take him up on it in a heartbeat.

"We're havin' a team meeting here in three weeks. Tristan, I understand you and Lyric have your heads together on potential sponsorships. Let's see who you've got, and then get 'em here. We'll call it a meet and greet, and see who fits."

Instead of feeling sad about leaving, she could look forward to coming back in less than a month. "Sounds good to me." A couple of days ago she would've felt as though coming back so soon would be imposing, but not now. She'd gotten used to Liv and Ben's open door policy. Everyone was welcome, at any time. Had she even suggested she stay anywhere else, Liv would've been insulted.

Plus, Crested Butte was quickly growing on her. She'd love to spend more time in the quaint town. In their agreement, they'd given Lost Cowboy access to the Flying R's plane, if it wasn't already in use by one of the rough stock partners, or by Ben's band or father. Even if she didn't make use of it and flew commercial, flying in and out of Gunnison was easier than going through Denver. There was a direct flight to and from LaGuardia a couple of times a day. It was the closest airport to her family's place on Long Island.

When Liv overheard Tristan talking about booking a flight, she called Ben. "Can you please check the log book, sweetheart?" Liv winked at Tristan, and put her hand over the phone. "I love this man so much."

Tristan couldn't help but smile. Being around them, and Billy and Renie, and Jace and Bree, and...all of them basically, made her yearn for a relationship of her own. It might be a long time coming, though. Isn't wasn't like she was in the position to meet anyone, other than cowboys. She looked around her. The very relationships she was envying were *with* cowboys. It couldn't be that *all* of the good ones were taken.

"Okay, great. See you later, sweetie." Liv turned to Tristan. "The plane is yours tomorrow. Ben said he needs to go to New York anyway. He'll stay a couple of nights, and then fly home. If tomorrow works for you, of course. I'm in no hurry for you to leave."

"Tomorrow is perfect. And, uh, we have plenty of room at our place for Ben to stay with us, if he doesn't mind driving into the city. There's an airport in Ronkonkoma, which is only a few minutes from our place in Holbrook. The drive into Manhattan is a little over an hour."

Liv hugged her. "I'm sure he'd love it."

Tristan probably should've checked with her father before she invited Ben to stay at their place, but they had plenty of room, and she was certain her father would agree to it.

"What's with the furrowed brow? Ben can stay in the city. It wouldn't be a problem."

Tristan's cheeks heated. "Oh, no. I was thinking how nice it would be to have him at our place. If anything, we don't make that kind of offer often enough."

She'd change that though. Maybe some of the Lost Cowboy-Flying R meetings could be held in New York.

The door opened and Bullet walked in carrying Grey. He'd been standoffish to her since the other night even though she'd tried to apologize more than once. Each time he'd waved her off.

"Mornin'," he said, more to Liv than to her.

"Good morning to you, too. How's my big boy today?" Liv walked over and took Grey out of Bullet's arms.

"You sure about this, ma'am?"

"There are at least two things I'm sure about. One, you know my name. It's Liv, and I expect you to use it. Two, Caden has been asking me for over an hour when her buddy Grey is going to be here. She'll be thrilled to see him, which makes my life much easier."

Liv unbuttoned Grey's jacket and went in the direction of the family room, where Caden was playing. Tristan heard the little girl squeal when she saw her playmate.

"He loves comin' over here." Bullet shuffled his feet. "And she's so great to make it seem like she ain't doin' me a favor when she watches him." He looked at the floor, then the ceiling, then over her head in the direction of the family room. Everywhere but at her.

"Bullet, I want you to know how sorry I am about what I said the other night. What you do isn't any of my business. I don't know the first thing about being a parent, or a bull rider. I'm in no position to judge you."

"I told you before not to worry about it." He still didn't look at her. "My life is a mess right now, and I'm workin' hard to get it right. As right as I can anyway, considerin' my son no longer has a mama."

Tristan's eyes filled with tears.

"It ain't nothin' for you to cry about. We don't need you feelin' sorry for us."

At least he finally looked at her. "I don't feel sorry for you, Bullet. Or Grey. It's just that I understand—"

"Forgive me for leavin' in the middle of your sentence, but if I don't, I'm gonna say somethin' I'll regret. I will say this though," he walked closer, his eyes boring into hers as he did. "You don't understand anything about my life, or my son's life. Nothing at all."

When Bullet stormed out of the front door, Tristan closed her eyes and waited for it to slam behind him, but it didn't.

It wasn't her fault. It was his. But he couldn't help it. Every time he looked at her, he saw his own shortcomings. He'd wasted a hell of a lot of the last couple years having fun, not thinking about the consequences of his actions. He had two kids to prove it.

He'd spent a half hour this morning trying to talk Hannah Pearl's mama into letting his daughter come and stay with him for a few days. She questioned him up one side and down the other about what happened with Callie, and why he was in Colorado with Grey. When he told her he couldn't tell her why Callie killed herself, the woman lit into him.

"Bullshit," she'd said. "I know how it feels when you lose interest. I've lived through it. Remember?"

He hadn't lost interest in Callie. He tried more times than he could count to make their relationship work. It didn't help the guilt he felt, especially since he was still dreaming about her pretty near every night.

"Ready to get to work?" Lyric asked. "You're leavin' tomorrow, right?"

"Right," Tristan nodded her head.

"You and Bullet have some powerful chemistry between you."

"What? No, we don't. We don't have anything between us."

"Uh huh. He's under your skin, and you're under his."

"You don't know what you're talking about. Bullet is..." What could she say that wouldn't insult his twin sister? She was about to say that he was immature. And pig-headed.

"Waitin'," Lyric drummed her fingers on the table.

"For what? Oh." Tristan pulled out her pile of notes.

"No, not for that. Bullet is...you didn't finish your sentence."

"He's a very nice young man, with a lot on his plate."

Lyric rolled her eyes. "I call bullshit, but let's move on anyway. Have you given any thought to what we talked about the other night? Lost Cowboy followin' his story?"

She had, but she didn't want to admit it to Lyric. She reminded herself that whatever decisions Bullet made in his life couldn't be because of a potential Lost Cowboy sponsorship.

"No," she lied. "I haven't."

"Too bad. 'Cause if you ask me, his story would make a good one."

"I don't think he likes me very much."

"That isn't it. It's more that he doesn't like himself when he takes a look through your eyes."

"You're overstating it. I hurt his feelings. He doesn't know how to get around it. Rather than accepting my apology, he's sulking."

Lyric rolled her eyes. "Okay, let's move on. Who ya got?"

Tristan spent the previous evening doing her own research. She had a handful of cowboys and cowgirls she wanted to run by Lyric, but looking at the list in front of her, Lyric had almost twice the number she had.

"It isn't as though you're going to sponsor 'em all. It's just a starting point."

"Good. You scared me for a minute."

Some they crossed off the list without much discussion. Others they debated, and others stayed on the list without hesitation. In the end, they had ten potentials. Six cowboys, and four cowgirls. Tristan wanted it to be equal, so they went back to look through the barrel racers one more time.

"What about a female bull rider?"

"I don't know of any other than Mags Parker."

"There are a few more out there. Some up-and-comers mainly. Maybe you should talk to your daddy about two levels of sponsorship. One for the guys and girls who are already at the pro level, and another for the ones just startin' out."

It was something they'd talked about many times. For Lost Cowboy to get big names on their team, they had to recruit them early in their career. Once they achieved a certain level, Cinch or one of the other major clothing sponsors would be all over them.

"Good idea," Tristan murmured.

"What's up? You aren't as focused as you were last night."

"I'm giving your suggestion some thought. It's a good idea."

"Yeah, I'm like that," smiled Lyric. "I'm full of 'em. But which one in particular are you talkin' about?"

"Where's Bullet living?"

"*Scre-e-e-e-ch*. Whoa, girl. You gotta give me some warnin' before you bounce off the subject wall."

"Sorry. He's just on my mind. I tried to talk to him before you came in, but he wouldn't listen to me."

"He rented a place in town yesterday. It's furnished, which is a good thing. He doesn't have time for furniture shoppin'."

Tristan assumed he didn't have the money either. Crested Butte was not an inexpensive place to live.

"I'd like to talk to him before I leave tomorrow. You know, clear the air."

"What are you sittin' here for? Go find him."

Tristan thought it over for a minute, and then grabbed her jacket from the coat rack and went out the front door. The ranch was a big place. Who knew where he might be working?

She caught a glimpse of someone leading a horse into the arena. The man was built like Bullet, but she couldn't see his face. As she got closer, she saw he was working with a bronc.

"Shh now," she heard him say, his hands holding the catch rope lightly. "You can let your guard down. I ain't gonna hurt ya."

She listened to him soothe the horse. "Come on now, let's be friends. Let ol' Bullet take care of you."

It was the tone of voice one might use with a lover. It was slow and sultry, reinforcing the care he'd give, the time he'd take. Tristan leaned up against the fence, and closed her eyes. He coaxed and cajoled. Sweetly.

"Come on now, darlin'. That's a girl."

He was working with a filly? Surprising. Geldings typically made better broncs. Maybe this was just a spirited horse, not one they intended to take out to rodeos.

Tristan climbed up on the fence and watched as Bullet continued to soothe the horse, murmuring to her as he took the lead, and walked her around the arena.

"She's a beauty, ain't she?"

Tristan hadn't realized he knew she was there.

"She sure is." The palomino paint didn't look to be much over two years old, and about fifteen hands.

"You takin' her out?"

"Not yet. Not sure they ever will."

"What's her name?"

"Holbrook."

Tristan grinned. How did he know the name of her hometown? "Oh yeah? You playin' with me, cowboy?"

When Bullet smiled, she almost fell off the fence. It had been a while since one had been directed at her. The blue eyes that had been so frosty, warmed again when he winked at her.

He dropped the lead and walked over to where she sat.

"I'd like to be friends again," she said before he could say anything.

"Friends huh? I didn't realize that's what we were."

Tristan cheeks flushed. "I'd like to be."

"All right. We can be friends. If that's what you'd like," he drawled. As he got closer, she could see his dimples.

God, he was dangerous. He knew just what to say, and how to say it. If she was a little younger, and a lot dumber, he could talk her into just about anything. He put his hand on her knee.

"I'm sorry I ran out of the house so quick. I'm runnin' low on sleep and high on anxiety these days." The devastating smile didn't leave his face. He squeezed her knee. "Forgive me?"

"Bullet...I..." What was she trying to say? She couldn't think with him caressing her knee.

"Come on now, darlin'. Say you'll forgive me." He was using the same tone of voice with her that he used with the filly. And it was working just as well on her as it had with the horse.

She brushed his hand away. "There isn't anything to forgive. I was the one that insulted you. You still haven't accepted my apology."

Bullet leaned in closer, so his body rested up against her leg, his hand came back to rub her knee. "I haven't? Well, now." His hand stopped moving and he looked up at her face. "Tristan, I accept your apology."

***

1965

It had been four years since he first set foot on what was now called the Double-P-Bar Ranch. The had changed soon after he arrived with Clancy, since there were now two Pattersons at the helm. It had also been four years since he'd seen his mama.

When Clancy offered to take him to Colorado Springs to see her, Bill didn't hesitate to take him up on it. He missed her so much. And his sister. There was something important his mama wanted to tell him, that's what Clancy had said. Bill hoped it wasn't more bad news. His family had more than their fair share of strife in the last five years.

It took them seven hours to make the drive. The weather over Loveland Pass was rough, which made Bill worry more. If Clancy was making this drive in the middle of winter, his mother's news must be mighty important.

Clancy slugged Bill's arm. "Stop worryin' so much."

"Can't help it. Did she tell you anything at all?"

"She did, but she made me promise not to tell. So you gotta wait."

Clancy was smiling. If it was bad news he wouldn't be smiling. Right? Bill continued to chew on his fingernails. He couldn't help it.

His mama came running out the back door of the house as soon as Clancy drove up. Bill had the truck door open and was running toward her just as fast.

"Oh, my boy," she cried, "how I've missed you."

His little sister wasn't far behind, with stears in her eyes. "Look how big you've gotten," he said to her.

"Me? Look at you!"

"Let me look at you," said his mama. "She's right, you've grown a foot or more." She started to cry again.

"Oh, Clancy," she reached out to him. "How can I thank you for takin' my boy in?"

Clancy tipped his hat. "No thanks necessary, Mrs. Flynn. Bill here is a real hard worker. We're happy to have him up at the ranch."

She put her hand on his arm. "It's more than that, and we both know it is. I don't know what we would've done without you." Bill swore Clancy's weathered skin reddened.

He had a million questions. For starters, whose house was she living in? He knew it was far nicer than she could afford. He wondered if she and his sister worked for room and board. He hoped not, but that was the most likely explanation.

"Come inside, it's freezing out here." She took his hand and pulled him the direction of the door, and then put her arm around his shoulders.

A man came out the same door they were heading in. "There's someone I want you to meet. Someone very special. Bill, this is Russ Snyder. Russ, this is my son, Bill."

"Nice to meet you," said Russ, shaking Bill's hand.

"You too, sir." There was something about the man that didn't sit right with Bill. Something in his eyes.

Clancy offered to find another place to bunk for the night, but his mama insisted he stay with them at Mr. Snyder's place. He had a guest room with two twin beds in it, she told him. He and Bill wouldn't mind sharing a room, would they?

After thanking Mr. Snyder and Bill's mama for their hospitality, Clancy suggested they call it a night. They'd had a long day of travel, he told them, and they were both mighty tired.

Bill wasn't tired at all, and he doubted Clancy was either. He hoped this meant they'd have a chance to talk. The longer Bill was around Mr. Snyder, the less he liked him. His little sister didn't seem all that fond of him either. The only person who seemed to like the man was his mama, and she liked him a lot.

"You didn't do a very good job of hidin' your feelings, son," Clancy said as he closed the bedroom door behind him.

"Should I have?"

"Yes, you should've."

"Why? You can't tell me there ain't somethin' 'bout the man that rubs you the wrong way."

"No I can't say that."

"Can't say what? There is somethin' or there ain't somethin'?"

Clancy opened the door a crack. "Let's wait a bit before we have this conversation. I think they're headed to bed too."

That was more than Bill wanted to think about. His mama was sharing a bed with this man, and they weren't married. If his papa wasn't already turning in his grave over his wife being with another man, this would have him clawing his way out of the ground.

A few minutes passed. Clancy told him to follow him outside, and to be quiet about it. They crept down the hall, and out the door by the kitchen.

"You're right, young Flynn. I don't like the man much," Clancy began once they were inside the cab of the truck. "Can't put my finger on why not, but there's somethin' about him."

"See? So why'd you say I shoulda' hid my feelings?"

"Listen to me now." Clancy looked over at him. "Are ya listenin'?"

"Yes, sir," Bill muttered.

"Your mama is fixin' to tell you that she and Mr. Snyder are gonna get married. That's the important news."

Bill put his head down. He didn't know what to say. She couldn't be planning to marry him. She just couldn't.

"I don't know yet what their timin' is. Could be next week, could be next year. Although considerin' she wanted me to get you down here right away, I'm thinkin' next week is more like it."

A terrible thought crossed Bill's mind. "She don't want me to stay here, does she?"

"I don't have a read on that yet. Seems if she wanted you to, she woulda asked me to bring your gear down with us. And she didn't ask me to do that. She just asked me to bring you."

"Maybe he doesn't want her son around. Maybe that's the bad feelin' I get from him, that he doesn't want me."

Clancy rubbed his chin. "Possibly, but I think it's more than that."

"Yeah, me too."

7

"Got a minute, Billy?"

"Ya know, I've been meaning to ask you somethin'. Is Bullet a nickname?"

"Uh, no. It's my name." Bullet couldn't always follow Billy's line of thinking. Sometimes the guy came out of left field.

"Pretty cool name. How'd you get it?"

"Uh, my parents. How'd you get yours?"

"Smart ass. I'm a junior. So come on, tell me. Your parents really named you Bullet?"

"Yep." Billy was working on his last nerve.

"You ever ask if there was a story behind it?"

"It's always been my name. Never seemed unusual to me."

"I mean, Lyric, that makes sense. Your dad bein' a rock star and all."

"Number one with a *bullet*."

The expression on Billy's face changed in an instant. "You couldn't have told me that ten questions ago?"

"Nope."

Billy laughed, and grabbed Bullet's shoulder. "You fit in right perfect, ol' Bullet. Damn smart ass, ornery bastard. So what did you wanna talk to me about?"

"Bull ridin'."

"That's what I figured. Been waitin' for you to bring it up. Everybody has. We got a deal all worked out for when you finally did."

"Oh yeah? What kinda deal?"

"Now don't get your panties all twisted up. It's a good one."

Bullet folded his arms across his chest and waited.

"Here's the thing. My daddy isn't too keen on the idea of raisin' rough stock up at his place in Black Forest. The truth is, he isn't too keen on what he refers to as *modern rodeo*."

"Why are you involving him if he doesn't want to do it?"

"Because we need the support in El Paso County. We're partnerin' with TZ Bucking Bulls in Larkspur, but that's just bulls. We need a bronc operation too."

Bullet shrugged his shoulders and looked off in the distance.

"You got an opinion? Now's the time to tell me."

"I'd say the land belongs to your daddy, and if doesn't want to do it, ain't nothin' gonna change his mind."

"That's where you come in."

"Oh no. No way. I'm not gettin' in the middle of this. I hardly know you, let alone your family. Go fight your own battles." Bullet walked away.

"Don't you wanna know how this involves gettin' you on bulls?"

He stopped. "How?"

"My daddy's gonna be your trainer, and Flying R is gonna be your sponsor."

Bullet turned around. "Is this another thing he ain't too 'keen' on?"

"Nope, he's all for it."

Bullet walked back over to where Billy stood. "This doesn't add up. If he's against raisin' rough stock because he's against rodeo, why would he train me on bulls?"

"Guess that's somethin' you're gonna have to ask him."

"I wouldn't walk in that water wearin' your boots."

"I don't know what the hell that means, but I'm headed to Black Forest tomorrow. Renie and Willow are comin' with me. You and your son can follow us. We'll talk to my daddy and straighten all this out."

Bullet didn't see he had much choice. He worked for Flying R, and if one of the partners told him he had to go to Black Forest, then that's what he had to do.

"Hey, Daddy, I'd like you to meet Ben Rice. Ben, this is my father."

"Nice to meet you Mr. McCullough." Ben stepped forward to shake hands.

"Call me Hugh, and it's nice to finally meet you in person. Can't thank you enough for getting my girl home safe and sound."

"And this is my grandfather, Hugh McCullough Senior, although everyone calls him Gramps."

"Hello, sir," Ben shook her grandfather's hand, who then turned to Tristan. "Fancy stuff, little girl, travelin' in a private plane."

Tristan smiled. "Not something I plan to get used to." She didn't want Ben to think she expected door-to-door plane service on a regular basis.

"My pleasure. And it was necessary. I'll do just about anything to put off comin' to New York City. Havin' another reason to fly east forces me to take care of business."

Ben told Tristan his agent had been threatening to withhold his royalty checks until he made the trip. "He wasn't serious. But that tells you how mad he's been at me for avoiding the business side of my profession." He told her how hard it was to leave Crested Butte. He hated being away from Liv, their little girl, and the two sons he had from a previous marriage. He knew touring was necessary for the band to continue to sell records, but anything else was easy to put off.

Tristan understood. Sometimes she felt as though all she did was travel. Having a place she never wanted to leave, having people in her life she never wanted to be away from was something she couldn't comprehend. Although, she was yearning to get back to Crested Butte too, and it hadn't been twenty-four hours since she left.

Her dad offered to let Ben use one of their ranch vehicles to drive into the city. He declined and took the train from Ronkonkoma instead. "I'm a boy from the mountains, used to wide-open spaces. I'm not built for city drivin'," he'd told them.

Tristan offered to drive him back to the train station a couple of days later.

"What do you think of Bullet?" she asked him.

Ben rubbed his hand over his face. "As Liv would say, 'Bullet is one hot mess.' I know, I was one myself. Cowboy Patterson seems to think spendin' time in Black Forest on their family's ranch will help rein him in."

"Cowboy Patterson?"

Ben laughed. "I was never a big fan of ol' Billy. Still can't say I am. Although now that he's my business partner, and my son-in-law, I suppose I should work on gettin' over it."

"Do you think being in Black Forest will make a difference?"

"Can't predict whether it will or won't, but if there's a woman alive Bullet might listen to, it's Dottie Patterson."

"Yeah? Why's that?"

"You know the type. Some people just have a way about them. Dottie is a second mother to my Livvie, and one of the most loving people I've known in my life. You should meet her. She'll look straight into your soul, and then wrap her arms around you in the best hug you can imagine."

Tristan looked away when her eyes filled with tears. Dottie sounded like her mother. She'd been that way too. She always seemed to know the right thing to say, even if it was nothing at all. When she was a little girl, getting a hug and a smile from her mom always made things better.

Miss Dottie's cooking reminded Bullet of his Gram's. Every time he walked in to the kitchen, she was cooking something that made his stomach growl. Her homemade macaroni and cheese was extra gooey, rich with butter, fresh cream, and a blend of sharp and mild cheddar cheeses. She added crumbled bacon to it as a twist. Grey ate two big bowlfuls and was asking for a third when Bullet swept him out of the high chair.

"He sure likes your cookin', ma'am. And so do I."

Dottie beamed at the little boy. "It's my pleasure, Grey. You're welcome at my table anytime." She opened her arms and Grey ran straight into them. It was another thing that reminded him of his Gram. Dottie's hugs.

"I love having little ones in the house. I miss my granddaughter when she's in Crested Butte," Dottie looked at Willow, Billy and Renie's three-year-old daughter. At a little over a year old months, Grey was almost as tall as the little girl.

"Say hi to my baby," Willow pulled Dottie toward Renie. Dottie obliged by rubbing Renie's belly. "Not too long before you have a little brother or sister."

"I'm having a brodder." Willow put her hands on her hips.

"Is that right?" Dottie asked Renie, who shrugged her shoulders.

"Willow changes her mind daily. Sometimes she's sure she's having a little sister."

"You didn't find out?" Bullet asked Billy.

Billy stood behind Renie and put his arms around her waist. "We decided it'd be more fun this way."

Bullet had never known that kind of easy affection. When he refused to marry his daughter's mother, and told her he doubted he was the baby's father, she stopped speaking to him. After the little girl was born, and the DNA test proved he was her biological father, they'd tried to be friends. Sometimes they managed okay. Not very often though.

Callie had done a good job of hiding her "dark side," as he liked to call it, until after they got married. Even then, their relationship wasn't like Billy and Renie's. Bullet told himself he loved Callie, but being around the Pattersons made him question whether what he felt was really love.

"Got a minute?" Billy's father asked Bullet.

"Go ahead, " said Renie. "I'll keep an eye on Grey. He and Willow can play."

"You sure?" Bullet felt as though he was always imposing on someone to watch Grey. Once he figured out where he was going to be based, he'd have to look for a regular babysitter or day care.

When Renie waved him off, he followed Billy's dad out the back door.

"I understand you're going to be working here with me."

"That's up to you, Mr. Patterson."

"Call me Bill, young man. And my son isn't giving me much choice."

"As I told your son, this here is your land. If you don't want to be involved with rough stock, you shouldn't be."

"Let's say I changed my mind. How would you feel about working here?"

Bullet wasn't sure what to say. As long as he had a job, he didn't really care where he was working. Being in Black Forest was convenient because he and Grey could stay with Lyric. The drive from her place here would take less than half an hour.

He'd have to give the place up he'd just rented in Crested Butte, but that wouldn't be hard to do. He hadn't gotten around to moving much of anything of his into the furnished apartment anyway. What had been there of his, he'd packed to bring himself and Grey here. He could make arrangements to give it up over the phone, and send the keys to the property management company. That's how transient his life was now; he could almost live out of two suitcases.

"The job comes with that place over there," said Bill, as though he was reading Bullet's mind. He pointed east, toward a house that sat closer to the road.

"Who lives there now?"

"Nobody's lived there on a regular basis for years. Dottie keeps it on the ready though. Just in case. It's the house we lived in when we were first married."

"My sister has a place in Palmer Lake. Grey and I can stay with her."

"Nah. Workin' here means livin' here. You managed a ranch before?"

Managed? *Hell no*. How in the world could he manage a ranch, take care of Grey, and get on bulls?

"Son, I asked you a question."

"No, sir, I haven't come close. I don't know what Billy told you, but I'm a ranch hand for Flying R."

"You think you could learn?"

"I know I could, but…"

"Go on, speak your mind."

"I got my hands full, Mr. Patterson. I still ain't figured out how to take care of Grey and hold down a regular job, let alone manage a ranch. I wouldn't know where to begin."

"You'd begin by learnin'. You'd be workin' with me, learnin' the ropes. For the time bein' you'll only manage the rough stock portion of the ranch. I got a guy been with me a long time that manages the cattle operation."

That was some relief. He understood rough stock. It was everything else that gave him pause.

"There's somethin' else isn't there, Bullet?"

"What's that, sir?"

"Bull ridin'. You're lookin' for trainer, aren't you?"

"Yes, sir. I am." Bullet took his hat off and rubbed his forehead. This conversation was giving him a headache.

"Let's go back to the house. We'll have a sit down with Dottie and Billy and see what we can figure out."

"Yes, sir," Bullet said again.

"My name's Bill, son, I told you that before. We're gonna be spendin' a hell of a lot of time together, and if you keep callin' me sir, it's gonna make me uncomfortable."

"Yes, sir. I mean, Bill."

There were three hundred photos waiting for Tristan to sort through, and her father had another pile he wanted her to look through.

The one on top was of a bull rider Lost Cowboy sponsored. The photographer had captured him flying through the air, just as the bull bucked him off. Her father had written the words, "It's not how good you are…it's how good you want to be," on a sticky note on the back of the photo along with the digital image reference number.

Tristan opened the digital file, and adjusted the highlights and shadows of the photo in an image enhancement software program. Next she added a blend near the bottom of the image, and then superimposed the words her father had written on top of the darkened area.

She repeated the same process with the rest of the photos her father had asked her to look through. She added a date to each one, and then sent them to a local high school student who interned for Lost Cowboy.

The images would be uploaded to social media sites on the dates Tristan indicated in the file name.

The only time the prearranged schedule varied was if something significant happened either with one of their riders, or in the world. In that case, no matter where Tristan was, her father would email her a photo along with his caption, and she'd prepare the image and upload it herself.

"Got some good ones the last couple of weeks," her father said, and sat down in the chair by her desk.

"Really good ones, Daddy. I especially like this one." The image was a silhouette of a cowboy sitting on a fence, watching the sun set. The caption her father wrote was, "Most people don't listen with the intent to understand. They listen with the intent to reply."

It was one of life's lessons she learned from him. "A conversation is like a game of catch," he'd say. "If you're not payin' attention, you're gonna get hit with the ball."

Bullet sat in a rocking chair in the kitchen holding Grey, who was sound asleep on his lap. He didn't have the heart to move him. Billy and Renie had gone back to their place, which was just up the road, but Dottie and Bill were close by, cleaning up from dinner.

"What do you think?" he heard Dottie ask Bill.

"About what?"

Dottie must've swatted Bill with something, and the two of them laughed.

"He reminds me of someone."

"He reminds me of someone too. And so do you."

"Me? I thought we were talkin' about Bullet."

"Clancy. The way you talk to him, Bill. It reminds me of the way Clancy used to talk to you."

"That's a right fine compliment, sweetheart."

Bullet could hear the emotion in Bill's voice, even from the other room. Who was Clancy, and what did he have to do with Bill and him?

***

1965

The weather was better for their drive back to the ranch. Not that Bill was thinking much about weather. Clancy had been right. His mama told him that she and Mr. Snyder were getting married. She didn't say a word about him coming to live with them, and he didn't ask.

"She gave me hell about your schoolin'," grimaced Clancy when they stopped for lunch.

She'd asked Bill if he was keeping up with his school work, and he'd muttered that he was, but nothing could have been further from the truth. There wasn't a school close to Double-P-Bar Ranch, and even if there was, as an employee of the ranch, he wouldn't have time to go to school during the day.

He and Clancy had talked about it a few times. There were other workers at the ranch with children who were home schooled. Clancy had been willing to let Bill give it a try by teaming up with one of the other families, but Bill hadn't done anything to make it happen. He was thirteen. Lots of kids whose families made their living on a ranch quit school before then.

"Your mama made me promise to get you back to learnin'."

"I already missed two years. Nothin' but a waste of time."

Clancy squinted his eyes and raised his index finger. "I promised her I'd do it, and we're gonna. Even if it means I gotta school ya myself."

"Oh yeah? You got somethin' past a sixth grade education?"

The index finger came back up, and Clancy reached across the table to poke him in the chest. "One thing you're gonna learn is respect for your elders, boy."

Bill hated that he'd just disrespected Clancy. The man had been good to him. "I'm sorry, sir. I know better than to talk to you like that. And I sure know you're a smart man."

"You're damn straight I am. And if you wanna know the truth, I got a college degree to prove it. I'm ashamed of myself in lettin' your education slide, but not anymore. We're gettin' you back on track, young Flynn."

Clancy hadn't been kidding. Before they went back to the ranch, they stopped in Glenwood Springs, where Clancy ordered a bunch of books and other supplies from the bookstore.

"This is where the others get their materials. You'll test at the school here too." They stopped by the office and registered Bill for independent study. With as many ranches as there were in this part of Colorado, home schooling was common.

Each day Bill was expected to get up at dawn, and do his chores, which had been greatly reduced. When he finished, he was expected to work on his lessons. Clancy would come back to the house they shared, have lunch, and review Bill's work. If there was anything Bill didn't understand, he had an hour of Clancy's time to go over it. There was more school work to do in the early afternoon, and then Bill was expected to do his afternoon chores.

Around six in the evening, he'd meet Clancy and the rest of the cowboys at the dining hall for dinner.

After dinner Bill had free time. He'd stopped writing a letter every night to his mama. Instead he used the time for reading, or getting ahead on his lessons.

It wasn't long before he'd made up the two years he'd missed, and was close to a full year ahead of his age level.

It had been embarrassing every time he showed up at the school and they'd asked what level he was there to test for. Now when they asked, he'd be able to hold his head high.

His grades were good too. He and Clancy had even started talking about colleges, although Bill didn't see how it would be possible for him to go. It wasn't just a question of how he'd be able to be away from the ranch, there was also the cost of it.

"You could get on a rodeo team," one of the cowboys told him at dinner.

"What are you talkin' about?"

"You aren't good enough now, but if you're willin' to put the time in, Western State has a good team."

"For what?"

"Junior Rodeo," he answered, as though Bill was a complete dumbass.

Bill had been getting on some of the smaller bulls and broncs for a few months. At first it had been on a dare, but he took to it like a fish to water. He didn't

have the money to enter any rodeos, but he still prac-
ticed whenever they had time on the ranch.

To him there wasn't anything like the thrill he felt
when he heard the bell ring indicating he'd stayed on a
bull the full eight seconds.

He was getting pretty good at bareback bronc riding, and he wasn't half bad at tie-down roping. Usually
to compete in the all-around competitions, a cowboy
had to focus on roping, either tie-down or team roping,
and steer wrestling, but the requirement was to compete in at least two events.

Bareback bronc riding and bull riding worked, and
if he added the tie-down roping, he'd be well-qualified.
Was it really something he could do in college? It didn't
seem possible.

"That's right," Sadie the cook said overhearing
their conversation. "My niece goes to Western State,
you remember Misty, don't ya?"

Bill nodded that he did, although it wasn't Misty he
thought about from time to time, it was her sister,
Dottie. And he thought about her more than from time
to time.

Dottie and Misty came back to the ranch one more
year. After that he'd heard Sadie say that the girls had
gotten involved in so many activities at home, they
didn't have time to visit. Instead, she'd visit them in

Gunnison, where her sister lived. Whenever she came back, she'd tell Bill that Dottie had asked after him.

"You should write her a letter," Sadie told him. He would, but he wouldn't know the first thing he'd say to her if he did.

"I think she's considerin' Western State, too."

She was? That changed everything.

"What's so interestin' to you about college all of a sudden?" Clancy asked.

"Just wanna better myself is all."

The phone rang and Clancy stood to answer it. There was only one phone in the ranch house, and it was in the kitchen. Bill was in earshot, and he didn't like the tone in Clancy's voice.

8

"I can't wait either, it seems as though it's been months since I've been to Crested Butte. Does that sound crazy? It's only been three weeks," Tristan said to Liv.

"I know. I've been pestering Ben incessantly about getting you back out here."

The two spoke a couple of times a week since Tristan left Colorado, although in the last few days, it had become daily. The two talked a lot about barrel racing, so much so that Tristan was beginning to miss it.

For the longest time barrel racing reminded her of things, and people, she'd as soon forget. She talked about the sport with Liv, not the lifestyle. They also talked about many promising young competitors.

Tristan had been working on new clothing designs that would serve as Lost Cowboy's first true women's collection. She hadn't shown her sketches to her father yet, she wanted to get feedback from other women in the industry first. She hadn't told Liv about them either. She wanted her friend's initial reaction to be authentic, not based on anything Tristan told her beforehand.

"How's the Black Forest operation going? Have you heard?"

"From what I understand it's going quite well. Renie told me Billy's nose was out of joint at how well his dad and Bullet are getting on already."

"Really? How interesting."

"I told her to tell him to be careful what he wished for," Liv paused. "I use that expression a lot. But it's so true. What we ask of the universe sometimes comes back to us more quickly than we anticipate."

Sound thinking, and very true words. Tristan began jotting down things Liv said while she was in Crested Butte. Things Ben said too. In fact, she took notes on many expressions she'd heard from the Rice and Patterson families. She planned to work them into Lost Cowboy's upcoming social media posts.

"They'll all be here next week."

"Who all?"

"Billy and Renie, Bullet, even Bill and Dottie are coming. I can't wait to see them…"

Liv was talking about Bill and Dottie, something about how much she missed them. But all Tristan could think about was Bullet. He'd be in Crested Butte next week. She was hoping he'd be there when she was, but wouldn't dare have asked.

"You're done for today," Bill told Bullet.

"What do you mean? Why?"

"Your head isn't in it. You're not paying attention to me or the two-thousand pound animal you're tryin' to ride. You'll get yourself killed that way."

Bullet couldn't argue. They were leaving for Crested Butte tomorrow, and that's where his head was instead of on the practice bull.

"I'm sorry, Bill."

"Don't apologize to me. You wanna quit training, just say the word. All I'm doin' is sittin' on the fence watchin'. You're the one who's got the work to do."

Bill might be sitting on the fence, but the bull hands weren't. And if he wasn't taking it seriously, he was wasting their time too.

"Ride the buck, not the bull," Bill had been shouting at him. "Think less, feel more. Quit tryin' to wrangle him. Ride the pattern."

Bullet knew all this. He heard Bill's voice in his head when he was in the chute mounting on. It was the time in between that got him today. Once he eased his toes down the bull's side, careful not to touch him with his spurs, he stopped hearing Bill's voice, and heard Tristan's instead.

"It's irresponsible for him to even try riding bulls. He has a child to raise." Those weren't the exact words he'd overheard her say, but they were close enough.

Once the chute opened he didn't have time to think about much other than staying alive, if only to prove her wrong. And Bill was right, that would get him killed.

Bullet and the partners were on their way to Flying R Rough Stock headquarters for a sponsored rider meeting. The cowboys and cowgirls who were already on the team would be there, along with new recruits being considered.

While Bullet was on the Flying R team, both as an employee, and as a rider, it was the Lost Cowboy team he was vying for. It didn't matter that Flying R was the bigger fish. If he was wearing the LC brand, it would mean he'd won Tristan over.

"We're leavin' at the crack of dawn tomorrow morning. Get some rest tonight." Bill climbed down the fence and walked in the direction of the barn. "Oh, and Dottie wanted me to tell you she left dinner on the back stoop."

"Thank her for me," Bullet shouted back.

Bill waved and went into the barn.

Bullet looked at his phone. He had another hour before he had to pick Grey up from the babysitter. He could stick around and pull gates for the other guys.

Miss Dottie made dinner for him and Grey almost every night. He'd thank her, and then tell her she didn't have to, only to have her shush him every time.

"No sense letting good food go to waste," she'd say. Bullet didn't dare suggest she not make as much.

Liv insisted she'd pick Tristan up at the airfield in Gunnison. She didn't have Caden with her this time, so she suggested they take the opportunity to have a quieter "girls' lunch."

Tristan brought her portfolio in with her. "Would you mind giving me your opinion on some new designs?"

Liv clapped her hands. "I'd love to. I'm so excited."

"It isn't anything that special, just a few sketches for a new line."

"Tristan, I spend most of my time listening to conversations about bull semen, and other equally disgusting rough stock minutiae. My girl talk is limited to making conversation with Caden and her dolls. Please, show me your work. I'm begging you."

"Remember these are preliminary." Tristan set her sketchbook on the table in front of Liv, and then watched her slowly turn the pages.

"Well?"

Liv flipped back to the beginning. "I absolutely love the riding jackets. I don't know if I can decide which one I like best. You'll have to make them all, and in my size."

"Really? You like them?"

"No. I love them. They're beautiful. So colorful. What's this?" Liv pointed to the detail on one of the jackets.

"Turquoise inlay."

"Yes! That would work perfectly." Liv flipped the page and asked more questions. "They're magnificent." She pointed to another sketch on the page. "What are these?"

Tristan had sketched out complementary riding pants as well as undergarments designed specifically for riding.

"I didn't realize Lost Cowboy was offering a new line."

"I haven't broached the subject with my father yet. I'm not sure—"

"Before you say another word, listen to me. You have to produce this line. There's nothing else like it. Even if I never rode again in my life, I'd buy all of it. Every piece."

Tristan was smiling from ear to ear. Liv's enthusiasm was authentic enough that she couldn't question her reaction.

"I wish I had one of your new jackets to wear to tonight's dinner. It's gonna be a serious shindig."

"I haven't heard anything about it."

"I'm not surprised. The boys aren't big on advance notice. I can tell you this much, Flying R rented out Tracker's Bar at Mountaineer Square, and Ben's band is playing after dinner. I hope you brought your dancing boots."

"Are you sure I'm invited?"

"Of course you are. Everyone is. All the partners, and you're a partner, plus all the riders. I warned Ben that putting that many cowboys and cowgirls together when his band is playing is risky." Liv winked at Tristan.

She'd been listening to CB Rice music since she left Crested Butte. Ben's music was definitely sexy, especially the records the band had released since Ben married Liv.

"You have heard that Flying R is sponsoring Bullet, right?"

"Is that your way of warning me he'll be there tonight?"

"Yes. Are you okay with that?"

"Why wouldn't I be? I mean, Bullet and I will likely cross paths often. I guess I didn't tell you we made up before I left."

"You didn't. What happened?"

Tristan told Liv that she and Bullet talked before she left, and he had accepted her apology. "I'm sure he'll be busy getting to know the barrel racers we invited to the meet and greet."

"Maybe. Then again, he did specifically ask if you were coming into town this week."

"He's just interested in Lost Cowboy's sponsorship."

Liv patted her hand. "You keep tellin' yourself that, girlfriend."

"How's this one look?"

"God, Bullet, would you stop changin' your shirt? The last five you tried on looked fine."

"I'm goin' for better than fine, Lyric."

"Why's that? Somebody gonna be at the dinner tonight you're aimin' to impress?"

"Heard there's a new batch of barrel racers gonna be there." He was lying. He didn't care about anyone invited other than Tristan.

When he brought Grey over to play with Caden this morning, he asked Liv if Tristan was arriving in time to attend the dinner, and she'd told him she was leaving in an hour to pick her up from the airport. If he hadn't had so much work to do he would've offered to go in her place.

"Tristan McCullough's the reason you're in such a state, and we both know it."

"Just tell me which shirt looks the best. This one or the green one?"

"The blue one. It makes your eyes look bluer." Lyric rolled her eyes at him. "You're not wearin' those boots are you?"

"Yeah, what's wrong with 'em?"

"They could use a good polish for starters."

"Shit. I don't have time to polish my boots now. Why didn't you say somethin' earlier?"

"For goodness sake. Take 'em off. I'll do it."

"No, I'll do it," he grumbled. Damn, this woman had him rattled. He didn't remember the last time he was this nervous. Maybe before the first time he got laid.

He saw her as soon as he walked into the bar. Tristan was across the room, talking to a cowboy he recognized. Stormy was his name, and he'd been bragging earlier about nailing a Lost Cowboy sponsorship.

She was looking mighty fine tonight with her Cowgirl Tuff jeans tucked into her deep red boots, her red and silver fringed shirt hugging her womanly curves. The other cowboys had to have noticed too.

Something Stormy said made Tristan laugh, which burned a hole in Bullet's gut. When he saw the guy reach out and touched her hair, it took Bullet all of five seconds to cross the room.

"Hey, asshole, I don't think the lady wants you mawlin' her."

"Bullet!" Tristan gasped, and then looked at Stormy. "I'm sorry."

"Don't apologize for me." Bullet leaned in closer to her. "Don't mind you talkin' with other fellas while you're waitin' on me, but I draw the line at them touchin' you."

"Waiting on you? Are you joking?" Tristan spun away from Bullet's grasp on her arm, but Stormy had already walked away.

"Hey, darlin', it sure is nice to see you."

"Give me a break, Bullet. I told you once before I'm not your darlin'. Now if you'll excuse me, I have a conversation to finish with one of our new riders."

She shouldn't have rubbed his nose in it like that, but he made her mad with his caveman antics.

"Can I buy you a drink, cowboy?" she approached Stormy, who was standing at the bar.

"Open bar, ma'am, but I'll take a rain check if you're willin'."

"It would be my pleasure. I'm so sorry about Bullet. I don't know—"

"It's okay, Tristan. Bullet's got a reputation for settin' his sights on a pretty lady and not givin' up until she's his, if you know what I mean."

"Yeah, I know what you mean, and I assure you, I'll *never* be his."

"Glad to hear it. Uh, does Lost Cowboy have a rule against the boss lady dancin' with a rider?"

"Of course not, and if we did, my daddy is a long way from here, and would never know."

She danced with Stormy for two songs, and then excused herself.

Had she really just told a cowboy that she'd bend the rules for him because her father would never know? What had gotten into her? It was Bullet dammit. She looked around the room and didn't see him. Maybe he left after embarrassing himself. She looked around a second time, but still didn't see him.

When Tristan turned back to the bar, Bullet was standing next to her. "Who ya lookin' for, darlin'?"

"No one," she scowled. "Just seeing who else is here."

He held out his hand. "Dance with me?"

"I don't think that's a good idea."

"Come on now, one dance won't hurt any."

Bullet was using the same tone of voice he had the last time she saw him. The same one he used with the filly. Why was it sending chills up her spine?

"You think you're pretty smooth, don't you?"

"Nah, I'm not like that, Tristan. You should know better." He leaned in, close enough that she could hear him breathing. "Dance with me," he whispered.

"Um, maybe one song." What was she doing? Getting closer to him was not a good idea. Why wasn't she walking in the opposite direction? Instead, she let him lead her to the dance floor.

"That's my girl," he whispered as he drew her close. Much too close.

* * *

1967

"Calm down now, and start over. What happened?"

Bill joined Clancy in the kitchen. When he did, Clancy shook his head. "I'll get there as soon as I can."

When he hung up the phone, he rested his hand on Bill's shoulder. "Son," he began, "there's some trouble with your mama."

More bad news. Bill was beginning to think his family was cursed. Clancy made two more phone calls after the first. Bill went up to his bedroom because Clancy asked for privacy.

"I'm goin' alone this time," he said after he asked Bill to come back downstairs.

"Are you gonna tell me what it's about?"

"I'm not, and I need you to trust that I'm makin' the right decision by not tellin' you."

"Did he hurt her?" Bill caught Clancy's wince.

"No, son, not in the way you think."

Bill didn't like it one bit that Clancy was keeping something from him, especially since it was about his mother and sister.

"I don't like it."

"I know you don't." Clancy put his hand on Bill's shoulder. "As I said before, I need you to trust me. Can you do that?"

9

The spring schedule was set. Bullet would be moving broncs from the Crested Butte operation to Patterson
Ranch in Black Forest later in the month. Next month
he'd move more broncs to Black Forest from Jace Rice's
place in Montana.

Doing it now would give him time to evaluate the
stock and determine which horses he and Bill would
take to each of the events before the rodeo season
kicked into high gear.

"You sure about this?" Bullet asked Bill when the
bronc meeting broke up.

"About what specifically?"

"All of it."

Bill smiled at Dottie, who had been in the meeting
with the rest of the Flying R partners. "Been a long time
since my girl and I traveled the rodeo circuit. We made
a lot of friends over the years, some we haven't seen
since Billy retired from ridin'."

Bullet shook his head. "I don't get it. Billy tells me
you aren't keen on what you call modern rodeo, yet
your son was a national saddle bronc champion.
Where's the disconnect?"

Before Bill could answer, Dottie rested her hand on his arm. "It's the timed events Bill has a harder time with."

"But aren't those events closest to what happens in a cattle operation every day?"

"No, son," answered Bill. "At least not in the same way. Sure, we rope. But it's different when you're tryin' to do it in a number of seconds."

"What's your stand on ranch rodeos?"

"I have to admit I prefer them, what about you, Dottie?"

"The Working Ranch Cowboys Association is goin' on twenty years in operation. We've participated in their Ride for the Brand cattle drive in Colorado Springs for ten years."

"I think it's been longer than that, but you're right. I'm much more 'keen' on ranch rodeo events than I am on the Professional Rodeo Cowboy Association's events, for example."

Bullet needed to have his head examined. Instead of focusing on the two rodeo circuits he'd need to compete on to achieve his own dreams, he was talking to Bill and Dottie about the ranch rodeos instead.

There was no way he could travel solely to ranch rodeos and compete in other events. He'd need to be in two places at the same time. And he was the stupid one who brought it up. *Why?*

If he didn't compete in enough PRCA sanctioned events, he'd never qualify for the Super Bowl of rodeo, the National Finals Rodeo held in Las Vegas in December. The same with the Professional Bull Riders, which was the organization Bullet wanted most to ride with. Initially was hoping to ride for the Touring Pro Division, considered the minor league of the PBR. As a Touring Pro rider, Bullet could compete in PBR-sanctioned events and start moving up in earnings to qualify for the bigger events.

But neither the PRCA or PBR had anything whatsoever to do with ranch rodeos.

"You got a problem now, don't ya, son?" Bill rested his hand on Bullet's shoulder.

He gave them a fake smile. "Nah. No problems. Only opportunities."

Bill and Dottie were good to him, and putting his desire to be a professional bull rider in front of what they were doing didn't sit right with him. At the end of the day, he needed a steady paycheck, and a home for Grey. He didn't need the thrill associated with covering a bull for eight seconds, he just wanted it.

Bill squeezed Bullet's shoulder. "Don't worry, son. We'll work it out. The Flying R partners aren't gonna be satisfied with ranch rodeos alone."

Bullet felt sick to his stomach, and more than anything, needed to go for a walk. He felt his dream slipping further out of his reach, and he didn't want Bill and Dottie to sense his frustration. He used the excuse that he was going to check on the filly he'd been working with the last time he was in Crested Butte.

"I get the prize for biggest mouth, that's for damn sure," Tristan overheard Bullet say to the horse. "Why in hell I can't learn to keep it shut I just don't know."

The horse reared, probably because of the tone Bullet was using. The filly could sense Bullet's anger and frustration just as well as she could.

She'd gone outside to stretch her legs, and feel the sun on her face. The back-to-back meetings all day were wearing on her, but the next one was hers, and that made all the difference. In a few minutes the Lost Cowboy sponsorship meeting would begin. She was equal parts nervous and excited about signing new team members. In years past, they hadn't signed five competitors. Today they were signing twenty. And Bullet wasn't one of them.

He hadn't brought it up last night either. She'd expected him to, particularly after the run-in with Stormy. Instead, he danced with her. Tristan lost count of how many times. After the first two songs, Bullet went to the bar and got them both a drink while Tristan talked to Lyric about today's meetings. Before she could get too deep into business mode, he whisked her back to the dance floor. Bullet was a good dancer. That hadn't been a surprise, but his graciousness, and their conversations, had been unexpected.

This morning Lyric told her about Bullet's late wife's struggles with bipolar disorder, and how hard Bullet had tried to make their marriage work. Tristan was beginning to think she'd been wrong in her initial assessment of him.

"You talkin' to yourself or the horse?" she shouted out to him. Bullet waved, slapped the horse's hindquarters, and walked over to her.

"Needed some time outdoors. Bein' inside all day was gettin' to me. I'm not one for sittin' in meetings."

"Me too." Tristan looked up at the mountains surrounding the ranch. The sky was so blue set against the green of the trees. No photo could capture its intensity.

"Beautiful here, isn't it?"

When Tristan opened her eyes, Bullet stood right next to her. "It's the same in Black Forest. Sometimes

Grey and I lie right down on the grass and watch the clouds move across the sky."

"Mmm, that sounds wonderful."

Bullet hopped the fence, and pulled her by the hand. "Come on, we got a few minutes before you gotta get back inside."

He didn't let go of her hand until he'd pulled her down on the grass with him. She expected it to be damp and cold. Instead it was warm from the sun.

"See that one there?" Bullet pointed to a cloud. "Looks a lot like the filly when she reared up on me a bit ago."

Tristan put her hand across her brow to shade the sun's glare. "It does."

"Reminded me of you."

"What?" Tristan started to sit up, but saw Bullet's grin and laid back down.

"Dada!" Grey came running across the lawn and jumped on Bullet's stomach.

"Sorry," said Liv, chasing after him. "He saw you out here and was through the front door before I could stop him."

Bullet lifted the little boy up in the air and spun him around until he giggled. "How's my big boy?"

Tristan couldn't understand any of what Grey said in response, but it seemed as though Bullet did. Watching him with his son made her think again that she had misjudged him. Perhaps she should invite him to the sponsorship meeting. If they could sponsor twenty, they could certainly sponsor twenty-one.

Bullet set Grey on his bottom on the grass and pulled his ringing phone out of his pocket.

"Yeah," he answered. "'Bout damn time." Pause. "Sure, I can meet ya. Just give me a couple of days to make arrangements."

When he hung up he picked Grey up again. "You ready to see sissy?"

Grey squealed and let forth another slew of unintelligible words.

"Sissy?" Tristan asked.

"My daughter. Her mama finally agreed to let her come visit. Been too damn long, hasn't it, Grey?" He set Grey down again, who laid down in the grass next to Tristan.

Her head was spinning with questions. Daughter? Mama? Bullet had another child? Had he been married before? Why hadn't Lyric told her that part of the story?

"Pearl just turned three," he said, as though that was all the explanation necessary.

"Time for my meeting," she stood and walked toward the house.

"Tristan?" he asked after her.

"What, Bullet?"

He was on his feet, striding toward her. "What's goin' through your head?"

"Nothing, why?"

He reached out and rubbed her shoulders. "You were relaxed for a minute. Now you're all tensed up again. What happened?"

"Break's over. Back to business." She turned away from him, and was almost up the porch steps when he caught up to her again.

"You got somethin' against kids?"

She felt the heat rise in her cheeks. "Kids? As in your two children? Or as in you, Bullet? I have no problem with the former, it's the latter that makes me shake my head."

"What's that supposed to mean?"

"Never mind. None of my business. See you later." Tristan closed the front door behind her, leaving him standing on the porch.

Bullet kicked at the dirt. *"Shit."* Between last night and just now, he'd felt Tristan easing up on him. When he took her hand, she'd come along willingly. She was smiling when they lay in the grass. And when he rested his hand close enough that his pinky touched hers, she hadn't moved it away. Even when Grey barreled on top of him, she hadn't tensed up. It wasn't until his phone call that she moved away from him.

It hadn't occurred to him that she didn't know he had a daughter too. Was it really so bad that he did?

"Damn judgmental woman," he mumbled.

"Damn, damn, damn," Grey sang as he ran around Bullet's legs.

"If I said a hundred words, you'd pick out the only curse word and make that your song, wouldn't you, Grey?"

His little boy smiled when Bullet picked him up. "Voom, voom?"

"Yep, that sounds good. Time for you and me to go for a ride."

Bullet strapped Grey into the buddy seat. "I gotta get away from here for a bit."

"Where's he goin'?" Lyric asked Tristan.

"No idea. He got a phone call about meeting someone. Something about picking up his daughter."

"Finally. I called Pearl's mother this morning and gave her a piece of my mind. He hasn't seen his daughter in almost two months. That wasn't the agreement. Not even close. But that isn't where he's headed now. She lives in Texas. It'll take a bit more plannin' for that meet up."

Tristan shook her head. She didn't care. She'd given too much thought to Bullet as it was. She didn't want to know any other details about his life. Her first impression had been spot on. What you saw with Bullet was what you got. Twenty new riders were plenty for her to sponsor this year. Adding one more wouldn't be happening.

"Course callin' her Pearl only made her mad. But I don't care. She can't keep his little girl from him."

Tristan wanted to put her hands over her ears. She didn't want to be curious about Bullet, or his kids. "Why did calling her Pearl make her mother mad?" *Dammit.* Why had she asked?

"Her name is Hannah."

"Then why does he call her Pearl?" Tristan shook her head again. She was getting further into his business rather than out of it. What was wrong with her?

"He wanted to name the baby Pearl. Her mother didn't agree. That was after he knew for sure the baby was his. I doubt he gave much thought to it before the DNA test."

He needed a DNA test to know the baby was his? Jeez. It was even worse than she thought. She often wondered if the bull rider who broke her heart had any kids. Probably. He and Bullet were so much alike. Hadn't she learned her lesson the first time?

"I can't do this," she said more to herself than to Lyric. "We've got a meeting." Tristan huffed off in the direction of the lower level of the house, where the meetings were taking place.

Two hours later, the contracts were signed. Liv helped her record the measurements of the barrel racers while Lyric helped Jace record the bronc and bull riders' sizes.

"Have you shown Lyric your new designs?" Liv asked quietly.

"No, just you so far. I don't know…" She'd pulled her sketch book out a half dozen times to show Lyric, as well as some of the barrel racers, and then put it away moments later. Were her designs as good as Liv said they were, or was her friend being polite?

"Show Lyric, at least."

"Maybe later."

"No, now." Liv walked over to Lyric before Tristan could stop her. "Ask Tristan to show you the new women's line, the designs are fabulous." Liv smiled in Tristan's direction.

"New designs? What? I'm so excited. Where are they?" Lyric looked around as though she was looking for the actual pieces.

"Right here," Tristan answered, holding up her sketchbook, which Lyric snatched out of her hand.

Ten minutes later, Lyric and Liv were still flipping pages back and forth, trying to decide their favorites. "When does production start?"

"I asked the same thing," Liv answered Lyric. "And then I told her to make one of each in my size."

Lyric high-fived Liv. "Right on! For me too."

"What are you looking at?" asked Bree, walking down the stairs.

"New designs for Lost Cowboy."

"Let me see." She took the book out of Lyric's hand the same way Lyric had taken it from Tristan.

"Hey," Lyric snipped. "You got a serious entitlement thing goin' on. You think I won't smack a pregnant woman? You're wrong."

"Give her a turn." Liv beamed at Tristan. "See? I told you to share them."

"None of these will look any good on me," groaned Bree. "Do you have any designs for *bigger* women?"

"You're pregnant, not big," insisted Lyric. "Before you know it, you'll pop that kid out and be back to a size two."

Bree cringed. "I've *never* been a size two."

Liv followed Tristan when she walked in the direction of the patio. "You should know Lyric well enough to realize she wouldn't hesitate to tell you her honest opinion. If she didn't like what she saw, she'd tell you. As I said, your designs are fabulous. Have you thought of a name for the line?"

Tristan had been thinking about it. She wasn't ready to share it yet. First she needed to present the idea to her father. She didn't know whether he would sign off on producing a whole new line of clothing. Telling Liv, or anyone else, the name she'd come up with seemed premature, and she didn't want to jinx it.

Bullet drove to the park in town, and let Grey loose on the playground. He sat on the grass, close enough that he could catch him if he climbed too high, or got into some other kind of trouble.

Grey was just like him. Gram would say there was never a minute in Bullet's childhood when he didn't have a scraped knee or elbow.

"You must take after your father," she'd tell him. "Your mama could go play in a mud puddle and come out of it clean as when she walked outdoors."

Bullet could see that. His mother didn't necessarily stand out in their group of friends, not visibly anyway. She looked and dressed the part of a rocker's wife. There was just something about her, her aura maybe, that set her apart. Gram said she named his mom after

Guinevere in the movie, *Camelot.* "Doesn't she look just like Vanessa Redgrave?"

Bullet had never seen the movie, and he didn't know who Vanessa Redgrave was, but when Gram showed Lyric and him the picture of the king and queen in the movie, he had to admit his mom looked a lot like the lady.

He wasn't sure about taking after his father. If he and Lyric weren't twins, Bullet might think he was adopted. He didn't seem to take after anyone in his family.

His father met his mother when he was touring with his first band. They were the opening act for a band that wasn't much more successful than his was. His dad would say he'd never doubt his wife's love, because she'd loved him when he was a starving, struggling musician. Unlike some of his bandmates' girlfriends, she'd loved him before he made it big, she loved him still, and would even if it all ended tomorrow.

Bullet wasn't sure if he would ever love a woman the way his father loved his mom, who he probably never cheated on. Unlike Bullet. He'd cheated on Callie. While she was pregnant.

When Bullet told Gram he was going to marry Callie, she told him she wouldn't try to talk him out of it, just like she didn't try to talk him into marrying

Pearl's mama. "If you're enough of an adult to make a child, you're enough of an adult to make a decision." She hugged him that day, and whispered, "Slow down, Bullet. Don't be in such a hurry to grow up."

He remembered feeling old that day, old enough to be considered a grown up. Looking back on it, he wasn't. He was pretending to be mature and responsible. He wasn't then, and he wasn't much more so now.

Gram's friends would say that Lyric got the responsibility gene when the two were in the womb together. They'd say Bullet didn't have a lick of the sense his sister had. Gram wouldn't say much in response, but she would look at Bullet and wink. "We know better, don't we?" she'd say later, when her friends were gone.

She may know, but he sure didn't. Bullet thought Gram's friends were right. Lyric was the responsible one. She never got in trouble, had good grades, and was already a successful businesswoman. What did he have? He'd had a lot of fun. And a couple of kids to show for it.

He pulled his cell phone out of his pocket when he felt it vibrate. He looked at the screen and saw Bill Patterson was calling.

"Hey, Bill. Uh, I'm at the park with Grey. Everything okay?"

"Just checkin' on you. It isn't like you to leave a horse out in the corral when you're done workin' it."

Shit. He'd completely forgotten about the filly. Another example of his lack of responsibility. Tristan probably told Bill, or one of the other partners that he'd left without thinking about the animal he was responsible for.

"I'll round up Grey and get right back."

"I took care of the horse, Bullet, but I think we need to talk."

"Yes, sir." Great. Now he was going to lose his job too. "I'll be right there."

* * *

1968

Clancy never told him what happened with his mama. All he'd say was everything had been taken care of, and his mother and sister were fine. Clancy went on two more trips during the last year, and wouldn't tell Bill where he was going. When Bill asked, all Clancy would say was that he had private business to take care of. And that wasn't like Clancy.

Tomorrow most of the ranch hands were driving to Gunnison for Cattlemen's Days. This was the first year Bill was able to join them. He'd been so anxious about going he hadn't slept too well the last few nights. He wasn't as nervous about competing as he was about seeing Dottie again.

At the ranch cook's urging, Bill had written Sadie's niece a letter. He'd fretted a whole week about whether she'd answer. When he and Clancy made their weekly trip to the McCoy post office, there was a letter from Dottie waiting for him. For it to get to him that quickly, she had to have written it the same day she received his letter.

They exchanged letters weekly. Bill didn't know what to expect when he wrote that he'd be coming to Gunnison. He worried she might have a steady beau, so he came right out and asked. She wrote back she did, and his name was Bill Flynn.

He'd done well that week on bulls and broncs. Tie-down roping too. Dottie was his girl, and he intended to do her proud.

10

What the hell was he going to do now? If Bill fired him from the Black Forest operation, he doubted if any of the Flying R partners would offer to let him work at one of the other ranches.

Bullet needed to pull his head out of his ass, again, and pay attention to what was in front of him. His kids. His job. And forget about women for a while. A long while. Especially one woman. Tristan. The more he tried to impress her, the more he did the opposite. Why did it matter what she thought of him?

Last night, as he held her in his arms when they danced, he imagined himself holding her all the time. She felt so good. Unlike Callie, who was more than a foot shorter than he was, Tristan was tall. Her head rested easily on his shoulder, and her body fit against his, as though it was made to.

When he closed his eyes, he could remember how she felt, her scent, his body's reaction to her. It had been a while since he'd been with a woman, but it was more than that. It was her. There were plenty of other pretty women at the bar last night. None of them did it for him. He'd danced with a couple. They didn't fit. Not like Tristan.

Maybe if he could seduce her, sleep with her, get a taste of her, he could get her out of his head. He was sure that was her allure, that he couldn't have her. When had he ever given up on the challenge of a woman he wanted? Never.

Bullet only hoped he was right, that once he had her, she'd be out of his head and he'd be able to pay attention to his responsibilities. He needed to get laid. It was that simple.

But in the back of his mind lingered the feeling he was wrong, that getting Tristan McCullough out of his head wasn't going to be simple at all.

"I can't believe you're leaving already," pouted Liv.

"You're the one who told me to hurry up and produce this line. In order for me to do so I have to get back and talk to my father."

"I know, I just like having you here."

Tristan understood. Her friendship with Liv meant more to her every day. She was easy to talk to. And fun. She loved her father and grandfather, but she missed being around another woman. Biologically Liv was old enough to be her mother, but their friendship wasn't based on that. She had more in common with Liv than she did with Lyric, or Liv's daughter, Renie, who were both her age.

"Damn stubborn," they overheard Bill say to Dottie.

"Yes, he is. Now go right back out the door you came in and apologize."

"Apologize? Over my dead body."

Dottie laughed. "I can arrange that."

They heard the front door open and close, and Dottie came into the kitchen.

"What's going on?" Liv asked.

"Bill and Bullet had an argument. Somehow Bullet got it into his head that Bill was going to fire him. I can't figure that out myself, but Bill told him he wouldn't accept his resignation. Bullet said something about not resigning, Bill was firing him. Anyway, the two of them are arguing on the same side, and neither one of them can set their stubbornness aside long enough to realize it."

Tristan felt as though there was a rock in her stomach. If Bill fired Bullet would she ever see him again? Would he go back to Oklahoma? "Why would Bill fire him?"

"He wouldn't. That's the point." Dottie turned and looked at Tristan. "Uh oh. You've got it bad for the cowboy. My oh my."

"What? No. I don't. That isn't it. Bullet has a child to raise, that's all. I'm just worried…"

Tristan stopped trying to explain when she realized Liv and Dottie were grinning at her.

"Stop it," she barked at them. "It isn't like that."

Dottie patted Liv's hand. "We've seen that look before, haven't we, Livvie?"

"We sure have."

"Stop it. I'm telling you it isn't like that."

"What isn't like what?" Lyric shouted from the other room. Tristan hadn't realized she was within earshot.

"Tristan and Bullet."

"Oh yeah, I know it. She's in love with him."

"*Lyric!*" gasped Tristan. "I am not. Don't be ridiculous."

"And what's better, my brother is in love with her too."

"That's absurd—"

"Oh, stop it," Lyric added. "Anyone with eyes can see it. Besides, twins know these things. Can't argue with a twin."

Tristan looked to Liv to defend her, but saw immediately that it was pointless. Liv, Dottie, and Lyric were grinning at her in a way that told her she shouldn't bother protesting.

"I'm not firin' you, Bullet. Although I should considerin' you can't keep your damn mouth shut long enough to listen to me."

Grey danced around Bill's legs singing at the top of his lungs, "Damn, damn, damn."

Bullet saw an opportunity by the look on Bill's face. "Now see what you did. You're teachin' my kid to curse."

"Well, shit. I'm sorry—"

Grey didn't miss a beat, although it was harder for him to pronounce. "Sit, sit, sit," he sang instead.

"For Christ's sake," Bill began again, quickly realizing his third error.

Bullet was laughing too hard to speak, but held up his hand.

"What's so da—, I mean, funny?"

"Nothin'," Bullet's hand was still in the air, but he was bent over holding his stomach, still laughing.

Bill folded his arms in front of him, and waited for Bullet to stop while Grey continued to dance around him, "Sit, sit, damn. Sit, sit, damn," he sang.

Bullet sat down on the porch, tears ran down his cheeks from laughing so hard. "You shoulda seen the look on your face." He pointed at Bill and started laughing again.

Bill sat down next to him, and laughed too.

"Like he ain't heard *those* words before." Bullet wiped the tears from his cheeks. "Damn, it's been a long, long time since I laughed that hard."

"Me too," admitted Bill. "Now where did you get the idea I was gonna fire you?"

"I left the filly out for starters."

"You think that's firin' grounds?" Bill shook his head. "You're mighty hard on yourself, son."

Bullet hung his head and let out a deep breath. "I'm feelin' like a screw-up lately. Wouldn't blame you is all I was sayin'."

"Put that foolish notion outta your head. We have work to do, startin' with loadin' broncs into trailers. If I was gonna fire you, which I'm not, I'd sure as hell wait until after that job was done."

"When we headin' back?" Bullet no longer felt like laughing. Heading back to Black Forest meant he wouldn't have any more time with Tristan. He needed her in his bed, and out of his head. He may have run out of time.

"Not until tomorrow mornin'."

Good. That meant he still had tonight.

"Livvie's got another shindig planned for tonight. Just partners and crew this time. No new riders."

Even better. He'd basically have Tristan all to himself.

"You can't leave until tomorrow. Stay one more night, at least."

"I don't know, I really should get back."

"If you stay until Tuesday, Ben can fly you back."

Tristan couldn't stay until Tuesday, and she couldn't ask Ben to fly her across the country again so soon.

"I appreciate it, but—"

"Go home tomorrow instead."

"Liv, you're being silly."

"There's a party tonight just for the partners. Billy and Jace are gonna be mad if you miss it."

Tristan folded her arms in front of her. "Really?" she smirked. "They're going to be *mad* at me?"

"As soon as the words came out of my mouth I knew you wouldn't buy it. How about this? I'm *begging* you to stay."

"Liv—"

"*Wait.* I've got one better. If you stay I'll invest in your new clothing line."

That got Tristan's attention. The idea had been in the back of her mind, and was one of the reasons she hadn't broached the subject with her father yet. She'd been contemplating producing the line on her own. Making it separate from Lost Cowboy.

"Aha! That got you thinking, didn't it?" Liv reached around and patted herself on the back. "I knew I could get you to stay."

"Are you serious, or do you just want me to stay?"

The expression on Liv's face changed. She was no longer joking. "I'm very serious. And I'm not the only one interested."

"Who else?"

"Lyric, Dottie, Bree, Renie. I'm sure Paige, who's Bree and Blythe's mother, would be interested too. She's the real businesswoman of the bunch."

"You're kidding?"

"I'm not."

"Why?"

"Are you kidding? There are a thousand reasons."

"Name a couple."

"You already know the first reason. We love your designs. Apart from that, it's *girly*. We're surrounded by cowboys and rough stock. Not that we don't love our cowboys. But investing in your line would give us a feminine outlet."

Tristan listened intently. Liv was serious. This wasn't a ploy to get her to stay longer, and Liv wasn't being polite. She believed enough to want to invest. And so did the others.

"Okay. I'll stay."

Liv let out a whoop and danced around the kitchen. "Call the lawyers, Dottie! We're startin' a clothing line."

"Let's finish making dinner first. Then we'll call the lawyers," Dottie answered.

"Spoilsport," Liv teased.

"Can I help?" Tristan asked Dottie, who put her flour-covered hand on Tristan's shoulder.

"Do you like to cook? I'd love to have more help." Dottie glared at Liv when she said it, but it quickly turned into a smile.

"I'm a great cook," answered Liv.

"You're a great baker."

"You're right. Ben is a better cook than I am."

"You got that right, darlin'." Ben walked into the kitchen, put his arms around Liv's waist, and kissed her cheek. "But I love you anyway."

Liv turned around and gave Ben a kiss that made Tristan blush. When she looked over at Dottie, the woman was smiling at her. Tristan's eyes filled with tears.

Dottie pulled her over. "What's wrong, sweet girl?"

"You remind me so much of my mother," Tristan whispered. When Dottie hugged her tight, Tristan couldn't stop her tears. "I miss her so much."

"How long has it been, sweetheart?"

"She died when I was fifteen."

Bullet turned around and went back downstairs, hoping no one saw him. Tristan lost her mama when she was a teenager? He remembered shutting her down the last time they were both in Crested Butte.

"You don't understand anything about my life, or my son's life," he'd said to her that night. She was trying to tell him she understood, because she did. Grey was too young to feel the pain of losing his mama, but there would come a day when he'd feel the same way Tristan was. He may not remember Callie, but he'd feel the loss of not havin' a mama.

His phone vibrated. Billy was calling him.

"Where the hell you at?"

"In the basement. Where are you?"

"I've been lookin' for you all day."

"You must not have been lookin' very hard. I was talkin' to your daddy just a bit ago."

"Get your ass to the barn." Billy ended the call.

Shit. What was up Billy's ass? Just when he decided he wasn't gonna get fired, now maybe he was.

When he walked in the barn door, he saw Billy and Jace talking to Renie. Bullet didn't know whether he should wait until they finished.

"Get your ass over here," Billy motioned at him.

"Billy!" Renie scolded her husband. "Don't talk to Bullet like that."

Bullet swore Billy looked embarrassed. "Like what? Jesus, Renie, this ain't no pansy-assed business we're runnin' here."

She reached up and kissed his cheek, "Play nice with the other cowboys, sweetheart." She smiled at Bullet on her way out of the barn.

"What' up?"

"Nothin'. Christ almighty. What's everybody's problem? I wanna talk to you about loadin' horses in the mornin'."

Instead of looking at Bullet, Billy looked at Jace. "What're you lookin' at?"

"Nothin'," laughed Jace. "You aren't acting any different than you usually do."

"You're damn right," Billy huffed and sat on a bale of hay. "If you can't take it, you can go back inside with the women." This time Billy was looking at Bullet.

"What the hell did I do?"

"He's just mad because Renie wants him to talk to you," Jace explained.

"About what?"

"Your wife dyin'."

"Why?"

"Exactly," Billy groaned. "I told her it wasn't any of our business."

"I gotta get off this ride before I lose my lunch."

Billy looked at Jace. "Now what's he talkin' about?"

Jace shrugged his shoulders.

"Never mind," said Bullet. "I'll tell her you talked to me. That it? Can I go now?"

"No, you can't go. And you can't lie to my wife. Now sit your ass down."

"How about me, can I go?" asked Jace.

"No, you can't go either. If Renie wants to know if I really talked to Bullet, you can vouch for me."

"Just get this over with, would ya?" Bullet was running out of patience. Either they were gonna fire him, or they weren't. They needed to make up their minds.

"You know Willow isn't Renie's biological daughter, right?"

Huh? No, he didn't. "What happened to her mama?"

"Car accident."

"Damn." Bullet put his head in his hand. "I'm sorry, Billy."

"Yeah, it was sad, but don't be sayin' sorry to me. Truth is, I didn't know she had a baby until after she died."

"Oh."

"Yeah, so, for the first few months of Willow's life, I raised her by myself. Renie and I weren't together then."

"She was with me."

Bullet was sure Jace was joking, but the look on Billy's face told him it was no joke.

"You don't have to bring that up ever again, you hear me?"

Jace just laughed. Bullet was confused. He thought Billy and Jace were best friends. But then he'd also thought Willow was Renie's daughter. "They look so much alike," he said out loud without meaning to.

"I know they do, but I'm tellin' you the truth."

"Okay, so…"

"Renie wanted me to tell you, so you know that nobody is feelin' sorry for you around here. It's more that we understand, or I do anyway. I been through it."

It explained a lot actually. Bill and Dottie acted as though it was perfectly natural for Bullet to be raising Grey on his own. They helped out, but they'd never done anything that made him feel uncomfortable about the situation.

"Thanks."

"Sure thing." Billy looked at Jace. "Did I cover everything she wanted me to tell him?"

"Nope."

"*Shit*. What did I leave out?"

"She wanted you to tell him that the right woman will love his baby too."

"Yeah. That." Billy stood and walked over to one of the stalls. "End of conversation."

When Jace started laughing again, Billy threw a curry comb at him.

"Dinner bell. You're both saved." Jace stood and walked out of the barn. Billy followed him.

"You comin' to dinner?"

Yeah, he was. All this deep conversation was making him hungry.

Lyric motioned at him when Bullet approached the table. She was standing behind the chair next to Tristan. When he got close, she stepped back and walked around to the other side of the table, next to Grey's high chair.

"Needin' a little auntie time," she explained.

"Thanks," he mumbled.

Before Tristan realized what was happening, Bullet was seated in the chair next to her. He leaned in close. "Hey, darlin', you don't mind sittin' next to me, do ya?"

His breath was warm on her skin. It made her want to lean closer still. "No, I don't mind." Why couldn't she resist him? What was it about Bullet, or was she destined to keep falling for the exact kind of men she didn't want to fall for?

"Good. I like bein' next to you," he smiled.

And with that, Tristan was toast. Putty. A heaping blob of hormones, all screaming at her to pull him away from the dinner table, take him downstairs, and into her bed.

He leaned in again. "Whatever you're thinking, I couldn't agree more."

He couldn't know what she was thinking, could he?

"Come with me," he said after dessert.

"No, Bullet, I can't."

"Yes, you can. Come on, let's go for a walk."

Tristan looked around the table. Everyone was engaged in conversation, not paying attention to her or Bullet. Lyric had Grey and Caden in a fit of giggles. Bullet leaned in close again, as he had throughout dinner. "Come on, darlin'," he whispered. She was powerless to deny him.

As the front door closed behind them, Bullet turned her back against it, and covered her mouth with his. And, oh, it felt good. Better than she imagined, and she'd spent more time than she'd ever admit imagining.

His hard body pressed against hers, keeping her pinned between him and the door. He slid one hand into her hair, keeping her lips where he wanted them. He leaned back and ran his eyes down her body. His hand tugged her hair, forcing her chin up, giving him open access to her neck, her throat, and down to where her v-neck shirt rested against her breasts. He ran his tongue back up and along her collar bone, stopping to kiss each of the freckles he found along the way.

"Wait," she groaned, putting each hand on his strong biceps. "Bullet, stop."

He couldn't stop, not with the way she just ran her tongue over her bottom lip. He leaned up against her, feeling her body with every length of his. Heart to heart, he could feel hers thundering. He trailed kisses along her jawline, back up to her lips. Her lips parted, allowing her to draw in a deep breath. He covered her mouth again, following the breath, deepening the kiss. He smoothed his hand down her side, feeling the swell of her hip, the curve of her spine. When he slid his hand into the waist band of her jeans, Tristan froze.

"Wait," she breathed. "I can't do this. Not here."

Not here. That's what she said. Not that she couldn't do this, but that she couldn't do this here. He peeled himself away from her, his body feeling the chill of the night air, after having her warmth seeping into his bones. He sunk back again.

"I have a place in town. We can be alone for a bit." The hand that was still in her hair kept her from turning away. Thank goodness he hadn't turned that key in yet.

No, no, no. What was she doing? One hand still in her hair, his free hand was on her waist, sliding back up under her shirt. He grazed the underside of her breast with the back of his hand before trailing back down, over her hip, where his fingers dug into the curve of her backside.

"God, you feel good. So good."

His voice. His breath. His hands. She wasn't imagining any of it. This time it was real. Tristan rested her head back against the door, taking another deep breath. Whenever she did, he took the opportunity to slide his tongue deep into her mouth. He kissed her hard, taking her breath into him. And then he groaned.

The sound made her head swim—dizzy with wanting him. She began to shake, and rested her hands on his biceps again to steady herself. He stopped.

"Tristan? Are you okay?"

She wasn't okay. She was the furthest thing from okay. Inside the door she was up against were people who had welcomed her into the family, offered her their friendship, and here she was, no better than a buckle bunny, letting a cowboy get into her pants on their front porch.

"No," she moaned, catching him off guard enough that she could push away from him. "I can't do this, Bullet."

He watched as the front door closed behind her. She was inside. He was out, an outsider, never to be welcome into her bed, or her life. He'd done the very thing he knew would push her the furthest away. Bullet lost control. He ran his hands over her body, the body he craved like a man dying of thirst craved water.

Instead of taking his time, seducing her, he attacked her. When Tristan's passions met his, he lost all sense of thought. He was consumed by his desire to feel her next to him, under him.

This wasn't just another girl he'd get between the sheets and then forget all about, this was a woman he wanted in his life as much as he wanted her in his bed.

* * *

1968

Every time Bill looked into the stands and saw Dottie sitting there, watching him, he felt his chest pump up. He didn't miss the way the other cowboys looked at her, or at him, when she'd wave and blow a kiss straight in his direction. They hadn't had much time to talk, but agreed to meet later, after today's events were over. When he asked her if there was a place they could walk to dinner, she told him Main Street was only three blocks away, and all the restaurants were staying open late during Cattlemen's Days.

Bill covered his bronc and his bull, which meant he'd be moving on to the semi-finals tomorrow. He had one more event tonight, tie-down roping.

Clancy had offered to let Bill borrow his roping saddle. It had a wide horn leaving plenty of space for Bill's rope. Clancy also offered to let him ride his Quarter Horse, Cisco. He helped Bill tape the horn for better grip, and then had another surprise—a new rope. It felt stiff in Bill's hand, but flexible enough to bend around the head of the charging calf.

He sneaked a look into the stands, to make sure Dottie was still there. When his eye caught hers, she blew him another kiss.

Three cowboys before him failed to keep their calf secure, which resulted in no points. There was one more before him, and then it would be Bill's turn.

He watched as the calf was loaded into the chute and a small piece of breakaway rope was fastened around its neck. The cowboy entered the box and backed his horse into the corner as the chute workers stretched a rope barrier across the chute entrance.

The cowboy grabbed his rope, readied his horse, and signaled the chute worker to open the chute. The calf ran forward, the barrier popped, and the cowboy followed.

The cowboy lassoed the calf, and leaped off his horse to wrangle and tie the calf. Bill heard an audible snap, and the audience reacted with a gasp. Then silence.

At the same time the cowboy turned and walked away from the calf, rodeo officials on horseback raced to the center of the arena and crowded around the downed calf.

Bill watched as rodeo officials loosened the rope from the calf's neck, covering its eyes and easing its legs to the ground.

"What happened?" he asked Clancy.

"Looks like the rope's knot landed square on the back of the calf's neck. The force of the horse's stop flipped the calf upside down and directly onto its spine. It's called a jerk down. And it's a move that was explicitly banned years ago."

"What are they doing now?"

"They're sedating the calf to get it out of the arena."

Bill wanted to believe Clancy, but the calf didn't look sedated, it looked dead. No cowboy ever wanted to see an animal of any kind hurt in rodeo. Regardless of whether it was hurt, or dead, Bill was devastated.

"I'm out."

Clancy turned away from watching the vets work on the calf, and looked straight at Bill. "You're quittin'?"

"Yes, sir. I am."

Clancy nodded his head, walked over to one of the officials, and then led Cisco out of the arena with Bill still in the saddle. As he passed Dottie in the stands, he almost couldn't bring himself to look at her. When he did, he saw she had her head in her hands, and she was crying.

What had begun as one of the best days of his life had sunk into a horrible nightmare.

11

When she went back inside no one seemed to have noticed she and Bullet were gone. Rather than sitting in her seat at the table, she began clearing dishes. Soon Liv joined her.

"Everything okay?"

She didn't want to lie, but she also didn't want to talk about it.

"I'm more tired than I thought," Tristan finally admitted. "And ready to go home."

Liv rubbed her shoulder. "I'm sorry I made you stay. It's just that I love having you here. If you promise to come back soon, I'll promise not to be so selfish next time."

"It isn't that." She smiled at Liv's apology. "I really am tired. But I'm also glad I stayed." For the most part. Liv didn't need to know what had happened with Bullet on the porch.

She heard the front door open and close, but refused to turn around to see if it was Bullet. Instead she excused herself and went downstairs to pack.

Bullet crept back inside and went straight downstairs. He could hear Tristan milling around in the guest room. He approached the door several times, but couldn't bring himself to knock. He felt terrible about what had happened, and wished he could find a way to tell her so.

What could he say, though? That she was more than just a lay to him? That ought to go over well. He'd tell her things had gone too far. That her friendship was what was important to him, but he'd be lying, and she'd know.

He wanted her, then and now. He rested his hand against the door, willing her to open it, and let him in.

The next morning they got the broncs loaded into the trailers, and were close to ready to leave. When Bullet packed Grey's bag, his son had a temper tantrum, lying on the floor, kicking his feet, and crying. Clearly Grey didn't want to leave. If Tristan hadn't left an hour earlier, he wouldn't have wanted to either.

Before she'd left, he couldn't decide whether to try to talk to her, or stay out of her way. He finally decided on the latter. If she wanted to talk to him, she'd know where to find him. She hadn't.

"Hey bro—" Lyric slapped him on the back and scared the crap out of him. It was something she used to do when they were little. She'd tell him he should practice "feeling her presence," so he wouldn't be startled when she came up behind him. He figured that was a load of crap, and she did it because she liked to see him jump out of his skin.

"What happened with you and Tristan last night?"

"Why? What did she say?"

"She didn't say anything, but the two of you avoided each other all morning."

So, she *had* been avoiding him. He was glad now he hadn't sought her out. It only would've made everything worse.

"Ain't like we have a reason to be around each other. Don't make more of it than it is."

"Whenever you start talkin' like a Oklahoma hick I know somethin's up. Good thing for you there's a surprise waitin' on you when you get back to Black Forest."

Bullet hated surprises, and Lyric knew it. As well as he knew there wasn't anything he could do to get her to tell him what it was.

"It's a good surprise."

Yeah, whatever. He knew what it wasn't. It wasn't Tristan waiting on his front porch for him and Grey to pull up. Any surprise other than that wouldn't be a good one.

Bullet pointed toward Grey, who was on the lawn playing with Caden. "Soon as I pick him up, he'll turn from the happy little boy he is at this moment, into a screaming, unhappy monster."

"I'll get him," Lyric offered.

He'd let her. Bullet had already had one unpleasant tantrum from Grey this morning. His auntie could handle this one.

"Come on, Caden, let's walk Grey over to his truck, so we can wave bye-bye when he leaves."

Bullet watched as Caden took Grey's hand and the two walked to the truck. Before Lyric could lift him up and put him in his buddy seat, Caden wrapped her arms around his neck, and plastered a loud smooch on his lips. Grey smiled from ear to ear.

Oh, Lord, thought Bullet. His boy was in for it. Girls were already kissin' on him, and he was happy as a pig in mud. If he kept this up, he'd be on the road to a hell of a lot of heartache. Grey could take that from his old man.

Bullet rubbed his hand over his chest. Yep, it hurt. Bad. He didn't dare ask anyone when Tristan might be back in Colorado. Even when she was, she wouldn't want to see him.

Tristan leaned back against the window seat on the plane, and lowered the shade. Part of her wished she'd asked Ben to fly her home, the other part was glad she hadn't.

Every time she closed her eyes, she could feel Bullet's hands on her. And his lips. She could hear his voice, and feel his breath as he leaned in close to her. She'd wanted him as much as she could feel he wanted her.

If they'd been anywhere else she wouldn't have stopped him. Thankfully, there were too many people at the Flying R last night, and the thought of them being inside the house while they were outside, brought her to her senses.

Bullet Simmons was dangerous with a capital D. In fact, dangerous should be in all caps. He was the kind of man who fathered children with different woman. And worse, he was a bull rider.

He was also playful, and sweet. He was close to his sister, a good father, and a hard worker. Bill and Dottie adored him, that much was obvious. He wouldn't have a job with the Flying R team, or a sponsorship, if he wasn't a decent guy. He was good with kids. And horses. And her. Especially her. She groaned and covered her face with her hands.

"Tristan?"

There were only two people on earth she really didn't want to see this morning. One was Bullet

Simmons. The other was standing in the aisle, putting his carry-on in the compartment above her row of seats.

After crying for twenty minutes when they left the ranch, Grey slept the rest of the way home, all six hours. Playing with Caden the last couple of days must've worn him out, and Bullet was thankful for it. He only hoped that he'd be tired again by bedtime. If Grey couldn't sleep later, Bullet wouldn't be able to either.

When Dottie called his cell to say they were stopping for something to eat, he told them he'd keep driving. He dared to stop only once, to give the horses a break, and Grey had slept through it. He wouldn't risk it again.

He was tempted not to answer his phone when it rang again, but knew he had to in case it was Bill or someone else from Flying R.

"You home yet?"

"You're always givin' me shit about not feeling the twin thing, how come you don't know if I'm home or not?"

"Ha, ha. You're funny. I guess you aren't yet."

"Nah. I'm close though. Why?"

"You'll see." Silence. Lyric had hung up. What the hell?

"Tell me you aren't sitting here," she demanded when he threw his jacket on the aisle seat.

He pulled his boarding pass out of his back pocket. "Yep, I sure am."

"Then I'm moving."

The flight attendant standing behind him in the aisle stopped her. "Stay where you are. These are the last two open seats. We have a full flight, and Mr. Jones is our last standby passenger."

Mr. Jones. Tristan turned back toward the window and rolled her eyes. Addressing him in such a respectful way was a waste of words. There wasn't a single thing about Harris Jones that was respectable. He was a dirty, rotten scoundrel. In fact, scoundrel was too good a word for the bull rider. He was the devil incarnate as far as she was concerned.

"Tristan McCullough. Fancy meeting you here," he said after he fastened his seat belt.

"If a stranger was sitting where you are, I'd ignore him the same way I'm going to ignore you."

Harris leaned over, resting his arm on the seat between them. "You can't ignore me and you know it," he drawled. The way he said it made her skin crawl. And it made her think of Bullet.

Since she met him, Tristan had been comparing Bullet to Harris. Having him seated near her showed her how wrong she'd been. Bullet was nothing like this slimeball.

The way Bullet spoke to her was seductive, and soothing. Bullet made her feel safe. Deep down she knew she could trust him. Harris made her feel sleazy. She couldn't wait to get off the plane and take a shower. Had he always worn cologne? And that much of it?

Since Grey was still asleep, snoring in fact, Bullet waited until he was out of the rig to call for help unloading the broncs. Dead tired though he was, he knew it would be hours before he could catch some shut-eye. As soon as Grey was awake he'd be rarin' to play, and Bullet would not be able to deny him.

Bullet recognized the SUV in the driveway as soon as he pulled up to the house. Lyric was right, it was a good surprise. There were lights on inside, so either one of the ranch hands let Gram in, or showed her where the front door key was hidden.

"Grey, time to wake up," he said softly to his son. "Gram is here to see you."

"Not just Gram, Yaya and Poppa are here too." Bullet's father came up behind him, a big grin on his face. "Now hand over my grandson," he smiled.

Grey buried his head in Bullet's shoulder. "Someone's shy," said his mother, coming up behind them. Grey peeked over Bullet's shoulder and held his arms out to his grandmother.

"It's her voice," Bullet's father said. "Soothes the soul."

Bullet hugged his dad after he handed Grey to his mother.

"Oh, my goodness, he's heavy. What have you been feeding him?" she teased.

"I'll take him Guinie," offered his dad.

"No, it's been too long since I held him. You wait your turn."

Bullet followed his parents into the house where Gram was waiting.

"I can't believe Lyric kept our secret. She did, didn't she?" Gram pulled him into a big hug, just like Dottie's. He wondered if he had remembered it right, how similar they were.

"She did," he answered, and rested his head on his grandmother's shoulder. She ran her hand through his hair like she did when he was growing up. "Long drive?"

"Yeah. Long week before it too."

"Have a seat, and let me get you a beer," offered his dad. "You still drink beer, don't ya?"

"You must not have checked the fridge, or you wouldn't be asking," Bullet answered. "There's plenty in there. At least there was when I left."

Gram had his favorite dinner waiting on him, and she and his mama whisked Grey off for a bath. His daddy sat down at the table with him.

"Not hungry?"

"You know your gram, she made sure I had three helpings before she let me leave the table," Nate rubbed his hands over his stomach. "You gonna ask what we're all doin' here?"

Bullet's mouth was full, so he nodded.

"You need a break, son, and we're here to make sure you take it."

"Listen, Daddy—"

"No, you listen. We're here because Bill and Dottie Patterson asked us to come."

"Why'd they do that? How did they even know how to get in touch with you?" Bullet had given Dottie Gram's phone number in case anything happened to him on the ranch, or while he was riding bulls.

"She didn't. Dottie asked your gram to come, and since we were planning to fly in yesterday anyway, she picked us up at the airport in Denver."

Bullet pushed his plate back. He'd lost his appetite. He'd been trying to be a good employee, to work hard for the Pattersons, and not let the fact he was raising his son on his own interfere with his job. If Dottie had asked his gram to come, he obviously wasn't succeeding.

"What am I doin' wrong?" he said to himself as much as he did his father.

"It isn't that. They asked her to come because they think you need a little time to yourself. And they know you well enough to know you wouldn't depend on their kindness if they offered to watch Grey for a few days. So they called in the cavalry...in the form of your grandmother."

Bullet still didn't understand. Between Billy telling him that he'd raised his daughter on his own, and Lyric always after him about following his dream, and now this, it seemed as though everyone was encouraging him to do the opposite of what he knew he needed to be doing.

Had he proven himself to be so undependable that even the smallest sign of responsibility made everyone believe he needed a break to get his head screwed back on crooked?

"Lyric said you were thinkin' about gettin' a place in Colorado."

"She's right. Not sure where yet though. Got any ideas?"

Bullet talked to his dad about the places in Colorado he knew well, and brought up other towns he'd like to visit.

"Lyric suggested Aspen. I don't know why. Seems like a sleepy ol' town to me."

"Lots of rockers maybe."

"Don't know about that. Unless you mean the chairs. I've been to Telluride a few times for their Blues Fest. Although outside of that and ski season, doesn't seem like too much is happening there either."

"Colorado ain't Los Angeles."

"It sure isn't. But it's all good. I'm done with LA anyway. Doesn't matter anymore where you're based. You can record music anywhere. You can set up a damn studio in your house."

Bullet told his dad about Ben's set up in Crested Butte. "You should check it out."

"I got a call from Ben recently. About hookin' up with Mark Cochran. Won't that be somethin'?"

Bullet remembered Ben talking about it several weeks ago. He was probably supposed to arrange it, or at least tell his dad, but he'd forgotten all about it with Callie's death.

"Sure would. Mark lives close to here. I don't know if Ben told you."

"Yep, and we're scheduled to get together day after tomorrow."

"Where?"

"Here, or at Mark's. Like you said, he lives close. Ben is comin' in tomorrow for dinner, and then the next day we'll see what kind of musical firecrackers we can light up."

How had all this been arranged without anyone mentioning it to him? Bullet was beginning to think they were right, he did need a break. Maybe he was already having a break—a mental one, and that was why so much of what was going on around him made no sense.

"How much of a break did Bill and Dottie say I needed?"

"A week."

What was he supposed to do for a week?

"And before you start over thinkin' it. Bill has a place lined up for you to go."

"Oh yeah?" Bullet laughed. "Am I bein' committed somewhere?"

His dad laughed too. "I told your mother you were gonna say that." Nate looked over his shoulder. "Hear that, Guinie? Bullet wants to know where we're committing him."

His mother came out of the bathroom wiping her hands on a towel. Bullet could hear Grey speaking his gibberish to Gram, who sounded as though she was loving it.

"She's soaked from head to toe, but with a big smile on her face."

Bullet looked his mother up and down. Gram was right about her. She didn't look to have a drop of water on her, but he knew she'd been right in there playing with Grey.

His mother looked herself up and down. "What?"

"Gram said you could play in a mud puddle and not get dirty. Looks as though you can give Grey a bath and not get wet either."

"Oh, I don't know about that." She sat down at the table and covered his hand with hers. "Bullet, it's hard work taking care of a baby boy. On top of that, you're running a big part of the ranch for the Pattersons. Don't start imagining anyone is unhappy with the job you're doing just because they care enough to want you to take a vacation."

"If I'd had some notice I might've been able to plan somethin', but I can't leave right now. I talked to Pearl's mama yesterday. She's supposed to call me back today about gettin' her up here for a couple of weeks."

"Your mama talked to Pearl's mama. We'll go get her the day before you get back. She'll be stayin' with us for a month."

"A month?" Bullet scratched his head. He wanted to see his little girl, there was no doubt about it. But first they were suggesting he take a week off, and then have two kids with him for a whole month when he could barely keep a handle on one.

"It's all settled. We're stayin' on to help with Grey and Pearl. Bill has made arrangements for you to visit the ranch he grew up on. And while you're there, you'll be riding bulls."

"*Are you serious?*" Bullet couldn't contain his smile. Was this really happening? A whole week riding bulls. This must be some kind of dream. Or there was a catch. Was he going there on behalf of Flying R Rough Stock? He'd call over and talk to Bill once he finished eating his dinner.

"Look, Guinie, he can't help grinnin'."

"Where am I going?" Tristan asked her father.

"It's a place in McCoy, Colorado. They want us to do private label work for them. Enough that it warrants a trip to see them."

But, she'd just gotten home. She hadn't had a chance to talk to him about her plans, or even show him and her grandfather the designs she'd done. She couldn't argue with him, though. If her father needed her to go, she'd go.

"Now don't get a pout on, little girl. You love traveling. Isn't that what you've been telling me the last few years?"

He was right. She did love to travel. Or at least she used to. Now all she wanted to do was spend a week at home.

"Yes, Daddy."

"You go get some rest. Your flight doesn't leave until noon tomorrow."

"Tomorrow?" she gasped.

"Yes, tomorrow. You're flying into Denver, and then taking a commuter flight to Edwards where someone from the ranch will pick you up. It's another hour from there."

She studied her father as he spoke. It wasn't like him to make arrangements without discussing it with her, especially when she'd just gotten home.

"This must be some deal."

"Yes, it is. And, Tristan, I expect you'll represent us well, as you always do."

"I better unpack, and then pack again." Tristan went upstairs without hearing the conversation that took place between her father and grandfather after she left the room.

"She's gonna be mad."

"I know, Dad, but she needs some time off. If I left it up to her, she'd get something else in the works before I could stop her. This was the only way I could get her to take a break."

"Mighty nice of Liv Rice to suggest it."

"She did more than suggest it, she arranged it. Tristan will have a cabin all to herself for the week. If she wants to hibernate and work on her designs, she can. If she wants to go on a trail ride, or hike, or sit in the sunshine, she can do that too."

"Has she shown you any of them yet?"

"No, and until she does, not a word that we know about it. Understand, Dad?"

Tristan's grandfather chuckled. "Hasn't been me peekin' at 'em when she wasn't lookin."

Bill warned Bullet the ranch was a long way off the main road. "I remember the first time Clancy took me there. It felt as though we were on that old dirt road for hours."

"It was a long, bumpy ride," smiled Dottie. "I still remember it, although it's been years and years since

I've been out there. Who knows, maybe they paved the road by now."

"Can't say what they've done to the old place. It's changed hands a number of times since Clive finally passed away. His kids didn't want anything to do with the place."

"In fact, when we heard Renie was workin' a dude ranch a couple years back, we didn't put two and two together until we heard where it was. Neither Bill or I knew it by the name Black Mountain Ranch," added Dottie.

Bill turned to Bullet. "Take some pictures for me, will ya?"

"Of course. And thank you again."

The smile left Bill's face. He stepped closer, and poked his finger into Bullet's chest. "You've got everything you need to be a champion bull rider. Take this week and get the hell out of your head for a while. Focus on the buck, not the bull."

Bullet could've finished Bill's sentence for him, he'd heard it so often. This week would be different though. He wouldn't be checking the time to make sure he wasn't late to pick up Grey. He wouldn't be worried about the broncs fighting, or anything else to do with the rough stock. This week would be all about bull riding, and nothing else.

"I'll say it again. I don't know how to thank you."

Dottie pulled Bullet into a hug. "You thank us every day, sweetheart, with how hard you work."

"Well, I best head over to the house, say goodbye to my family, and get on the road. What time am I meeting the flight in Edwards?"

"You need to be there by 3:30. If you leave in the next half hour, you should have time to stop for lunch on the way."

Bill told him the folks at the ranch asked if Bullet would mind picking up another guest from the local airport. Since there were few guests visiting this early in the year, their staff was short-handed. Bullet didn't mind. The fewer people who were there this week, the better. Now that he'd accepted he was going on vacation, the peace and quiet appealed to him.

"Uh, how will I know who I'm picking up?"

Dottie went back into the house. "I almost forgot. She'll be looking for this sign." She handed him a sign that said *Black Mountain Ranch*. "She'll find you."

She? Now this was an interesting development. One other guest, and he was meeting her at the airport. The week was looking more and more promising. Bullet could use a romp with a pretty cowgirl. Maybe then he'd be able to get his mind off Tristan McCullough.

Tristan's father told her to look for someone holding a sign saying *Black Mountain Ranch*. She was the only person they were meeting, and the airport was small, he'd told her. She shouldn't have any trouble finding her ride.

"Daddy, when I get home, there's something important I want to discuss with you. So please don't make any other travel arrangements for me until we've had time to sit down and talk."

"No problem, little girl. You have a safe flight, and a good time."

A good time? That was odd. She had business to conduct. He'd walked away before she could ask him about it. Must have just been a slip. Usually he told her to come home with a pad full of orders.

Tristan breathed a sigh of relief when the flight attendant closed the cabin door, and no one had claimed either of the empty seats in her row. It was bad enough that she was on an airplane again so soon. It would have been much worse if she'd been stuck with another boorish passenger who wanted to talk the entire flight.

Yesterday had been a nightmare. Harris spent most of the flight trying to chat with her. When she put on her headphones, snuggled under her cashmere pashmina and closed her eyes, he moved into the center seat, and offered his shoulder for her to rest her head. She didn't answer, just turned her back on him.

When he thought she was asleep, Tristan overheard him flirting with the all-too-willing-to-flirt-back flight attendant. Listening to them made her sick to her stomach. She turned the volume all the way up on her music, and it still wasn't enough to drown them out entirely.

When they landed and were waiting to depart, Harris tried again to woo her into having a drink with him. Instead of bothering to be polite, she simply answered "no" to each thing he asked. He hadn't been polite when he slept with half the women at every rodeo he attended, not giving a second thought to his "girlfriend." She didn't need to be polite to him now.

His parting words when he walked by her in baggage claim were, "This isn't over, Tristan. I want you back. I need you back." He leaned and whispered, "We were so good together, baby. I know you want me as much as I want you."

She'd rolled her eyes, but he had walked away. They might see each other at various rodeos, unless she saw him first.

Once they were airborne, Tristan closed her eyes. Today was going to be a long one. A nap would do her good, if she could only fall asleep.

"We're getting ready to land, miss," the flight attendant touched her arm. How could it be? Hadn't she just closed her eyes? Had she really slept the entire flight? Usually she couldn't sleep at all on planes.

Tristan had a one hour layover in Denver, but needed to get to the other side of the airport to catch the regional flight to Edwards. Fortunately many of her flights changed planes in Denver, so she was familiar with the airport.

An hour later she landed at the small airport near Vail. There would be no baggage carousel. Someone would bring the luggage on a cart. Once she had her bag, she'd look for her ride.

Bullet dozed off sitting in the airport waiting for the flight from Denver to arrive. He woke with a start and realized he'd dropped the sign on the floor beneath his chair. He reached down to get it and when he straightened up, he saw a woman looking out the window on the other side of the small terminal. He rubbed his eyes. From behind she looked so much like Tristan. *Wow.* He really needed to get laid, and get his mind off the elusive Miss McCullough.

He stood, holding his cardboard sign in front of him. He looked around the airport for any women who looked lost. So far everyone who had walked through had done so with the determination of someone who knew where she was going. The woman by the window turned, as though she was looking for someone. Bullet met her eyes at the same time she recognized him.

She approached him. "I don't understand."

"Hi, Tristan. How are you?" he smirked.

"I'm *fine*, Bullet. Now, please explain yourself."

"Explain myself?"

"Don't pretend you don't know what's going on here. How did you arrange this? A better question would be why did you do this? How in the world could you have thought this was a good idea?"

"I don't have any idea what the hell you're talkin' about." He was annoyed now, so he stepped around her, out closer to the walkway. "I'm meetin' someone here to give her a ride. If you'll excuse me, I'll see if I can find her."

"Uh, Bullet. You're looking for me. Or I'm looking for you. Black Mountain Ranch. That's what your sign says, right?"

"Oh. Shit."

"Yeah, that's right. You're caught. If you'll excuse me, I have to go find out when I can catch a flight back home."

"Wait a minute," Bullet tried to catch Tristan's arm, but she yanked it away. "Hold up a sec." She walked faster down the short length of the terminal.

Bullet sat in the closest chair. One way or another, she'd be back. He checked the board at the desk when he came in, there were no other flights scheduled in or out today. He crossed his arms in front of him, and waited.

"You really didn't know you were picking me up?" she asked as Bullet threw her bag into the back seat of the cab.

"Nope."

"And what are you doing here again?"

"Bull riding."

"I don't understand. My father said the owners of the ranch wanted to meet with me about private labeling some of our clothing. This is quite a coincidence, don't you think?"

"Yep."

He opened her door for her, and held his hand out to help her up. She was used to getting in and out of trucks, so she ignored his offer and climbed in on her own.

"Where is this place?"

Instead of answering, Bullet handed her the sheet of paper with directions to the ranch.

"Read 'em to me."

"You ever heard the word 'please'?"

"Nope."

What was his problem? It was logical for her to assume he was in on this. Did he really expect her to believe he didn't know she was the one he was picking up? Irritated, she set the map back on the seat of the truck, folded her arms, and looked out the window. She turned back and glared at him. "I don't know why *you're* mad."

"I don't know why anyone has to be mad," he grunted at her. "I didn't know, okay? That's the last time I'm gonna say it. And listen here, we're goin' to a ranch. If they call it a ranch, it means there's lots of land. You can't stand the sight of me? Keep away from me, and I'll do the same."

"I didn't say I couldn't stand the sight of you. What makes you think I feel that way? I just don't think you're telling me the truth. The two have little to do with each other."

"You callin' me a liar and you not being able to stand the sight of me are the same thing in my book. Now I suggest you stop with the accusations if you still want a ride. You be quiet, I'll take you to the ranch. Deal?"

She didn't answer.

"I asked you a question, McCullough."

"I heard you."

"Then answer me or I'll pull this truck over and you can fend for yourself."

"Deal."

"Good. Now read me the directions."

***

1968

"Your mama asked me to come get her and your sister," Clancy said at the dinner table.

"You don't mind? Couldn't her husband drive her here, or am I that bad that he can't bring my mama to my high school graduation?"

"Bad? Where'd you get that idea?"

"I ain't seen my mama more than twice in the last few years. Gotta be somethin' wrong with me."

Clancy dropped his fork and looked at Bill. "There isn't anything wrong with you. The problems are his fault, not yours."

In all the years he'd known him, Bill rarely saw Clancy angry. And this time, he seemed very much so.

"It's time you knew the truth about what's been goin' on."

Bill sat still and waited. Over the last three years, Clancy had been called away from the ranch at least a half dozen times without offering explanation. It bothered Bill. Clancy was never secretive. When the first phone call came and Clancy told him he was going to Colorado Springs to help Bill's mama with something, he asked Bill to trust that he knew best. Clancy wouldn't say more. After all the man had done for him and his family, Bill couldn't argue.

"Your mama isn't married to Mr. Snyder any longer."

"She isn't?" Bill felt the heat rising in his cheeks. His mama had gotten a divorce and he hadn't known anything about it? A sense of betrayal was forming in his chest, making it hard for him to breathe. "What else have you been keepin' from me, Clancy?" Bill stood and stepped away from the kitchen table.

"It's a recent development. I just found out myself, so sit yourself back down and I'll tell you the story."

12

"I'm sorry," Tristan said, over a half hour into the drive.

"Yeah? What for?"

"For, uh...I'm not sure...whatever I said that offended you."

"You have no idea?"

"No, not really. I know you said I called you a liar, but I didn't."

"Did you believe what I was tellin' you?"

"No."

"And what do you call someone who tells you somethin' you don't believe."

"I doubted what you were saying. That's different than saying I thought you were lying."

"Tristan, come on. Listen to yourself. It's the same thing."

Tristan shook her head. "You're right. And I am sorry, Bullet."

"For two people who haven't spent much time together, you and I say we're sorry an awful lot. You notice that?"

Now that he mentioned it, she did. "I think it's more me apologizing to you rather than the other way around."

"You're forgiven."

"Will you talk to me now?"

"Yeah. I'll talk."

"Tell me why you're here again."

Bullet told her about finding Gram and his parents at his house when he got back from Crested Butte, and then about Bill and Dottie arranging for him to spend a week at the ranch.

"Didn't it seem strange?" she asked.

"Hell yeah, it did. But my whole life is strange right now. I questioned it, sure. But then when Bill said I'd spend the week training and gettin' on bulls, I figured what the hell? Why are you here?"

"I told you. I'm meeting with the ranch owners about our clothing."

"Bet that isn't the real reason."

"What does that mean?"

"I just wonder why you're really here." Bullet laughed.

"I'm not here because you're here. That's for damn sure."

He laughed again and shook his head. "Let me ask you this," he began. "Is there something you want for yourself? Something someone knows about, and also knows that you never put what you want before everything else in your life?"

"Yes, there is," she murmured.

"What is it?"

"I don't want to tell you."

Bullet raised an eyebrow in her direction.

"It isn't that I don't want to tell you specifically. It's just not something I'm ready to talk to anyone about."

"So you haven't told anyone what it is?"

"I didn't say that. I did tell someone."

"Who?"

"Liv. And…"

"Who? Come on, just tell me."

"Your sister. And Dottie knows too."

"I'm here to work on my dream. Maybe you are too. What's your dream, Tristan? Just tell me."

It took her a long time to answer, but finally she had to admit it wasn't anything to make a big deal of. What would it hurt to tell him? "I'm designing a new line of clothing."

"That doesn't sound much different than what you're already doing."

He was right, clothing was her business. But this was different. This was for her.

"It's a women's line. Not necessarily for Lost Cowboy. I mean, maybe. I don't know." She looked away from him. "I haven't had time to discuss it with my father." she murmured.

"Why not?"

Well, she'd planned to, until he shuffled her off on a plane this morning.

"It's nothing, really. Just designs at this point. I rarely have time to work on it."

"Makes sense then."

"What does?"

"You'll have plenty of time to design stuff if you're hangin' out here for a week."

"But why here? My father could have put me on a plane to just about anywhere."

"Renie and Jace used to work this ranch. That's where they met. Liv probably suggested it to your father as a good place to get away."

That made sense, although she doubted Liv was this manipulative.

"She just wants you to be happy."

Tristan studied Bullet. "How did you know what I was thinking?"

"I don't know. I just do."

"And what am I thinking right now?"

Bullet covered her hand with his. "You'll make me blush, Miss Tristan, askin' me to say it out loud."

Tristan pulled her hand away and crossed her arms. She couldn't hide her smile, or the heat she felt creeping into her cheeks. That hadn't been what she was thinking about, but now it was.

They had their own cabins, next door to each other. Bullet unloaded Tristan's bags for her, and waited while the female ranch manager explained the schedule to them.

"You're both experienced riders, so just call this number when you want to go for a ride," she handed them each a business card. "I make breakfast and dinner for the ranch workers. It's served in the dining hall which you passed on your way in. You're on your own for lunch, but there's plenty you can grab and take with you at breakfast. If there's anything else you want, just leave me a note and I'll get it for you as soon as I can, usually it's the same day."

She gave Bullet another card, with a number on it for his trainer. She told him to call him right away and let him know he'd arrived. They'd start work that afternoon.

"Any other questions?"

Bullet and Tristan shook their heads.

She pointed to another building, south of the pond. "There's a steam room and sauna, workout equipment, and you can schedule massages or facials. We have folks on staff year round for the spa."

A massage sounded really good to Tristan, especially after spending the better part of two days on an airplane.

"Is there a hot tub?" Bullet asked, looking at Tristan when he did. He winked at her when her gaze met his.

"Yes, there is. And a lap pool."

"This is quite a setup. I didn't expect it to be this elaborate," Tristan commented.

"People pay big bucks to spend a week with us. They come over from Vail and Aspen, or fly in like you did. A few years ago business started to fall off. Research told us we had to offer the spa services along with gourmet food, dancing, hot cowboys, easy and healthy horses, and loads of options for daily activities. The owners paid attention. Now we sell out just about every week we're open."

"Do you know anything about a private clothing line?" Tristan ventured.

"Oh, I'm glad you mentioned that. Yes, I'm supposed to arrange a meeting with you, me, and Stewart. He's the owner. I understand your company has a new woman's line in the works. We'd love to be among the first to offer it." She picked up a catalog that had been sitting on the coffee table in the cabin. "This is the majority of what we offer now. We sell to folks around the world through this and our website. Take a look through it and see if you think your pieces would be a good fit, although from what we've heard from Liv Rice, they will be."

Tristan glanced at Bullet who had an "I told you so" look on his face. She looked again at the card.

"Thank you, Piper. That's you, right?"

"Oh goodness, didn't I introduce myself? Yes, I'm Piper."

Tristan and Bullet shook hands with her, and she left.

"Guess I'll see you around." Bullet walked toward the cabin door.

"Sure, see you."

"If you're interested, I can let you know where I'll be practicin'. When I know, that is."

Once again Tristan was reminded how different Bullet was from Harris. Seeing the lecher who broke her heart really put their differences in perspective. Bullet was his own man, but she'd never let him be. Instead she thought of him as Harris Jones' clone.

"I'd like that," she said after too long a time. She saw Bullet visibly exhale as though he was waiting for her answer to breathe again. "Maybe we could check out the hot tub later too," she added.

If only she had a camera to capture the stunned look on Bullet's face. It was priceless.

"Yeah? Did you bring your bathing suit?"

When Tristan walked closer to the cabin door, Bullet stepped over the threshold. "Nope, I sure didn't." She could only imagine the look on his face now was even more priceless as she closed the door behind him.

She wasn't sure what had gotten into her, other than she felt like giving him back a little of what he gave her. It had been a long time since she let herself flirt so brazenly with a man. It felt good. Instead of feeling like a nun, she felt like a woman.

Bullet could barely walk let alone remember how his phone worked. The last thing, the very last thing, he expected from Tristan was for her to flirt with him, and so *brazenly.*

How the hell was he supposed to focus on bulls now? Maybe he should go back, knock on her door, and wait a few hours to call his trainer. In fact, maybe he should wait until tomorrow to call him.

"Hey there, you Bullet?" a man shouted from down near the corral.

"Yes, sir, I am."

"I'm Buck Bishop. I understand you're quite the young bull rider."

The two met halfway on the path between the cabins and the corral. "Don't know about that, but I sure want to be."

"Let's get to work then."

He'd heard of Buck, he was known as one of the best bull riders and trainers in the world. But Bullet had heard he'd retired.

He'd taken Tristan's bag to her cabin, but his was still in the truck. "I'll stow my bag and grab my gear."

"I'll be waitin'. Don't dally."

Dallying would be the last thing he'd do. Having an opportunity like this was once in a lifetime.

As he walked back to his truck, he could hear music coming from Tristan's cabin. Talk about an opportunity of a lifetime. He'd have two this week. And he intended to take full advantage of both.

Tristan unpacked her clothes and put them in the rustic-looking wardrobe. Everything in the room was designed to look old-time western, but upon closer inspection, the fabrics used, the construction of the furniture, even the fixtures, were the best of the best. She was beginning to understand that while those vacationing at the ranch wanted an authentic experience, they also wanted high-end comfort.

She ran her hand over the granite counters in the over-sized bathroom, and was pleased to see a jetted soaking tub big enough for two.

Back in the main room of the cabin she found a docking station for her smart phone, and chose the playlist she listened to most often when she was designing.

She heard the door of the cabin next door close, and peeked out the window. Bullet was on his way to the corral, carrying most of his gear. He'd already put on his chaps and vest, and in his hand he carried his bull rope, leather glove, and protective helmet. She was happy to see it had a mask attached similar to those worn by hockey players. It would be downright sinful for a face as perfectly rugged as his to be injured. His jeans hugged his butt as he swaggered more than walked down the pathway.

The chaps he wore were relatively plain compared to most she'd seen. They were made of black leather, with fringe along the sides and bottom. Tan leather accents dressed them up a bit, but Tristan knew for certain that Bullet would want flashier chaps for actual competitions.

Perhaps she'd sketch a few designs for men's chaps this afternoon too. She was sure her father expected her to be working on the Lost Cowboy line this week. She'd go home with some for him, along with more for her.

First she'd spend a few minutes making notes for Bullet's Lost Cowboy story. It was another thing that came out of her run-in with Harris. Comparing the two had made it so clear. Bullet *was* a Lost Cowboy, and he was working damn hard to find his way back. He was a flirt, no question, but the more she got to know him, the more she realized he was a decent man. The story was a go, and soon, so would the sponsorship.

There wasn't anything Buck told Bullet that he hadn't heard before from Bill. The difference was Buck was harder on him than Bill had ever been, and there wasn't anyone or anything else to distract him from seeing every single mistake Bullet made. He was patient though, and while he pointed things out to him, Buck didn't seem frustrated.

"Good first out," he patted him on the back. "That's enough for today. I have a good idea what we'll focus on this week." Buck handed Bullet a folder. "Here's your workout schedule." He pointed toward the same building Piper had. "You'll find a workout room in there. When you finish your sets, I want you to hit either the steam or the sauna, but not both. Then get yourself into the hot tub."

"Yes, sir," Bullet said, perusing the sheets of paper in the folder. He'd never worked out this hard in his life, not even when he was in high school and played football and baseball.

"You swim?"

"Yes, I do."

"In the back you'll see some workouts you can do in the lap pool. That'll be less hard on your joints on days you're feelin' sore."

Bullet saw Buck had a schedule for each day he would be at the ranch. It started right after breakfast, and ended right before dinner. It looked as though he'd have time to himself in the evening, if he wasn't too exhausted to move.

"Thank you, sir," Bullet shook Buck's hand. "I don't know who set all this up, but I sure do appreciate your time. I guess I should ask what I'm gonna owe you."

"That's all taken care of. Don't give it another thought."

Bullet figured as much, which is why he hadn't asked earlier. Could be that Flying R covered it as part of his sponsorship. Bill could've too, in which case, he'd pay him back every penny, either in cash or in damn hard work. There was a possibility it was his parents, but that was the least likely option.

Both he and Lyric were raised to make their own way in the world. His gram's house was nice, and they never wanted for anything they needed, but they were expected to earn their keep. As far as he was concerned, learning the value of a dollar, and the importance of having a good work ethic were the best things his family taught his sister and him.

He knew if he ever really needed financial help his parents would give it to him. So far, he hadn't. Even with paying child support to Pearl's mother, and providing for Callie and Grey while they were still in Oklahoma and he was in Colorado, he'd made it work.

He did it by living simply, not extravagantly. And always working. He'd gotten his first ranch job while he was still in high school. While his buddies were still in bed, he was at the ranch helping with morning chores. If he didn't have sports practice after school, he'd be over there again. They paid him a good wage, but he earned it. Along with it, he earned a reputation that had ranches competing over him when it came time to hire for calving season, or branding.

It was his off-hours that got him into trouble. When he'd go out after work, he and his buddies would dare each other to do just about anything. They'd have drinking dares, who could pick up certain women dares, who could come up with the best pickup line that actually worked dares.

He'd won that one hands down one night, with three different women. All he'd done was walk up, look'em up and down, and say, "Nice shoes. Wanna fuck?" It said something about the caliber of women they ran into at the bars in his hometown. Looking back on it, Bullet was ashamed of the way he acted.

If he ran into one of those buddies now, they'd have a hard time believing it had been over two months since he'd been with a woman. There had been a time when he couldn't go two days.

Maybe he was finally growing up. And maybe he wasn't quite as irresponsible as everyone else believed.

"See ya in the mornin'," Buck waved. Bullet had forgotten he was there.

"Yeah, see ya. And thanks," he waved back. He pulled his phone out of his pocket. He didn't have a signal way out here, but he saw he had about an hour before dinner. Time enough for a shower and sprucing himself up for what he hoped would be a dinner date with the lovely Tristan McCullough.

She was already there when Bullet walked into the dining hall. She stood at the bar talking with the cowboy behind it pouring her a drink. She looked mighty fine in her sleeveless blouse and flowery short skirt. It had been warm today, unseasonably so, and it looked as though she'd spent some time in the sun. Her long legs were tucked into her calf-high boots, and her toe tapped to the beat of the music.

She turned then, and looked at him. Once again her cheeks pinkened, as they often did when she smiled at him. Behind her ear, tucked into her flowing, long blonde hair, was a daisy. He remembered seeing the vase full of them sitting on the desk in her cabin. He didn't remember seeing flowers in his.

Strands of her hair fell forward and curled around her cheeks. She moistened her lips and he remembered how soft they'd felt when he kissed her on Liv and Ben's front porch.

Her gaze fell when he got close, her lips curved into a sweet smile. "You looked good out there."

"You were watchin'?" Once again her cheeks gradually turned a faint pink.

"For a little while." She looked up at him. "Would you like to join me for a drink?"

He sat on the stool next to hers. Her body was close enough that he could smell her natural scent—sunshine and the outdoors mingled with something else, roses maybe. Or daisies. When she moistened her lips again, something passed between them. He felt it, and knew she did too.

"You smell good," he said, leaning in close.

"So do you," Tristan rested her hand on the bar. He longed to cover it with his, but he'd wait. He'd be in no hurry tonight, instead savoring every minute he could be alone with her.

"I was afraid I'd smell like horses, or bulls," he laughed.

"No, it's more leather, and freshly cut hay. I like it." When she reached up and touched his hair an electric current surged through his body. He breathed in slowly as her fingers toyed with the curls that formed around his face when his hair was wet. He reached over and touched her hair too.

"We both have curls." He could feel the heat spreading through him. He'd barely touched her, yet his heart thundered. He wanted to kiss her so badly. He hoped he could make it through dinner.

"Bullet, I've judged you unfairly…"

"What's this about?" he soothed.

She shook her head. "I had a bad experience with a bull rider—"

"Shh now, we don't need to talk about that." He longed to draw her close, and make her forget any other bull riders existed.

"No, I do need to talk about it. I haven't been fair to you because of it. I saw him a couple of days ago, and I realized then, you're nothing like him."

Bullet felt his stomach muscles tighten. It wasn't what she was saying, it was the idea that she'd just spent time with someone she'd had a bad experience with.

"What did he do?" His heart tightened. Why was the idea of her with another man, any other man, painful?

"When? I mean, originally, or a couple of days ago?"

"Either one."

"I met him when I was competing. He was a bull rider, I was a barrel racer. He swept me off my feet, and then broke my heart. It didn't happen that quickly. It was long and drawn out and miserable."

Bullet leaned forward. He couldn't bear to hear another word. Before he could think better of it, he kissed her. He waited to see if she'd pull away, but she didn't, so he kissed her again, this time more deeply.

"Bullet—"

"Shh," he soothed again. "Don't pull away from me."

He put his hand on the nape of her neck, and rested his forehead against hers. "I can't resist you. No matter how hard I try to go slow, I get close to you and I can't help but kiss you."

"I know," Tristan rested her hands on his chest. Bullet didn't know if anyone else was in the dining hall, and didn't care. "I feel the same way."

"Do you want this, Tristan? I mean, really want it? You've been sendin' me some mixed signals, girl."

"That's what I was trying to tell you. It was never you, Bullet. It was my past, haunting me. I let an experience I had with someone else cloud my judgment of you. It was unfair, and I'm sorry."

"So, does that mean yes?"

She smiled. "Yes, I do want this. Right now, more than anything."

He groaned at her admission, tightened his grip on her nape, and kissed her again.

Bullet's lips on hers felt so good. He alternated between ravaging her and kissing her softly and slowly. His mouth moved against hers with warmth. He was tender with her, and loving.

She opened her mouth to him, but her hands remained on his chest. His muscles were hard beneath her fingers, and she longed to slide inside his pearl snaps and feel his skin.

"Oh, sorry. Oops."

Tristan moved away from Bullet when she heard Piper's voice. "Wait," she said, pulling further away from Bullet.

Piper turned around, and Tristan saw a tray in her hand.

"Is that dinner?"

"The first course anyway. I can keep it in the back if you're not ready to eat yet," she looked between them and smiled.

Tristan felt the heat in her cheeks once again. At this rate she'd spend the entire week in a state of embarrassment.

"I'm ready. What about you Bullet?"

"I'm famished."

Tristan met his gaze. It was obvious he wasn't talking about dinner.

"Shall we then?"

"You have your pick of tables," said Piper.

Bullet took her hand and led her to a table by the front window. "How's this?"

"It's perfect."

Bullet held her chair for her to sit.

Piper placed an appetizer plate in front of her, and then placed the other across the table. Bullet picked it up, and brought it to the place next to her instead.

"Don't mind if I sit next to you, do you? I want to be as close as I can."

He ran his fingers up and down her bare arm. She closed her eyes and concentrated on his touch. He leaned closer and kissed her shoulder.

"I thought you were famished."

"I am. And you know what I meant, don't pretend you don't. You're famished too, I can feel it."

Chill bumps covered her arms, and she trembled under his touch. There would be no pretending with Bullet. He read her perfectly.

"Seriously, you must be starving."

"Uh huh," he murmured, his teeth gently grazing the skin on her shoulder.

Piper approached their table with a bottle of wine in hand. "I can bring dinner to your cabins. Or cabin, if you'd prefer."

"No," gasped Tristan. "We're, uh, fine."

"Would you like a glass of wine? It's a Chardonnay, but if you'd prefer something else—"

"No, that's fine." Why did she keep saying everything was fine? "It's perfect, thank you." Tristan held her glass out for Piper to pour.

"Sir, would you like some wine?"

"I'll have whatever the lady is having," he answered. Tristan could feel his gaze on her. She doubted he'd even looked at Piper.

"Enjoy your first course. Pear and goat cheese on crostini with fig confit, in case you were wondering."

"Mmm," Bullet moaned. "It sounds amazing. Thank you, Piper."

He was using that tone of voice again, the one she'd heard him use with the filly. When Bullet talked that way, women seemed to melt around him. Tristan didn't miss the way Piper's cheeks turned pink the same way hers had.

Bullet lifted his crostini to her lips. "Take a bite."

"Don't you want it?"

"Sure I do. We're gonna share."

Tristan took a bite. Bullet popped the other half in his mouth. "Your turn," he said.

She lifted her crostini to his lips and instead of taking a small bite as she had, he took the whole thing, his mouth catching her fingers as he did.

"Hey, that isn't fair."

"I take what I want Tristan. That's meant as a warning." His deep voice reverberated through her. Her breath quickened as he continued to trail a finger softly down the length of her arm. When he reached her hand, he clasped it, and brought it to his mouth. He licked each finger where she'd held the crostini. "I don't know which tastes better. I think it's you," he murmured. "And I want more. A lot more."

****

1968

Bill sat at the table and waited for Clancy to continue. Instead of talking, Clancy stood, went to the refrigerator and took out a beer. "Want one?"

Bill didn't drink often, but cowboys didn't pay much attention to him bein' underage. This was the first time Clancy had offered him one at home though.

"Sure." He tried to sound nonchalant, while inside he wanted to scream at Clancy to tell him what was going on with his mama. Maybe that's why he offered him a beer, to calm him down some.

"You remember the first time we met Russ, right?"

Bill nodded.

"Neither of us had a good feeling about that man. And we were right."

"What did he do to her?" Bill felt as though the top of his head was going to blow off. His anger had reached a boiling point. If that man had laid a hand on his mama, he'd kill him.

"It isn't what you're thinkin'. What he did brought more trouble on himself than it did on your mama and sister."

"Just tell me for Christ's sake," Bill stood and paced the kitchen floor.

"The first time I was called down there, was because Russ ended up in jail, and your mama asked me to come and bail him out. She didn't have the money to do it."

"What was he in for?"

"He got into it with some fellas he was playing cards with. That's the root of the problem right there. Russ Snyder is a gambler."

"You get arrested for that?"

"Nah, but you do get arrested for assault. When he gambles, he drinks. Drinkin' is what brings on the violence."

Bill set his beer on the counter. Just the thought of it was turning his stomach. "What did you have to do?"

"I got him out of jail and got him a lawyer. The lawyer got him off for time served, and probation. Russ promised your mama he'd quit gamblin', but it wasn't six months before a friend of your mama called me again."

"What happened then?"

"Pretty much the same thing, only this time your mama was too ashamed to call me. When I got there, I talked some sense into her. The next time it happened, she called me herself."

"How many times?" Bill was trying to remember how many times Clancy left the ranch with no explanation.

"All together, it happened six times. Not every circumstance was the same. A couple of times he left for several days, and your mama had no idea how to find him. She was afraid he was gonna turn up dead."

"Did you have to bail him out each time?" Bill couldn't believe his mama would rely on Clancy that way. It wasn't up to him to give her money. Bill had money. He could've helped.

"What happened to the money we've been sendin' her? Does he take it from her?" Bill was spitting mad at the thought that his hard-earned money was being gambled away. That money was for his mama and sister, not for Mr. Snyder.

"He doesn't know about that money, somehow she's managed to hide it from him. And she refused to use it to bail him out. After the first time, I wouldn't bail him out either, and she didn't want me to. I figured spendin' a few nights in jail might scare him enough to quit."

"What took her so long to divorce him?" This didn't sound like his mama. Before his daddy died, and the whole while he was sick, his mama managed things all on her own.

"Well…that's complicated. Each time he promised it would never happen again. And she loves him, or at least she did. Sometimes you wanna believe the best about someone you love, even though they keep provin' themselves unworthy."

"What's gonna happen to my mama and my sister? I have money saved up. I can get them a place in McCoy. Maybe she could find a job here."

Clancy rubbed his face with his hands. "No son, your mama owns the house in Colorado Springs now."

"I don't understand. Whose house? Mr. Snyder's?"

Clancy nodded. "The last time Russ got into trouble, it was bigger than before. And this time, they weren't just threatening him. They were comin' after your mama."

Bill felt the blood drain from his face. "What'd you do?" He could barely get the words out.

"I paid the money he owed, but only after he signed the deed to the house over to your mama. Then I gave him the money to get the hell out of town. I told him if he showed his face around again, I'd be waitin' with a shotgun."

Bill slunk down into his chair. All this time he'd been working the ranch, riding bulls and broncs, writing letters to Dottie, and not worrying about his mama at all. He was a terrible son.

"Your mama and sister are comin' to your graduation, Bill. Once we get you settled at Western State, I'll be leaving the ranch."

"What? I don't understand." Why would Clancy leave the ranch? If this had something to do with his family, Bill would never forgive himself.

Clancy leaned forward and rested his elbows on the table. "I made your daddy a promise that I would look out for his family after he passed. I haven't been doin' too good a job of it."

Bill hesitated. Clancy couldn't give up his share of the ranch because of a promise he'd made his daddy. He had his own life to live. No, that wouldn't be the way it would go. Instead of Clancy going to live with his mama and sister, he'd go. If he could get into Western State there had to be a college near Colorado Springs he could get into. It hurt his heart to think he wouldn't be attending college with Dottie, but his heart hurt more knowing he hadn't been there when his mama needed him.

The other thing it meant was that it was time to give up rodeo. He was at a crossroad. If he went one direction, he'd continue living life as a selfish ingrate. If he went the other way, he knew in his heart he'd be doing the right thing.

"I'll go," he said finally. "It's time I started takin' care of my family, Clancy. You've been better to us than anyone could ask, and I appreciate all you've done, but it's time for me to take responsibility."

Clancy smiled. He looked different tonight. Weary, yet not stressed. "That's the other part of the story, young Flynn. You better get yourself another beer to hear this part."

13

Being alone in the dining room wasn't necessarily a good thing. Bullet tried to keep his hands off Tristan so she could eat, but he couldn't. If he wasn't touching her, the yearn to do so overpowered his ability to resist.

She'd lean into him, as though her body yearned for his in the same way.

"Finished?" She'd barely set her fork down when he asked.

She drew a deep breath, and her eyes turned hazy. "I'm either finished, or just getting started, depending on how you look at it."

Bullet felt the blood leave the rest of his body and settle in his groin.

"Let's go," he stood and held his hand out to her.

"Do we need to let Piper know we're leaving?"

"I think she knows, darlin'."

Bullet watched the flush spread up her cheeks.

"I'll walk you back…"

"I hope you plan to do more than that, Bullet."

Oh, he did. Much more. Starting with picking her up, tossing her over his shoulder, and running up the hill to the cabin. Instead, he held her hand, and his breath, until they reached her cabin door.

Tristan reached for the doorknob, but couldn't bring herself to open it. Instead she turned around. Bullet was so close, their bodies would soon fuse. Tristan stared into his eyes, her cheeks warmed. "I want you to know, I don't do this…"

With a quick nod, he pressed her up against the door. "I do." He brushed his nose against her hair, and trailed kisses down to her temple, her ear, her neck.

"Bullet, we should talk."

His lips found hers, and oh, God, he tasted good. He slid his hand into her hair, and slanted her head, nudging her lips open. His tongue pierced deeply, as his lips devoured hers. Tristan held on to his biceps, so hard and sexy, and pressed up against the flexing muscles in his chest. She could feel her affect on him as she pressed her body closer. The idea of having him inside her made her dizzy. She gripped his arms more tightly, her fingers digging into his flesh.

"We'll talk later. Now open the door," he demanded. Tristan turned her hand on the knob, and Bullet turned her into the cabin. His hand went back into her hair, clenching hard enough to hold her in a possessive embrace.

He tugged her hair, tipping her head back, to gain access to her throat. He ran his tongue down further, tasting her skin.

"Wait—"

"No. No more waiting." Bullet brought his lips back to hers, and delved his tongue in deeply. He wanted to consume her. All of her.

She groaned, igniting him further. His fingers hooked the strap of her bra through her shirt, and released it in one quick motion. He slid his fingers along her buttons, releasing each as he went, until she stood before him, shirt open, bra drooping. She shimmied the shirt from her arms, and Bullet pulled her bra first off one arm, then the other. He could see the outline of the curves of her breasts by the light of the moon through the window. But he wanted more.

He pulled her toward the bed, and eased her against it. "Sit for me." He walked to the nightstand and turned the low light of the lamp on. "I want to see you."

He knelt on the floor next to her, and cupped one breast with his hand. "And feel you." Her eyes closed, and she leaned forward.

"Look at me. Watch me," he demanded.

When her eyes reopened, he covered her taut nipple with his mouth, his tongue swirled around it, until it beaded. When she rested back on the bed, he followed. He ran his hand up the inside of her thigh, and under her skirt. He eased her panties down, and tossed them aside.

"I want to taste you." He teased his tongue along her inner thigh, and up, licking as he went.

Tristan ran her fingers into his hair, holding him where he was, yet feeling as though she should stop him. She was naked, he remained fully clothed. Since the night in Crested Butte, when they sparred at the hot tub, she'd fantasized about seeing him naked again. She'd seen then, but hadn't been able to touch. Her fingers craved his body, his skin.

He stopped, as though he sensed what she was thinking. He stood between her legs that hung off the end of the bed, and opened the pearl snaps on his shirt in one swoop. His gaze ran over her body, his hands rested on his belt buckle.

"Please hurry," she gasped.

"On no, I've imagined this too many times to hurry through it." He leaned forward and lifted her arms over her head. "Leave them there for me, so I can see you stretched out, waiting, welcoming me into you."

She wanted to beg him to look later, but knew her protests would only result in him taking more time. He'd take what he wanted, that's what he'd told her at dinner.

"I've thought about this since the night in the hot tub, fantasized about having your body laid out before me so I could look and taste my fill."

He knelt down again, and brought her foot to rest on his shoulder. He trailed kisses from her ankle, up her calf, and to her knee. She squirmed when he reached her inner thigh. His kisses quickened, and soon he reached her apex. He took turns bringing her pleasure with his lips and fingers. "Let me take care of you, Tristan. Just relax," he stroked into her, teasing, playing.

"*Please*," she moaned, and arched against his hand and mouth.

"Tristan, darlin', I'm not gonna last too long," Bullet breathed. He'd spent too many nights imagining being inside her, now that he was about to, he knew he wouldn't be able to control his response. When she wrapped her long legs around his waist, and her thighs tightened around his hips, he knew he couldn't dare even move. Tristan shifted, just a slight motion with her hips, and he could feel her tighten around him. He drew in a shaky breath, and covered her moan with his mouth.

He held her there, until the last of her aftershocks squeezed him. Gently, he rolled until he was under her, and still inside her. He needed to ease away from her, get up, and dispose of his condom. If she was feeling the way he was, they'd both be ready again in no time.

Tristan had to watch closely to see the rise and fall of his chest, he slept so deeply. It was another way he was different from Harris.

The differences showed themselves daily if not hourly. Bullet didn't snore, Harris sounded like a chainsaw. Bullet took care of *her*. Everything Harris did was for himself, for his own pleasure. Until last night, Tristan had no idea the kind of pleasure Bullet gave her was possible. Over and over again, he brought her to the brink, pulled back, and then sent her soaring again. Remembering, she squeezed her thighs together—and winced. She rolled over, and discovered more muscles that needed soothing, but all in a good way.

Soft light filtered in through the curtains on the cabin window. It was early, she should let Bullet sleep. If she drew a warm bath, would it wake him?

Sliding gently from the bed, she tiptoed into the luxurious bathroom, quietly closing the door behind her. Warm water ran softly from the far rim of the tub, like a waterfall. She shook the bath salts she found on the counter into her hand, and ran it under the water in a sweeping motion. The scent of lavender and eucalyptus filled the air. Tristan took a deep breath, and sank into the warm water.

Thinking about last night, she ran her hands along the inside of her thighs. Bullet's hands on her had been strong, yet gentle. They didn't have sex last night, he made love to her. He took his time, soothing her with his words as he explored her body. Over and over he told her how beautiful she was, and how much he wanted her.

Her fingers trailed up her body, and she ran her hands over her breasts. Just the skim of fingers over her nipples revealed how sore they were this morning.

"I should be doin' that," Bullet whispered in her ear. "You startin' without me this mornin'?" He covered her mouth with his, and eased her lips open, his tongue playful against hers.

"Let me in," he breathed. Tristan opened her eyes, and realized he meant the tub. She scooted forward and Bullet climbed in behind her. He slid his long legs on either side of her, and pulled her back into him. "Relax against me."

She reached over, turned the water off, and then rested her back against his chest. He put his hands on hers and brought them back to her breasts. "Now where were you when I interrupted you? Were you imagining it was me doin' this to you?"

He tightened his grip, and his fingers slid over hers, and squeezed each of her nipples, hard. Briefly, pain from their soreness shot through her, quickly replaced with pleasure that shot down the length of her body. He released her hands, and she started to move hers away.

"Leave them there," he demanded. "I want to watch." She continued what he'd started, while his hands explored other parts of her body, making their way down until his fingers found her sex. She jolted when they found their target, but his strong arms around her kept her still. "Relax and let me take care of you." His voice was raspy. His fingers read the subtle nuances of her body.

His arms were tight against the sides of her body, pinning her between his legs. She couldn't move, let alone squirm away from his incessant touch. Her orgasm came on so quickly, it surprised her. "That's what I like to see." He continued to soothe, bringing her down from her release.

Her thoughts drifted as she once again relaxed against him. He was good. Really good. How many women had experienced such pleasure from his strong hands, his body?

He trailed his fingers up her arms, and squeezed her shoulders. "Thought I told you to relax." His tongue followed his words into her ear, and she was powerless to do anything but his bidding. She pushed the intrusive thoughts of other women out of her mind, and focused on what his hands and mouth were doing to her. "That's better." Could he really read her that well?

He reached over and lifted the jar of lavender scrub. "What's this?" he asked, but Tristan doubted he expected an answer. Next he picked up the loofah she had unwrapped and set on the edge of the tub before she'd drawn the bath.

"Does this hurt?" he rubbed the scrub-coated loofah along her arm.

"No, it feels wonderful," she crooned. He continued, carefully washing each of her arms before scooping more of the scrub onto her breasts.

"I'll be careful of these," he promised, tapping her nipples with his index fingers. He continued to loofah her tummy, and the tops of her thighs. Tristan felt him rise from the water, and turned around to see him sitting on the tile on the edge of the tub. He wrapped his arms around her waist, and pulled her back, so she rested where he'd been sitting.

"Lean forward, and let me scrub your back." He moved her long hair out of his way, and she felt him spread the scrub across her shoulders. He was gentle as he pampered her, the same way he'd been when he made love to her. A groan of pleasure escaped her lips.

He smiled. "I guess I'm doin' this right."

"So right." Tristan closed her eyes and let her mind enjoy the sensations of Bullet washing every part of her body.

"Slide further in," he gently pushed her shoulders. "Get your hair wet for me."

He shampooed her hair, and then ran conditioner through it. With both hands, he massaged her scalp. His hands were strong, yet he knew how to be gentle.

"Have you ever considered a career in massage?"

Bullet laughed, but his voice was serious. "I haven't done this to any other woman, and Tristan, in the future I don't intend to have my hands on anyone but you."

She didn't really believe him, but smiled anyway. It didn't matter. For now, she was the one enjoying his caresses. At the end of the day, or the end of the week, they'd eventually make their way back into their own lives. She wouldn't allow herself to think about his hands on other women, and spoil the time she had with him.

Harris had done a number on her, and for a long time, she allowed the past hurt to keep her from living in the present. She had grown up a lot since her time with the philandering bull rider. Her heart had toughened, and at the same time, she'd matured.

"You still here?" Bullet teased. He'd shifted so he was facing her, his back against the other side of the tub. His hands continued pampering as he lavished the scrub on her feet.

"Yes, I'm still here," she purred.

"Good, 'cause I don't want your mind driftin' anywhere else. I want your full attention right here, knowin' it's my hands makin' you feel this way."

Did he think her mind was on someone else? How could it be? Not with the way his hands were making her feel. He rested her foot in the water, and stared into her eyes.

"I like you this way."

"Which way is that?"

"Open to me." He put his hands on her knees and opened her legs. "Put your ankles on the edge of the tub," he said, as he helped rest them where he wanted them. "That's better."

Tristan's natural response was to cover herself, but she didn't do it. Instead she met his gaze, and looked into his eyes as he again brought her to the release he was so good at coaxing from her.

"Your turn," she said after she'd recovered from the orgasm that shook her to her core.

Bullet closed his eyes and slunk his body deeper into the water. When he joined her in the bath, he'd planned to hold her while they soaked, but having her in front of him, naked, was more than he could resist. He wanted his hands on her, everywhere at once. His brain wanted him to take his time, but the rest of him refused to listen.

He'd watched her last night, every time she climaxed. The look on her face was addictive. Five minutes after he saw it, he wanted to see it again. Her body responded to him as though it had been his to enjoy forever. In the same way they fit when he held her, or danced with her, their bodies were a perfect fit when he made love to her.

As she reciprocated the care and nurturing he had given her body, he felt his heart slipping deeper into feelings he'd never experienced before. This was far more than lust, far more than he'd ever felt for anyone, including Callie. Bullet knew for certain, he was falling in love with Tristan McCullough.

"I wish I had time to have breakfast with you, but I'm late, and I have a feeling no one is ever late to a training session with Buck Bishop," Bullet sighed.

"Buck Bishop? *The* Buck Bishop? That's who you're training with?"

"Yes, ma'am. Isn't that somethin'?"

"And it's just you. No one else is training with him this week?"

"I got him all to myself." Clearly Tristan understood the significance of what that meant. He had to pinch himself to make sure he wasn't dreaming even as he said it.

"I'm really happy for you, Bullet. This is a once in a lifetime opportunity." He appreciated the sentiment from her, but couldn't help but wonder if he still wouldn't be good enough for Lost Cowboy, even after a week with Buck.

"Can I watch?"

"Of course you can. But if Buck catches me flirtin' with you, don't be surprised if he chases you off."

"Don't worry. I'll watch from the dining hall porch. I won't be in flirting distance."

"You'll be in viewing distance though, which means my body radar will be registerin' the whole time you're there."

"If you'd rather I didn't—"

"I didn't say that. You watchin' will just make me try harder to be the best damn bull rider you've ever seen." He pulled her close and kissed her hard. "I hate to say this, but I gotta run."

Bullet went out her door and into his cabin. A few minutes later she heard the other door close and couldn't help but look out the window. He was a sight to behold, unclothed and clothed. He wore the same chaps he had yesterday, and this time, a crisp white shirt with his wranglers. Tristan watched him walk away, and counted the hours on her fingers until he'd be done training.

Part way down the trail he stopped and looked in the direction of her cabin. Before she had a chance to move away from the window, he tipped his hat to let her know he knew she was watching.

She checked the time on her phone. She had a half hour to get to the dining hall if she wanted breakfast. While she was there she'd pick up a few things for lunch, and extra for Bullet, who hadn't had time to eat. She wondered if Buck would give him a break, and felt guilty that she'd kept him occupied so long this morning.

After breakfast she sat at a table on the porch of the dining hall, and pulled out her sketch books. She had two—one for Lost Cowboy designs, and the other for her own collection. Along with sketching, Tristan wanted to jot down notes for Bullet's Lost Cowboy story. She needed to remember to thank Lyric for the idea, and tell her father about it.

She hoped the story would culminate with Bullet making it to the annual National Finals Rodeo.

* * *

1968

Bill walked from the house down to the corral after Clancy gave him the news. It wasn't that he was upset by it necessarily, it was just a lot to get used to.

Clancy had dated his mama in high school, he'd told Bill. After they broke up, and she started dating Bill's daddy, the three remained friends. Clancy visited his friend when he heard of his illness, and that was when Gene Flynn asked Clancy to look out for his family after he died.

Nothing happened between Clancy and his mama while she was married to Mr. Snyder, but when she told Clancy she was divorcing him, Clancy took the opportunity to confess his true feelings for her.

"Your mama is fine woman," he said to Bill. "I reckon that's why I never married anyone else. No one came close to holdin' a candle to Jane." Bill's daddy always called her Janie. He was glad Clancy hadn't.

Clancy told Bill he had two questions for him. The first was to ask if he wanted to ride down with him tomorrow to pick up his mama and sister. The other was to ask for Bill's blessing to marry his mama.

Clancy didn't need Bill's permission, and neither did his mama. If needing his permission had been the case before, he would've refused to permit her to marry Mr. Snyder, that was for damn sure. But now, things were very different. This was Clancy.

He had to admit it was getting harder to remember much about his daddy. He still missed him. But Clancy had become like a second father to him.

He had no doubt Clancy would love his mother, and care for her and his sister. If he hadn't stepped in these last few years, Bill didn't know what might've happened to them.

When he asked about his leaving the Double-P-Bar, Clancy assured him he felt ready to go. "In addition to the house, Russ Snyder owned a lot of land. It belongs to your mama now too." No matter how much land there was, Bill doubted it could match what Clancy had at the Double-P-Bar.

"You sure about this?" he'd asked him again. Clancy told him he was, and then asked Bill to go down to the barn and check on the horses. The horses didn't need checking on, Bill knew that as well as Clancy knew he needed time to process what he'd just been told.

When he got back to the house, Clancy was waiting for him on the front porch.

"I'd like to talk to my mama tomorrow, if that's okay with you. And my sister." Bill felt as though he hadn't been a very good son or a very good brother these last few years. He wanted that to change.

Clancy nodded.

"And I want to look into colleges closer to Colorado Springs."

Clancy didn't argue with him about it, and Bill was relieved. As much as he had his heart set on going to Western State, where Dottie would be attending college, he knew in his gut it was time for him to put his family before other things in his life.

When they got back from picking up his mama, Dottie would be at the ranch. She had asked her Aunt Sadie if she could stay with her while she was in town for Bill's graduation. As soon as he could, he'd let her know he was changing his plans.

He couldn't allow himself to hope that she'd understand, or be willing to continue their long distance relationship. She'd given up a lot in high school, like going to the prom, or dating local fellas in order to be his girl. He couldn't ask her to wait for him any longer than she already had.

Now that he was graduating from high school, it was time for him to give up rodeo too. Clancy needed help with the land that his mama now owned. Between working that land and going to college, he wouldn't have time to travel the rodeo circuit.

He rubbed his chest, knowing doing so wouldn't ease the pain he felt. He was about to let go of the only two dreams he'd had in life. One was to be an all-around rodeo cowboy champion, and the other was to marry Dottie.

He wouldn't speak of either dream again. If only not thinking about them were as easy.

14

Bullet could sense Buck's frustration with him, and he felt terrible wasting the man's time. Heck, he wasn't just a man, he was a legend. Instead of doing the work Buck asked him to do, Bullet got lost in Tristan McCullough.

He had every intention of waking up early, and getting his workout done this morning, but the lure of Tristan's naked body in the bath was more than he could resist.

When Buck offered to let him break for lunch, he said he'd go get his workout done instead. Buck told him that wasn't a good idea, and to wait until they were done. He also suggested they wrap up early so Bullet would have time to work out and get to dinner, but Bullet asked him not to do that.

As hard as it was going to be, he wasn't here to court Tristan, he was here to practice bull riding. A lot of people made sacrifices both personally and financially to get him here. He wouldn't feel right wasting their money or their time.

"Give me a minute?" he asked after he dismounted the last practice bull. It had been a good ride, which only reminded him again why he was here. Buck nodded, waved, and went back to his conversation with the guys pulling gates.

Tristan appeared lost in whatever she was working on, and didn't raise her head as he approached. If he had the time, he'd stand right where he was and watch her. He could watch her for hours. She tilted her head as she studied what was in front of her. At that angle, the way her neck rounded open, he could sink his teeth into her, run his tongue—*what was he doing?* He came up here to tell her he wouldn't be joining her for dinner tonight, not fantasize about what he wanted to do to her neck or any other part of her body.

"Hi," she said as he walked closer and she noticed him. "The last ride was your best so far."

"Thanks." He didn't think she had been paying that much attention. "Uh, listen…"

"Buck wants you to focus less on me and more on bulls. Is that what you're trying to figure out how to tell me?"

Damn, she rattled him. "I guess. But not entirely. There are workouts he wants me to do after we're done each day. I didn't get one in last night, or this morning." He regretted his words as soon as he spoke them. He made it sound as though it was her fault, and it wasn't.

The responsibility rested solely on his shoulders, and in his usual fashion, he'd shirked it.

"What did he say about 'post-workout activities'? Anything?"

"Hmm, let me think about that," he smiled. "He did mention something about getting in the hot tub when I finished."

"I see. And what about meals? I doubt Buck would be happy if he knew you skipped both breakfast and lunch today. What about after your workout? Think Buck would care if you ate then?"

Oh man, the visuals she was giving him with her questions. How the hell was he supposed to concentrate on bulls now? He might as well tell Buck he was done for the day.

Tristan closed the book in front of her and stood. "Come here, cowboy," she motioned him closer. "If you promise to do everything Buck tells you, I'll deliver supper to the hot tub later. Sound good?"

Hell yeah, it did. "Uh huh," were the only words he could think to say out loud.

"And if you're a really, *really* good boy, I'll join you."

Bullet almost bit his tongue as he watched her walk away. He *never* rode shotgun, but there was no question, Tristan had taken control of the wheel.

On the walk back to her cabin, Tristan stopped herself from looking back at Bullet at least a dozen times. She opened her door, and quickly closed it behind her, resting her back against it.

Who was she? She barely recognized herself. Exactly when had she become so *wanton*? And she wasn't the only one surprised by her behavior. Poor Bullet had been tongue-tied.

The thought of it made her giggle. Bullet was clearly used to being the seducer, not the other way around. Warmth spread over her when she thought about the effect her words had on him. She only hoped that once he got back to the practice pen, he'd be able to focus. At least she'd given him incentive to.

After rinsing her face with cold water, she took her sketchbook and walked outside, going in the opposite direction from where Bullet and Buck were working. She saw a large boulder a little higher up that would make a perfect place for her to sit in the sun and sketch.

She settled on the rock and opened the sketchbook containing the Lost Cowboy designs. She turned page after page, and studied the chaps she'd worked on most of the morning.

She usually sketched just the clothing, as opposed to the clothing on a model or mannequin. But this time, she'd drawn the chaps on a faceless cowboy. Face or not, her model was Bullet.

It hadn't been necessary to sketch the upper half of the body, the chaps were for the lower half. But she hadn't been able to stop herself. She added detail to the shirts the cowboy wore, so when she showed the designs to her daddy, he wouldn't wonder. She really didn't care about the shirts though, just what was under them. She'd drawn them snug, so the outline of the cowboy's pecs, flat six-pack abs, and powerful arms were evident. She even took the time to draw hands. In every sketch, they were Bullet's.

Tristan fanned her face. Perhaps she should've considered taking a cold shower before she left her cabin. She slammed the book closed and set it on the rock. For the rest of the afternoon she'd focus on the women's collection, and try to keep the sexy-as-all-get-out cowboy off her mind.

Piper had outdone herself with the picnic supper she packed for Tristan and Bullet. Grapes, strawberries, different types of cheese, and dry salami were tucked in the basket with a baguette, and a terrine of foie gras drizzled with a port wine sauce. She'd even included a bottle of Pinot Noir and two glasses. For dessert she gave them chocolate truffles covered in raspberry dust.

Tristan hadn't felt hungry until Piper began describing the basket's contents. Now she was famished. She ran into Buck earlier, after he'd finished with Bullet, who told her Bullet's workout would take approximately ninety minutes.

Piper promised they'd have complete privacy afterwards. The spa staff was gone for the day, and the ranch employees weren't allowed to use the spa if guests were in residence.

"Here," she said, handing Tristan a key. "It locks from the inside too," she winked.

Bullet closed his eyes and did the final set on the glute machine. Imagining Tristan naked and waiting for him in the hot tub was all the incentive he needed to keep going. Rather than feeling tired, each set he finished only energized him. One step closer to his goal. And tonight, his goal was Tristan.

He'd done as she'd told him, and listened to every word Buck said. At the end of the day he was rewarded with "great work today," and a pat on the back from the cowboy.

As tempting as it was to let the shower's hot water beat down on his sore shoulders, something, *someone* more tempting was waiting on him. He scrubbed away the sweat and grime from his day's work as quickly as he could, wrapped a towel around his waist, and walked through the locker room door that led to the hot tub.

The sight before him made him stop short. Tristan placed lit candles all around the water's perimeter. The table behind her was laden with food, glasses filled with wine, and more candles. But that feast had nothing on the one that waited near the in-ground spa.

Tristan was seated on the edge, leaning back and propped on her elbows. Only her toes touched the water. Otherwise, his eyes rested on nothing but her skin and the curves of her body.

Bullet entered the spa from the opposite side and sunk into the water. He reached out and grasped her ankles, pulling her to him until her naked body straddled his lap. The chill of the air outside of the warm water made her nipples pucker tight. Holding her still he bent to lick first one, and then the other. He went back to the first and closed his mouth around her.

The groan emanating from somewhere deep set him on fire. He brought his mouth back on to hers, easing her into a kiss intended to soften her, help her relax. Her body was coiled tight, as though she was ready to strike.

He explored her body with his fingers, finding her flesh hotter than the warm water, with a slick and heavy dampness. He stroked her open and slipped his fingers inside her folds.

Tristan responded by gripping his shoulders, digging her nails into his flesh, and kissing him with starving hunger. He deepened his fingers and she cried out, clamping down hard around him.

Within minutes he was rewarded with that look, the one he craved. She shuddered and he felt the wet warmth spill out on his hand. He continued to watch as she came down from her climax, the sensation fading quickly, she went limp against him.

Bullet gathered her close, and held her tight. No matter her bravado today, she'd told him what he needed to know yesterday. "I don't do this," she'd warned. Allowing herself to give in, in this open, public place regardless that no one else was here, had to rattle her.

"Bullet?" her insecurity was a siren in her voice.

He gave her a tongue-twining kiss of reassurance, and lifted her from the water. His hands supporting her bottom, he brought her to the table and sat her nakedness in a chair.

"Time to eat."

"But what about—"

He had to interrupt her. As much as she thought she was ready, the idea of taking her on the cold concrete of the spa left him as chilled as she'd be. When he took her again, it would be in the warmth of her bed, where he could hold her against him, and get lost in her lusciousness.

* * *

1968

Dottie was perched on the fence rail when Bill got out of the truck. Her long, blonde hair waved in the wind, and her smile dimmed the sun.

"Who's that?" asked his sister, who rode with him while Clancy and his mama followed in the car that had belonged to Mr. Snyder. Bill hadn't wanted them to drive it here, but there wasn't any choice. The four of them wouldn't fit in the truck, and Bill was insistent he ride down with Clancy rather than wait until they returned to talk to his mama.

"That's Dottie," Bill answered, unused to having someone around who asked so many questions. The entire ride from Colorado Springs had been an endless Q&A. At first he wanted to tell her his life was none of her business, as he would've anyone else, but his determination to be a better son and brother, made him answer her questions as honestly as he could.

He wasn't sure what else to tell about Dottie. Bill didn't know how to define their relationship. She was a friend, but so much more than that. However, after he told her he wouldn't be attending Western State in the fall as planned, he doubted they'd continue to be more than friends, if that.

"She's your girlfriend," his sister stated.

"I guess." Bill's shoulders tensed up, and he dreaded the conversation he'd soon be having with Dottie.

It was three hours before they could excuse themselves and go for a walk. Every minute had been torture for Bill. Each smile she bestowed when she took his hand in hers, even when she hugged him hello, worsened his guilt-laden dread.

"You seem preoccupied." The trail had narrowed and they had to walk single-file along this section, so he couldn't see the look on her face.

"I am." No sense beating around the bush, he might as well get it over with. "I'm not going to Western State."

He'd hoped she'd keep walking, so he didn't have to face her, but she didn't. She stopped, turned around, and put her hands on her hips. "What do you mean you're not going?"

Bill could see the clearing a few paces ahead. He suggested they continue walking and he'd explain further when they could sit down and talk face-to-face. Dottie, in her usual way, walked to the clearing with a smile on her face, and sat down on the warm grass. "Explain yourself, Bill Flynn."

Bill wished she'd stop smiling at him. Couldn't she sense his agony? What if she cried when he told her his reasons? He'd only seen her cry one time, and that was when the calf died during the tie-down roping event in Gunnison. And that hadn't been up close.

"Bill," she said softly. "Please tell me what's going on."

He wasn't sure how far back to go, so he began the night he met Mr. Snyder. When he told her how uneasy he'd felt about the man, the smile left her face. When he told her how many times Clancy had driven to Colorado Springs to help his mama, she grimaced. And then, when he told her about Clancy asking his mama to marry him, her smile lit up her face once again.

"I need to help out," he explained. "And that means living in Black Forest, just outside of Colorado Springs. That's where the ranch is."

"What about college?"

He told her he still planned to go, he might get a later start than he hoped, but Clancy assured him he'd help him get into the state college.

"So I guess you've waited all this while for nothin'." He couldn't look at her when he said it. He braced himself for the break-up he felt sure was coming.

"The last thing you are, Bill Flynn, is 'nothin'. But you're right, I'm done waiting."

"I understand." Bill's voice shook in a way he couldn't control. He only hoped he could keep the rest of the emotions he was feeling at bay, and not embarrass himself too much.

"I don't think you do."

"We're breakin' up. I get it. And honestl,y Dottie, I do understand. I'm just sorry you've wasted—"

"If you're about to say I've wasted my time, I'll stop you right there. I'm in love with you, and the last thing we're doing is breaking up."

Bill raised his eyes and looked into her smiling ones. He had no idea what she was thinking, but if it meant she was still his girl, he couldn't wait to hear about it.

15

Their week was coming to an end. Tomorrow they'd leave the ranch, and go back to their respective lives. Her time had been more productive than she could've dreamed. She was leaving with twice as many designs for Lost Cowboy and her new venture than she initially anticipated.

She also felt ready to discuss her ideas with her father. Deep down she knew he'd support whatever she wanted to do. Being in Colorado gave her time to think it through, and realize it was ridiculous believing otherwise.

Each day Bullet became a better bull rider. Without the distraction of everyday life, his focus was intense. Buck was an intuitive trainer, and managed to pick up on Bullet's areas of weakness, and get him to work straight through them. Depending on how much time Flying R gave him to compete, it was conceivable that he could earn enough to make regional finals this year. Buck believed he could go further than that.

Neither talked about when they'd see each other after they left the ranch. The rodeo season would be fully underway inside of a month, and they'd both be busy traveling the circuit. And when they weren't, they each had a lot of work to do. He with Flying R, and her with Lost Cowboy and her new venture.

Tristan rested her eyes on his now sleeping form. They'd worn each other out, making love every chance they got. It was as though they could never get enough of each other's bodies. When they came together after spending their days apart, their need for each other was frantic.

It was more than that for her, though. Bullet had intrigued her from the moment she'd met him in Liv and Ben's hot tub. On one hand, he was the epitome of a bull rider—arrogant, cock-sure of himself, and an experienced handler of ladies. Tristan wondered now how much of that was for show.

Conversely, he'd treated her with respect. He cared as much about what she'd done with her day as he had with his. He asked to see her designs, and talked to her about them. He'd tell her about his time with Buck, but never once monopolized their conversations.

He was nothing like Harris Jones. Nothing at all. The way Harris treated her was intentional—premeditated even. He'd falsely declared his love for her all the while knowing that tomorrow he'd be in someone else's bed, likely making the same declaration. Bullet gave her no empty promises, no professions of love, and she was glad he hadn't. It would've been difficult for her to believe that he could fall in love with her after only a week, even though she knew she'd fallen in love with him.

Tristan was sitting up in bed, her back to him. If he had the ability to read her mind, he wouldn't allow himself to. Bullet knew what she was thinking, and it made him mad. Furious, in fact. But not at her, at himself. She hadn't said one word about seeing him again once their week was over. Nothing at all.

He'd stupidly believed he was winning her over, but instead, he felt like a nick in her bedpost. The irony would make him laugh, if his gut wasn't burning.

How many women had he done this to? Sure he'd tell them they'd see each other again real soon. Meanwhile, he'd already forgotten their name. A week with any one woman would've been unheard of, except for Callie. He'd spent more than a week with her, but even then, it wasn't just her he was with. He never thought himself capable of committing himself entirely to one woman. Until now.

Tristan didn't come right out and say it, but he sensed she was biding her time. Once he delivered her to the airport and she was safely on the plane, she'd breathe a sigh of relief that she'd dodged him. This time he was the bullet, not her.

The question now was how would their final day together play out? When he leaned over and trailed kisses down her spine, he was rewarded with a heated smile that told him she wanted to spend their last few hours at the ranch the same way he did.

He should be the happiest man on earth. He was riding better than ever, and Buck Bishop told him he'd called Bill Patterson and said Bullet worked harder than any other rider he'd trained. He went on to tell him how proud Flying R Rough Stock should be to sponsor him, and his prediction that he'd be their top rider this year.

Instead of walking on air, he was downright miserable. Tristan had been at breakfast when Buck came in to report on the phone call. She was happy for him, smiling from ear to ear, congratulating him, even gave him a big hug and kiss.

But the two things he wanted to hear her say, she never said. Other than telling him how happy she was *for him,* there was no mention of either a Lost Cowboy sponsorship, or any talk of when they'd see each other again.

There were twenty times on the way from the ranch to the airport that he thought about bringing one or both up, but he stopped himself. He already felt like a fool, no need to make himself look more pathetic.

He walked her to the jet way, and waited, holding his breath, wishing she'd say something, *anything*, about when they'd see each other again, but she didn't.

His mood only worsened after her plane took off. When a fella decided to tailgate him on the highway, Bullet slammed on the brakes, and sent a slew of curse words in the driver's direction that would make a hard-core rocker blush. When he stopped to fill his gas tank and get a snack, the flirty cashier only annoyed him. Instead of wishing her a nice day too, he snarled, grunted, and walked back to his truck.

His attitude sucked, and he knew it. He spent the rest of the drive reining himself in so he didn't insult the people who had worked so hard to help make his dream come true.

Sure, Tristan McCullough had broken his heart, but no one needed to know that.

As much as she tried not to, Tristan missed Bullet. She'd been home several days, and no matter how hard she worked, she couldn't fend off the distraction that came when her mind drifted to something he'd said, or they'd done.

Bullet had an unexpected way of looking at life. He often surprised her with his views on a variety of subjects. Sometimes he'd play dumb, but if she pushed the conversation, his acumen would show through.

He'd been the first to predict her father already knew what she was up to in developing a new clothing line, and he'd been right. Her grandfather told her that his son had been sneaking peeks at her designs for weeks. When she confronted him about it, he scowled, and wouldn't own up to his espionage.

Her weekly, sometimes daily, phone calls with Liv resumed when she returned from the ranch. While she would admit the role she played in suggesting Tristan's father send her to there for some much needed time off, she insisted she had no idea Bullet Simmons was going to be there at the same time.

Liv pressed her on when she'd be back in Crested Butte, and how plans were coming for the new line. Tristan told Liv her father said he'd be happy to support her new venture with seed money, but he thought it best if she developed the brand separate from Lost Cowboy, which led Liv to suggest a meeting of potential investors.

"You could hold an informational meeting in Black Forest, and invite the women I already know are interested in investing. Depending on what you're looking for, we could open it outside of our Flying R circle as well."

Tristan's gut clenched. If she showed up in Black Forest, Bullet would believe for certain that she'd arranged the meeting with the ulterior motive of seeing him. She couldn't do that to him, or to herself. It would be mortifying if he ignored her in front of everyone.

"I think Crested Butte would work better."

Liv held firm, saying the reason she'd suggested Black Forest was because most of the key players lived there or close by. "It will be easier on everyone if we meet there. I'll have to travel, and so will you, but everyone else is based there."

With no choice but to relent, Tristan began planning the first investors' meeting for the new clothing brand, *McCullough Cowgirl*. The name was a hit with everyone she told, almost all of whom suggested the line would soon grow to include McCullough Home, McCullough Cowboy, even McCullough Kids.

She'd been tempted several times to call Bullet, or text him to alert him she'd be in town, but since she hadn't heard from him, she figured he wouldn't care one way or the other.

Obviously Bullet had forgotten all about her. Out of sight, out of mind. Too bad that wasn't working for her.

"What the hell do you mean she'll be in Black Forest tomorrow? How long have you known this, Lyric?"

"There isn't any reason to yell at me, Bullet. I got the call from Liv day before yesterday. How was I supposed to know Tristan didn't tell you?"

And here he was in Montana. He wasn't due to leave for Black Forest until Tuesday. Today was Friday. Tristan would be long gone by the time he got home.

He was so angry, he felt like putting his fist through something. Too bad the only thing close was the side of the trailer. The last thing he needed was to break the bones in his hand, and the way he was feeling, that was how hard he'd hit it.

"Steam's comin' outta your nose and ears, Bullet."

Billy Patterson was the last person Bullet wanted to have a conversation with right now.

"What's got ya all fussed?"

"Nothin'." Bullet walked away, but Billy followed.

"Renie told me there's a big meeting goin' on at Patterson Ranch tomorrow. Somethin' about a new business she wants to invest in. You know anything about it?"

"Nope."

"I heard Tristan McCullough has somethin' to do with it. That ring any bells?"

It was looking more and more like Bullet was going to punch something, and if Billy didn't back off, it would be *someone* instead.

"I said no. I meant no. Now leave me the hell alone, Billy."

"Okay then. I'll call Renie back and tell her to expect me home tonight. And here Jace and I were gonna offer to drive this load of broncs to Black Forest so you could be the one to leave early."

"Wait, what?"

"But if you don't know anythin' about it, and don't care to know, then I guess ol' Jace and I will get to see our wives a few days earlier than planned. Okay by me."

"*Shit.*" Bullet couldn't hold back any longer. At least now the closest thing for him to hit was the side of the barn. It still hurt like hell, but he doubted he'd done any real damage to his hand.

"What the hell was that all about?"

Bullet wanted to wipe the shit-eating grin off Billy's face. He knew damn well what it was about. It was why he'd spent the last five minutes giving him grief.

"She doesn't want to see me," Bullet muttered.

"What's that? I couldn't hear you."

"Fuck off, Billy. You heard me."

Jace was sitting on the fence near the barn, chewing on a piece of straw. "I don't know about that. Bree told me she overheard Tristan ask whether you were around.”

“You two tag-teamin’ me now?”

Billy put his hand on Bullet’s shoulder and squeezed. “We’re old and married, son. And both our wives are pregnant. We gotta live vicariously through someone.”

“I’m married, but I’m not old, Patterson. You’re the old one in this crew. And Bree isn’t anywhere near as pregnant as Renie is. What’s she goin’ on, month fifteen?”

Billy rubbed his hand over his face. “Sure as hell feels like it. They’re sayin’ she’s at thirty-six weeks.”

Bullet felt for the guy. He remembered when Callie was in the last month of pregnancy with Grey. She was *miserable*. He doubted Renie was the same way though. She didn’t seem like the miserable sort.

“Your time’s comin’, asshole,” Billy glared at Jace.

“That why you’re offerin’ to let me be the one to go back early? You don’t wanna be around your pregnant wives?”

He didn’t doubt Billy knew exactly how far he was getting under Bullet’s skin about Tristan, but he knew how to push back. If anyone said a single thing about Renie that could be construed in a negative way, Billy went near ape-shit. Bullet smiled at him and winked.

"You think you're so damn smart, don't ya?" Billy snarled. "But I ain't the one punchin' the side of a barn."

"Let's have a girls' night," suggested Liv.

"We don't have much choice, Billy and Jace are in Montana, Tucker's off at a watercolor workshop somewhere in New Mexico, Ben is on tour with the band. Who does that leave?" asked Renie.

"Dottie's Bill, Mark, and my dad and brother," answered Lyric.

"Mark and your dad are with Ben and the band," Liv responded.

"Just like my family not to tell me anything," sulked Lyric. "Does anyone know where my mom and Gram are?"

"At Bullet's," answered Dottie, walking in Renie's back door. "I came over to ask if we should invite them to the meeting tomorrow."

"Of course we should. Don't you agree, Tristan?"

Tristan nodded. "Of course." All that chatter and no one said a word about Bullet's whereabouts. Since no one mentioned Bill Patterson either, maybe that's who he was with.

"What about you, Dottie, are you able to join us for girls' night?" she asked.

"I sure can, Tristan. My Bill is at the PRCA board meeting tonight. When their meeting's over the guys usually break out the cards. I don't expect him back much before midnight."

Damn. Still no clue as to where Bullet was. Maybe if she volunteered to pick Bullet's mother and grandmother up at his house…no, that wouldn't work. Lyric would pick up her own family.

Tristan would just have to be patient and see if anyone else worked him into the conversation. No way she'd dare ask where he was. She'd never hear the end of it if she did.

She was three of Lyric's cocktails in when she heard Renie's back door open again.

"Who could that be?" whispered Bree whose idea it had been to watch the entire last season of *American Horror Story* on Billy and Renie's big screen television. "Who are we missing? Blythe, my mom, Lyric's mom and grandmother are here. Who else did we invite?"

Tristan hated horror shows anyway, which was the main reason she'd downed the three cocktails. But the fact that whoever had come in the back door, still hadn't shown him- or herself, was giving her the quivers. And not the good kind.

"Oh, for goodness sake," said Lyric's grandmother. "I'll go look." Tristan wanted to beg her not to, but then again, maybe she'd turn some lights on.

Grey, who had been in the bedroom with Willow, Caden, and Hannah Pearl, supposedly sound asleep, came padding through the living room and followed his great-grandmother. When he turned the corner into the kitchen, he let out a shriek that almost had Tristan peeing her pants.

"*Dada,*" he screamed. Tristan froze. *Bullet was here.*

"Well, well, well. Look at all the lovely ladies. What's goin' on tonight?" Bullet picked up a glass on the kitchen counter and sniffed. "Smells like one of Lyric's five ingredient cocktails, where all five ingredients are alcohol."

"Girls' night. Except for Grey," Liv giggled.

Tristan was sitting furthest away from where he stood. She had no idea whether he'd noticed her yet.

"Billy asked me to drop this off," he said to Renie, placing a duffle bag on her kitchen counter.

Tristan watched him walk around Renie's gourmet kitchen, tasting the hors d'oeurves spread out on the marble-topped island. "I am downright famished. You ladies wouldn't mind if I crashed your party, would ya?"

had every right to be. Her reaction to him even baffled her.

Lyric stood next to her on Billy and Renie's deck. "I'm mad at you too."

"It really isn't any of your business, Lyric. I'm sorry I hurt your brother's feelings—"

Lyric walked back in the house before Tristan finished her sentence. A minute later, Liv came outside.

"If you're going to scold me too, don't waste your time."

"My, my, aren't you in a tizzy?"

"He shouldn't have done that." Tristan waited, but Liv didn't respond. "Especially in front of everyone." Still nothing from Liv.

Finally, she spoke. "Did you know this used to be my house?"

Tristan hadn't put it all together, but yes, Liv had told her Billy bought her ranch before he married Renie.

"I love this house. My parents built it when I was a teenager. My father was a retired Air Force colonel, and prior to this house, there wasn't one I lived in longer than four years."

"It's a very nice house," Tristan murmured. "Especially the kitchen." She hadn't seen much more of the house than that and the family room, but just those two areas were beautifully designed.

"I was out here on the deck late one afternoon, and I saw a black bear, over there near the forest." Liv pointed to the edge of the clearing. "I believed it was a sign that I was meant to be alone." Liv paused, and shook her head. "I can't tell you how many times I almost lost Ben because of my fear. And my stubbornness."

Tristan didn't know what to say, so she listened.

"I was watching you. All evening you were wondering about him, but were too stubborn to ask. When he came in, your eyes twinkled like Christmas lights."

She *was* happy to see him, but then he took it too far. He toyed with her, and he did it in front of everyone. She hadn't heard from him since he dropped her off at the airport. Not even a text. Did he really think he could waltz in and she'd fall into his arms like some lovesick cowgirl? She'd done that once before in her life, and vowed never to be that naive again.

"Is it really so hard for you to give him a chance?"

"A chance at what? A chance to make a fool of me?" Tristan's eyes filled with tears.

"Oh, honey. I don't know who hurt you so badly that you've closed your heart at such a young age. But please listen to me. It's time to open it again." Liv wrapped her arms around Tristan and hugged her tight. "If there's anything I know, it's love is worth it."

"Love? God, Liv. Are you kidding? He's a cowboy, a *bull rider*, for God's sake."

"I'm confused. Do you think bull riders are incapable of loving someone?"

That wasn't the point. Of course they were. But not her, that was a lesson she'd already learned.

"You make him want to be a better man," said Lyric who Tristan hadn't heard come back outside.

"Do I? Why? So I can get him a Lost Cowboy sponsorship?"

"You know better than that," she heard Liv murmur.

"He doesn't even need it," she said softly.

"Why not?" Lyric asked.

"Your brother is on the fast track to championship bull riding. Between now and October he won't have time to think about anything else. Do you know who he trained with? Buck Bishop, that's who. You know as well as I do that Buck would never invest that kind of time in someone he didn't believe was world champion material."

Besides, she had her own dreams to chase, to coin Lyric's expression. Tomorrow's meeting would determine how much money she'd have to produce her line. The more she had, the faster she could do it.

As much as she tried to stop them, tears fell from Tristan's eyes.

Liv rubbed her shoulder. "What is it that's got you so riled up. Be honest."

"You really want to know? I'll tell you. We had a great time at the ranch. I did some of my best work and so did he. We had amazing sex, and then we both went home and I haven't heard from him since."

"I can't speak for Liv, but that was *way* more than I wanted to know."

Tristan couldn't help but laugh. Leave it to Lyric to say something to diffuse her anger.

Liv shook her head. "Not me. I want details."

"*Ew.* You're talkin' about my twin brother. Come on." Lyric covered her ears. "No details, please."

Liv put her arm around Tristan's shoulders. "You've got a big day tomorrow. Let's call it a night."

Tristan followed Liv inside. Other than Lyric's mother and grandmother, who were waiting for Lyric to head back to Bullet's, everyone but Renie was gone. Liv led Tristan downstairs to the guest rooms.

"Get some rest, and I'll see you in the morning."

She'd see Liv in the morning, but she doubted she'd get any rest.

* * *

1968

"If you aren't going to Western State, neither am I."

"But, Dottie, you have to. You can't give up a chance to go to college on account of me. I won't hear of it."

"Listen to you, Mr. Bossy. *You won't hear of it.* Well I won't hear of waiting another minute for you. And I'm not giving you up either."

"Is that right?"

"Yes. That's right."

"What do you propose we do?"

"I'm not the one doing any proposing, Bill Flynn, but you better be."

Just a couple of days ago his mama had given Bill the ring his daddy gave to her. Now that she was marrying Clancy, she didn't feel right having Gene Flynn's ring. He'd carried it with him in his pocket, but sure hadn't planned what he was about to do.

Bill pulled it out, and got down on one knee.

"Bill—"

"Now don't interrupt me, Dorothea. I have somethin' important to ask you."

Dottie grinned, and put her hands on her hips. Bill reached out and brought her left hand closer to him.

"I've loved you since the day I met you. Will you marry me, Dottie?"

16

Tristan was a nervous wreck, and it wasn't because of the meeting planned for that afternoon. Bullet called and asked if they could talk. He wouldn't elaborate over the phone, but she could guess how the conversation would go.

She'd hurt his feelings last night, and while it was unintentional, there was something to be said for the way she pulled away from him. It had been a knee-jerk reaction, literally, and once again she was faced with the realization that when it came to Bullet, even she didn't understand her feelings or the way she reacted to him.

He invited her to join him for breakfast. There was a place in historic downtown Monument, the town located northwest of Black Forest, called Cup of Coffee, that he liked. He thought she might too.

In fifteen minutes he would be picking her up. In the meantime, she couldn't sit still.

"What are you gonna say to her?" Lyric had spent the night at Bullet's after her mother had driven them there saying she was in no condition to drive to Palmer Lake. After having three of her five-ingredient cocktails,

Lyric agreed. Her mama had never been much of drinker, so it didn't surprise Lyric when her mother opted for tea.

"I haven't figured that out yet."

"Why'd you invite her to breakfast then?"

Bullet wasn't sure why he had other than knowing the time they had together was short, and he didn't want to waste it being mad at her. He didn't know when she was scheduled to go back to New York, but beginning next month, he'd be busier than he ever had been in his life.

Flying R had hired another hand to travel with Bullet, Bill, and Dottie. They were going on the road to help, but not in the way Bullet would need it most, with the broncs.

Kingston West, the guy they hired, was a bulldogger, which meant he was strong and tough as all get out. Steer wrestling took timing, speed, and strength. The cowboy needed to be a damn good rider to chase a steer, dismount his horse, mount the steer, and then wrestle it to the ground. Good bulldoggers could do it all in three or four seconds.

There were no historical records that connected this event with every day ranch life. Bullet remembered Dottie saying it was the timed events in rodeo that Bill had the most trouble with. Had Billy or the other Flying

R partners consulted Bill before hiring Kingston? Bullet sure hoped so since Kingston would be traveling with them pretty near non-stop the next six months.

Bullet shook his head and looked at his phone for the hundredth time that morning. He had five minutes before he had to leave. Instead of thinking about the new hand, he should be thinking about what he planned to say to Tristan.

He parked the truck, and before he could get out and knock on the back door of the house, Tristan was walking toward him. He got out anyway, to open the passenger door for her.

"Good morning." He couldn't really understand why he was feeling sheepish this morning; it had been Tristan who pulled away from him. There had to have been a reason though, and it had to have been his fault. It seemed almost everything was, one way or another.

She nodded, but didn't answer. When he opened the door for her, she wouldn't look at him. So Bullet did the thing that came natural to him, he spun her around and kissed the daylights out of her. The tension he felt in every part of her body quickly released. Her arms went around his neck, and she kissed him back.

"I'm sorry," they pulled back and said simultaneously. Then they both laughed.

"I'm the one who should be sorry, Bullet. I don't know why I reacted the way I did last night."

"Wasn't fair of me to put you on the spot the way I did. I understand if I embarrassed you."

Tristan looked in the direction of the house from where they stood next to the truck. "Let's go, okay? We can talk about this better over breakfast."

There was a part of him that wondered if Tristan was trying to hide being with him. Did she look toward the house to see if anyone was watching? He leaned down and kissed her again. When her mouth opened to him, he knew he'd won this battle, if there was a war.

"How's Grey this morning?" Tristan asked once they were seated.

"He's fine. I think he was startled more than hurt last night."

"I felt terrible. I still do."

"The thing that upsets me the most is I left in such a huff that you didn't get to meet my daughter."

Tristan looked away, and hoped what she was thinking wasn't showing on her face. Did he really care whether she met his daughter, or was he just saying that?

"I know what you're thinkin'."

"You do?"

"Yeah, I do. And neither of us needs to say it out loud."

"Bullet, I don't think—"

"Look, Tristan, there isn't anybody who knows I'm not good enough for you better than I do."

Is that what he thought? Is that what she was somehow leading him to believe?

The shame she felt hearing him say those words mortified her. If her father knew she'd ever made another human being feel that way, that would disappoint him more than anything else she could do. He had raised her with compassion, and the belief that anyone who was willing to work hard and do the right thing, could make anything they wanted of themselves.

The words she'd said when they'd first met came back to haunt her. She'd called him irresponsible, and she had been judgmental. Her embarrassment heated her cheeks.

"You're wrong, Bullet," she said finally. "The better I get to know you, the more I think I'm the one who isn't good enough for you. I'm sorry for everything I said in the past that made you feel that way."

He smiled. And she melted. Bullet was meant to smile. Frowning didn't suit him.

"God, you're beautiful."

Tristan dipped her head and felt her cheeks heat for a completely different reason. Not only wasn't she good enough for him, she didn't deserve him. He had every right to be mad at her, or even dislike her. Instead, he told her she was beautiful.

"Thank you."

"Come on now, give me one of your sweet smiles."

What choice did she have? When he talked to her that way, she was powerless to do anything but what he asked of her.

He stood and came to her side of the booth. When she slid over to give him room, he smiled again.

"Now that's much better." Bullet reached around the back of the booth and put his arm around her shoulders. "I like you close as I can get you."

Tristan looked at her phone, it was almost noon. She couldn't believe she and Bullet had been talking for over two hours.

"I have to get back. I'm sorry."

"You gotta stop sayin' you're sorry all the time. I know you have a meeting. It isn't something you should be sorry for."

"I know. I can't help it. I never realized how much I say it."

"Wasn't there some old time movie that had a line in it about love meaning you never say you're sorry?"

That took the smile off her face. "Bullet—"

"Now don't go gettin' all in a snit. I was just teasin' you."

"Oh. Okay. I'm—"

Bullet put his hand over her mouth. "Nope, I'm not lettin' you say it. Every time I think you're about to, I'm gonna do this." He leaned forward and covered her mouth with his kiss.

"And just so you know, I ain't ever gonna say I'm sorry for kissin' you. Even in the middle of a crowded restaurant."

Tristan looked around her. She hadn't noticed the empty tables were all full, and there was a lunch crowd lined up waiting.

"If you didn't have a meeting, I'd sit here with you all afternoon, maybe stay for dinner too."

"We close at three," said the waitress as she dropped their check on the table.

"I'm so embarrassed." Tristan covered her face with her hands.

"If that's all it takes to embarrass you darlin', you're in for quite an awakening."

Tristan didn't doubt the truth of his words for a minute.

"How'd the writing session go?" Bullet asked his dad.

"So good that we're getting together again tomorrow, and probably the day after too."

"That's terrific, Dad."

"Mark Cochran is so damn funny. Ben and I spend as much time laughing as we do making music."

"I don't really know him." Bullet had only seen Mark and his wife, Paige, a couple of times, and even then, he hadn't been introduced to them.

"That'll change later tonight. I invited everyone to dinner."

Bullet looked around his kitchen, and wondered what his dad meant by "everyone." More than six or seven people would overflow this room, and the dining room wasn't much bigger. Did his dad give any thought to the size of the house Bullet was living in? It was about one-tenth of the size of his parents' house in Los Angeles.

"Not here, dumbass." His dad gave him a playful punch and smiled. "I reserved a restaurant in town."

"The whole restaurant?"

"Well...yeah."

Bullet shook his head. He'd forgotten how his dad was. If he wanted it, he got it. Yep, Bullet hadn't fallen far from the tree after all.

"I want you to invite the girl Lyric has been telling us so much about."

"Tristan?"

"Yeah, that's the one. Lyric says she might become the newest member of our family."

Bullet almost choked on the drink of beer he'd just taken. *Jesus.* He knew better than to trust Lyric not to blurt that out in front of Tristan. Nope, he wouldn't be inviting her tonight. If he did, it might be the last time she agreed to go anywhere with him.

"You don't have any choice. Most of your investors will be at dinner tonight, and we want you there."

Lyric made Tristan laugh. She was as bad as Liv, who told her Billy and Jace would be mad at her if she didn't come to the partner dinner the last time she was in Crested Butte.

"You don't have to twist my arm, I'm happy to join you. I appreciate the invitation."

Tristan couldn't be in a better mood. She and Bullet "made up" over breakfast, where they also "made out".

Not to mention, each of the women associated with Flying R Rough Stock invested more money in

McCullough Cowgirl than she'd expected collectively. With their backing, the new line would be ready for a fall launch, which also meant a lot of press at the PBR finals in October, and NFR in December.

Lyric volunteered to handle the media through press releases and scheduled interviews. Tristan had a lot of experience with media herself, but her attention would be better focused on the clothing. Bree's sister, Blythe, worked for Lyric at RodeoChat, and volunteered to start promoting the line in international markets. Her first push would be in Australia, where she predicted it would explode.

Liv had been right about Paige Cochran. Mark's wife, and Bree and Blythe's mother, was the real business-person in the bunch. They had a meeting scheduled the next day to hammer out the new brand's business plan.

Wait until her father heard all this. She knew he'd be proud, and as long as she continued to design for Lost Cowboy, he'd be happy too.

When Tristan walked into the restaurant with Liv Rice, Bullet was surprised, happy, and anxious. He was happy she was here, but Lyric had gone too far in suggesting to their parents that she'd soon be their newest family member.

He walked over and pulled his sister aside. "Keep your comments about Tristan to a minimum tonight. You hear?"

"Let go of me." Lyric pulled her arm out of his grasp. "Don't worry. How dumb do you think I am? It's a prediction that I know won't come true if Miss McCullough thinks she's being rushed. She's not like the other women you've been involved with Bullet. I hope you realize that."

Bullet wanted to make a joke about Lyric not already knowing what he thought, but now wasn't the time for joking.

"Of course I do. She's a whole different caliber of woman."

"You're good enough for her. I hope you realize that too."

Bullet wasn't so sure, but he'd never completely win her over if he wasn't confident in himself. He sensed that the only type of man Tristan would ever fall for would be self-assured.

He walked over to the table where she and Liv were being seated.

"Well, damn. I didn't expect to see you tonight, Tristan. I sure am glad you're here."

Her cheeks turned their usual shade of pink. "I hope I'm not intruding. Lyric invited me."

He held out his hand to her. "Intruding? Heck, no. Come on, there's some folks I want you to meet."

Tristan put her jacket on the back of the chair in front of her, and was about to leave her bag on the seat.

"Bring it," Bullet pointed to the jacket.

"Why?"

"'Cause you're sittin' with me," he grinned.

"Whether I want to or not?" she teased.

"Yep. I told you I get what I want."

"No, you didn't. You told me you take what you want."

"Same difference."

Bullet introduced Tristan to his parents, who thankfully didn't mention Lyric's prediction about her joining their family. He saw Gram with Lyric, putting Grey in his high chair, and Pearl in a booster seat. He hoped Tristan wouldn't mind sitting with his kids. As busy as he knew he'd be, he didn't want to miss a night with them, or with her.

"This is my Pearl," Bullet said, walking over to his little girl whose face lit up when she saw her daddy. She held out her arms, and Bullet unfastened the clip keeping her in her seat. He picked her up and brought her closer to Tristan. When Grey saw what was going on, he raised his hands too. Lyric went to distract him, but

Tristan, much to Bullet's surprise, walked over to his little boy and took him out of the high chair.

"How's your noggin'?" Tristan rubbed her fingers over Grey's head.

Grey pouted a little, but then smiled at her. "Hurt," he said clearly, followed by a sentence even Bullet couldn't follow.

"He said it's okay," Pearl told them.

Tristan smiled. "He did? I'm so glad."

"Yeah, it's okay," Pearl said again.

Tristan motioned to two empty seats at the table. "Can we sit here?" she asked Bullet.

He nodded and smiled, his heart too full to speak.

* * *

1968

There was something important Bill wanted to take care of before he and Dottie were married. He talked to his mama about it, but he hadn't talked to Clancy yet, or Dottie.

His mother assured him that Clancy would be honored by his request, after she also assured him his daddy would understand. "He's been watchin' from heaven, and he would approve," she told him.

Dottie's eyes filled with tears when he told her his idea. "Oh, Bill, you are just the finest man alive," she'd said.

He had a meeting the next day with a lawyer, and then tomorrow night, he'd asked Clancy to have dinner with him. Bill hoped he was doing the right thing, and Clancy would go along with his proposition.

"Fancy," Clancy said when Bill pulled into the parking lot of the restaurant.

"Don't worry, they serve beer," Bill laughed. He knew Clancy really didn't care whether they did or not.

Bill gave his name to the hostess, and thought about the irony of it.

"I have something I want to ask you," Bill said after they'd ordered their dinner. "There are two things actually."

"Well, get on with it, son," Clancy smiled at him.

"About that. You call me son a lot, and I want you to know how much it means to me when you do." At first Clancy's grin faded, but his smile returned as Bill finished his sentence.

"Here's the thing. My mama told me a story the other day. She confessed that she sent you out lookin' for me that night that I was walkin' on the side of the road."

"Yes, she did."

"She also told me that you didn't have to partner up with your brother, or take me in, but you did it because you cared about our family."

Clancy was quiet, and his eyes clouded over. Bill knew the man well enough to ascertain he was doing his best to tap down his emotions.

"Before Dottie and I get married, I want to ask your permission to change my name."

Clancy looked up, startled. Bill held up his hand.

"Let me explain. About the same time Dottie and I get married, you'll be marryin' my mama. After you're married, her legal name will be Jane Patterson." Bill's eyes filled with tears and it took him a minute to continue. "When Dottie and I marry, I'd like to be Mister and Missus William Flynn Patterson. And I hope you understand why."

Clancy put his hand over his eyes, but Bill caught a glimpse of the tears that filled them before he did.

"You told me once that the thing you regretted most about never marryin' was that you didn't have any youngens. Well, you raised a son, Clancy. The man you see before you today had two men raise him. My daddy took care of the first half of my upbringing, and you've been responsible for the second half."

It took Clancy a minute to answer, but Bill understood why. He was feeling just as emotional.

"I'd be honored," he said solemnly. "I can't tell you how much this means to me, son."

"I have somethin' else to ask you."

Clancy nodded and smiled. "You need to borrow some money?"

Bill laughed too. "Nah, you've made sure I start my new life as a married man with a significant bank account."

"You earned every penny." Bill could see the pride on Clancy's face. "Now what's the second thing? I'm stumped."

"I want you to be my best man."

"Only if you'll be mine," Clancy clamped Bill's shoulder.

"Of course, I'd be honored."

"We're gonna have one hell of a bachelor party," chuckled Clancy.

"Not if Dottie and my mama get wind of it."

17

"Who's that?" Lyric asked Bullet.

"That there fella is Kingston West," he answered. "New hire, and soon to be my travelin' companion."

"What's he do?"

"He's a hand. Like me."

Tristan smiled. Bullet often referred to himself that way, but he was hardly a "hand." He was an integral part of the rough stock business. The partners were also convinced he was on the road to a bull riding championship. If not this year, next year for certain.

"What else does he do? A man doesn't get a body like his from ranchin' alone."

Tristan looked over at the man they were discussing. He was a big guy. Taller than Bullet, who had to be at least six foot four. Kingston had broad shoulders and a build that could be described as husky.

"Bulldoggin'," Bullet finally answered. "I hear he's also a country singer of sorts."

"I knew it!" exclaimed Lyric. "You can't have power like his and not do somethin' with it. Damn, that man is hot as a branding iron. I bet he can ride a woman even better than he can a horse."

Tristan laughed out loud and Bullet looked embarrassed. "She's done this my whole life," he explained. "Doesn't care what she says or who hears it."

"Get over it," Lyric looked between her and Bullet. "As if the two of you aren't doin' the nasty every chance you get."

It was Tristan's turn to be embarrassed. And she hadn't needed Bullet to explain Lyric's lack of filter.

"Jesus, Lyric, people are always sayin' how I'm so irresponsible. Your *mouth* is irresponsible. You can't keep sayin' everything you think whenever the hell you think it. Ever hear of keepin' some of your thoughts to yourself?"

Lyric was still studying the cowboy standing across the room. Tristan thought he looked just as uncomfortable as she felt. He'd be even more so if he could overhear what Lyric was saying.

"I gotta meet him." Lyric was out of her chair and halfway across the room. Heaven help him, thought Tristan.

"Sorry about that."

"Lyric? Don't be. It didn't take me long to get used to her. I'd be disappointed if she didn't say something embarrassing every time I see her."

"Yeah, you might think it's funny now, but wait until you're part of our family. You'll get sick of her right quick."

Tristan was sure Bullet misspoke. And she couldn't think of a single thing to say to change the subject. By the look on Bullet's face, he couldn't either.

"I don't know why I said that," he shook his head. "Gettin' a little bit ahead of myself."

"It's okay."

"Is it?"

Tristan hated how hopeful the words he spoke made her feel. Didn't he know how devastated she'd be once he lost interest in her? And he would. It was inevitable.

"Tristan…" he leaned in close. She thought he'd kiss her, but he stopped short of doing so. "Do you know how damn much I want you to be a part of my life?"

"Bullet," Tristan scooted back, and put her hand on his. "We hardly know each other." She tried to make her voice sound light, as though his words weren't setting her heart on fire.

But it didn't work. Bullet's eyes grew dark and his nostrils flared. He pulled her chair back closer to him. "You're wrong about that, darlin'. We know each other very well. When I close my eyes there isn't a single part of your body I can't picture. I memorized the look you get on your face when I take you over the edge. I know every freckle on your nose." He ran his finger over her collar bone, and then downward. "And the ones that are sprinkled here, and here." His finger dipped inside her v-neck to touch the lacy edge of her bra.

"There are other things I know about you too." He leaned forward and put his lips against her temple. "I know how damn smart you are," he kissed across her forehead. "And how creative." Bullet put his fingers on her chin, and tilted her head up. He looked straight into her eyes. "I also know that you haven't figured out how to let go, and let this thing happen between us. You don't wanna care what other people think, but you can't help yourself."

She opened her mouth to speak, but Bullet put his finger on her lips. "And you know me," he continued. "You know you can trust me, and you know exactly how I feel about you. You're just not ready to hear it."

He was right. She wasn't ready to hear it. Every word he said terrified her. She'd experienced the gut-wrenching pain of a cowboy breaking her heart one too many times already.

"Just wait," she warned. "Wait until you're on the road. Night after night pretty cowgirls will invite you into their bed, and you—"

"No, Tristan, I won't. I'm not him. I'm Bullet. I'm not the asshole who put this fear of trust in you."

"Can you honestly tell me you don't have a trail of broken hearts in your wake? Honestly?"

She knew by the way his expression changed that she was right.

"What'll it take for you to trust me, Tristan?"

"I don't know." She was being honest, too. She *didn't* know. Time, she supposed. But even with time, how could she know for sure? There were times she couldn't be on the road with him, and then she'd wonder if he was with other women. That's how it was with Harris, and it tore her up.

Bullet lifted her hand and rested her palm against his chest. "Feel that? It's my heart, and it belongs to you."

Those words. She'd heard them before, almost verbatim. Harris told her the same thing, and she'd been stupid enough to believe him. She'd vowed never to make that mistake again. Her eyes filled with tears, and she tried to turn away from him, but he wouldn't let her.

"What? Tell me what just happened. Is it so wrong that I want to give you my heart?"

"It isn't that—"

Tristan froze when her eyes met Liv's. Something was wrong, terribly wrong. It was as though everything and everyone around her came to a complete standstill as she watched Liv walk toward her. Tristan looked down and saw the Liv was carrying her phone. Why did Liv have her phone? Had she left it on the table? What in God's name was happening?

"Tristan, sweetheart, I'm so sorry. It's your dad," she heard Liv say. "We need to get you home."

"What's happened?" Bullet heard his mother ask Lyric, who had rushed over as soon as she saw Liv approach Tristan.

"I'm not sure," he heard his sister answer.

Liv was standing in front of Tristan, with her hands cupping her shoulders. When she said, "It's his heart," Tristan literally crumpled in his arms. He caught her the moment she lost consciousness, and held her until she came to. The pale gray color her skin had turned terrified him.

She looked back and forth between Liv and him. "Will he be okay?" she asked, not more than a whisper.

"We don't know much at this point, sweetheart," Liv told her. "Ben is making arrangements to fly you home now."

When Ben came back inside and walked over to the table where Bullet still held Tristan as close to him as he could, and reached out to take her hand, Bullet wanted to hold on, and not let her go.

"The plane is ready for us," Bullet heard him say. "We'll get you home."

Tristan stood and let Liv and Ben take her away from him. She didn't say a word, she didn't look back, she just kept walking.

His heart seized and he brought his hands to his head. *What was happening? Should he follow? Should he offer to go with them?* He had no idea what to do.

His father rested his hand on Bullet's shoulder and squeezed.

"I don't know what to do, Dad," he whispered.

"Let her go, Bullet."

Let her go? *No.* He couldn't let her go. Not ever.

Bullet shook his father's hand away, and sped out of the restaurant in time to see Tristan climb into the back seat of Ben's SUV.

"*Wait!*" he yelled as Liv climbed in after her.

He ran over and held the door open. "Tell me what I can do."

"We'll call you as soon as we know something. I promise."

Bullet stepped back and let them drive away.

Tristan went wherever Liv led her, in a daze every step of the way. When she encouraged her to close her eyes and rest once they were on the plane, Tristan nodded, but couldn't keep her eyes closed. Whenever she did, all she could see was her mother, and the way she looked the last time she saw her, before she died in the car accident. Was the reason she kept seeing her mother because she was there to take her father to heaven?

"Have you heard anything?" Lyric asked when she walked into where Bullet stood looking out the kitchen window at the sunrise. She'd stayed up with him most of the night, waiting for word, until she finally drifted to sleep on the couch. He hadn't slept at all.

"Not yet."

He thought about calling, or texting, or driving to the airport and getting on the next plane to New York. But he didn't do any of those things. He just waited.

* * *

1972

Bill had been premature in asking Clancy to be his best man, but four years later, it was finally happening. Tomorrow afternoon he and Dottie would be man and wife.

Dottie insisted they wait to marry until after they both graduated from college. As it turned out, they didn't have much choice.

She started out at Western State, even though Bill was going to school in Colorado Springs. Two years later, Dottie was awarded a scholarship, and was able to transfer to Colorado College, the prestigious liberal arts institution. It wasn't far from where Bill attended the Engineering School at University of Colorado at Colorado Springs.

Unfortunately, Bill transferred to Colorado State College in Fort Collins right before Dottie found out about her scholarship.

He'd been approached by the school that was Clancy's alma mater. They offered him a spot in the College of Agricultural Sciences, and his own scholarship, as a rider for the CSU College Rodeo Team. They competed from March to May, which didn't take much time away from his academics.

When he gave up rodeo after he graduated from high school, he turned to the only other thing he knew and loved—ranching. Now he'd be able to do both.

As part of his degree, Bill studied Agricultural Economics, Animal Sciences, and Soil and Crop Sciences. With all he was learning, he and Clancy could modernize the operation in Black Forest and work the land to it's maximum potential while at the same time preserving it's natural resources.

Right before he and Dottie graduated, Clancy finished construction on the three-story ranch house he designed for Jane and him to live in.

Bill's younger sister had married her high school sweetheart the previous summer, and the two made their home in Cheyenne, Wyoming, where he'd gotten a job in management with what was known as the "Daddy of 'em All" in the rodeo world, Cheyenne Frontier Days.

Clancy and Jane gave Bill and Dottie the original ranch house that had belonged to Russ Snyder as a combined wedding and college graduation gift.

The house didn't look much like it had when Bill first saw it all those years ago. Clancy had added a front porch that spanned the entire front of the house, along with bricking over the original wood siding. "Gets damn cold out here on the prairie," he'd said when he talked to Bill's mama about it.

Over the course of the last four years, Clancy had either remodeled or repainted every room of the house. Bill lived in the house and helped with the work the first two years he was at UCCS. That was when the major renovations were done. It didn't have to be spoken between them, Bill understood as well as Clancy did, that they were eradicating all signs of the former owner.

Apart from what little Bill remembered of the time before his daddy got ill, he'd never seen his mama as happy as she was with Clancy. He remembered what Clancy told him years before, about women trying to tame him. He didn't seem much different now than he was then, just happier. And he didn't seem to miss the attention he'd gotten at the dude ranch from all the ladies. The only lady he seemed to care about was Bill's mama.

The day of Bill and Dottie's wedding was what was known as a "Bluebird Colorado Day". The sun shone brightly, the sky was blue as a bluebird, and the only clouds they saw were soft, white, billowy ones that gently drifted across the sky.

Bill and Clancy had constructed a gazebo near the new house, both of which had an unobstructed view of Pikes Peak, the fourteen-thousand-foot mountain that defined the Colorado Springs area.

The backdrop of the majestic mountain, the wildflowers in the meadows of the ten-square mile ranch, and the babbling stream that ran through it, set the perfect tone for the wedding.

Dottie wore a simple white dress that her Aunt Sadie made, and Bill wore a black suit, white dress shirt, and black cowboy hat. The bouquet Dottie carried was made of a collection of the wildflowers found on the ranch, held together by a thin, leather tie-down.

Instead of going on a honeymoon, the couple wanted to spend their first few days as a married couple in their new home. After being apart so much of the previous four years, they wanted to spend their time walking the ranch land, riding horses, and planning their future together.

Bill woke and saw the note from Dottie resting against her pillow. She'd gone up to what they now called the main house, to pick up a few ingredients she needed to make breakfast.

He didn't know how long ago she left, so he decided to take a shower before she got back. She'd shoo him away from the kitchen anyway, if she was cooking something she wanted to be a surprise.

As he turned the water off, he heard the phone ringing. He grabbed a towel, and walked down the hall and into the kitchen, dripping water as he went. He knew he better get it cleaned up before his wife got back, or she wouldn't be too happy with him.

The phone stopped ringing before he got to it. He was five paces away, headed back to the bathroom to dry off, when it started ringing again.

"Good morning, Patterson Ranch, this is—"

Before he could finish, his mama stopped him. "Bill get over here quick. Something's happened to Dottie. I called the ambulance, but Clancy needs your help."

Bill left the phone receiver dangling in the kitchen. He grabbed his pants and boots, and flew out of the house. He was halfway across the meadow by the time he pulled his shirt over his head. He could see Clancy kneeling on the ground with a person that had to be Dottie.

Two days into their perfectly idyllic life, Bill feared it was coming to a horrible end.

18

By the time they landed, Ben made arrangements to rent a car, and he, Liv and Tristan arrived at the hospital, it was close to four in the morning. While she hadn't slept at all, for some reason, she was able to think far more clearly than she had on the plane. Second only to her father, the person she was most worried about was her grandfather.

When they checked in at the information desk in the lobby of the hospital, they were directed to the third floor, to the Cardiac Trauma Center.

Liv kept a tight hold on her hand as they waited for the elevator. Tristan looked back and forth between her and Ben. "I can't tell you how much I appreciate you being with me."

"You're family." Ben told her, and Liv squeezed her hand.

When they approached the room where they were told her father was, the door was open. Tristan's father was sitting in a chair near the window, and her grandfather stood next to him.

He looked fine. There were no wires connected to him, he didn't even have an IV. "Daddy..."

"Sweetheart," he answered. "I'm so sorry you had to rush back here."

"How are you feeling? What happened?"

"He collapsed," her grandfather began. "We were on our way back from a trail ride, almost to the barn, when this one slunk over…" Her grandfather's eyes filled with tears, and he looked away from her.

"It's okay," she murmured and put her hand on his arm.

"I thought we lost him," he said, so quietly his words haunted her. He wiped his tears with his handkerchief, and turned to face her.

"I called 9-1-1. He was breathing, and his eyes were open, but he wasn't there…"

"We don't have to do this now," Tristan offered.

"No. It's all right, sweetheart. Anyway, the damn fool came to and told me to hang up the phone."

Tristan looked back and forth between her father and grandfather, both of them were smiling.

"I though I just passed out for a few seconds," her father explained. "Turns out it was a lot longer than that."

"Four minutes and twenty-seven seconds," added her grandfather. "He tried to dismount, but then he got woozy again, so I told him to stay put. A few seconds later the ambulance pulled up and they took over."

"Did you have a heart attack?" she asked.

Her father's smiling face turned sullen and he shook his head. "Not a heart attack."

"The doctor came and talked to us a few minutes ago," said her grandfather. "Your daddy here needs part of his ticker reworked."

"What does that mean?" she asked both of them. "Do you need bypass surgery?"

Her father shook his head. "Valve replacement."

Instead of trying to explain further, her father handed her a piece of paper. "The doc said to have the nurse give her a call when you arrived and she'd come back and talk with you."

Tristan leaned forward and kissed her father's cheek, and then hugged her grandfather. When she walked out of the room to go to the nurses' station, she found Ben and Liv waiting a few feet away.

"I'll know more soon," she said, approaching them. "You don't have to wait around here. I know you need to…uh…" She wasn't sure what to say. They probably didn't want to hop back on the plane after landing just a couple of hours ago. "Do you want to go to the house? I can give you directions."

"We'll wait a little while longer," said Liv, linking her arm in Tristan's. "So tell me what you do know."

They walked arm-and-arm to talk with the nurse, who told Tristan the doctor would be right up, and directed her to a family waiting area. "She'll explain."

While they waited, Tristan told Liv and Ben what her father and grandfather told her.

"It's a miracle he didn't tumble off the horse," Ben commented.

Tristan shook her head. "I was thinking the same thing."

"Miss McCullough?"

"That's me." Tristan went to stand, but the doctor motioned for her to stay seated.

"I'm Dr. Perry and I'm a cardiologist." The doctor shook her hand. "What has your father told you so far?"

"Not a lot."

"Essentially, he needs aortic valve replacement." She took a piece of paper out of her pocket and drew a simplistic human heart. "Most of us have what's called a tricuspid valve, but your father's is bicuspid instead." She sketched a couple more images. "It's a genetic condition. We rate the risk of this particular diagnosis on a scale of one to five. Your father is as close to a five as I've ever seen. It's a wonder he hasn't had any episodes previous to this one."

Tristan wondered. As stubborn as her father was, it was certainly possible that he had fainted before, and not told anyone.

"What is the treatment?" she asked.

"Aortic valve replacement. There are a couple of options that we'll discuss in depth with a cardiac surgeon, but I have to stress there can be no delay with your father having this surgery."

Tristan nodded. "What are the options?"

The doctor explained the difference between a mechanical valve and one from a bovine. "In some cases the bovine's are larger, which means it'll last longer. At your father's age...well, we'll let the surgeon give us his opinion first. His name is Dr. Fredericks and I've specifically requested him. In the world of aortic surgery of any kind, he's the rock star."

Tristan smiled at Ben.

"I'll warn you, though, he looks like he's in his early twenties, but I assure you, he's much older, and the best-qualified surgeon I know. Of course you're also welcome to get a second opinion."

Tristan wasn't sure what her father would want to do, but if Dr. Perry was telling her that the surgery had to be performed as soon as possible, did they really have time for a second opinion?

"I'll call Dr. Fredericks and ask him to come down as soon as he's available."

Tristan thanked the doctor, and then again asked Liv if she and Ben wanted to go back to the house.

"How's your grandfather?" Liv asked. "Maybe he'd like something to eat, or a cup of coffee."

Tristan hadn't thought of that, and now that she was here, he could go home for a while, and get some rest.

"Is there anyone you'd like us to call?" asked Ben.

Tristan shrugged. "I don't know who. I mean…"

"What about Bullet?"

"I guess, although, I'm not sure he…I don't know. Would he…"

"Yes." Liv smiled. "He would."

Her grandfather took Liv and Ben up on their offer to go back to the house, and left Tristan the keys to his truck

"Do you want to get back in bed, Daddy?" she asked after they were gone.

He didn't answer right away, but after a few minutes, stood, walked over to the bed, and sat on its edge. "I'm sorry about this, sweetheart."

Inwardly Tristan rolled her eyes. This wasn't a condition he could done anything to prevent. He'd been born with this deviation, from what the doctor said.

"You need to get checked out too," he told her. "All these years I've had a heart murmur and not a single doctor told me to get what's called an echocardiogram."

"What's that?"

He explained that it was essentially an ultrasound for the heart. If he'd had one, they would have been aware of his condition. In the event it worsened, he could have been on the proactive side of surgery. He also warned her that if she ever heard the words "heart murmur" to get one done herself.

Bullet jumped when he felt his phone vibrate in his back pocket. He pulled it out and answered without bothering to see who it was.

"Bullet, this is Liv Rice calling."

"How's Tristan?" Bullet guessed he should've asked about her daddy first, but he was more worried about her. He still hadn't been able to sleep, he was so concerned.

"She's better now that she's seen her father."

Liv explained as much as she knew, she told him, and said that whenever there was an update she'd let him know.

"He needs surgery soon, so I should be able to give you an update tomorrow."

"Can I talk to her?" he asked.

"We're not at the hospital now, but you can call her, Bullet. I'm sure she'd be glad to hear from you."

He thanked Liv, hung up, and immediately called Tristan.

"Is that a call you need to answer?" her father asked when she looked at her phone.

"Not now. I can call him back."

"Him?"

"It's just one of the riders, Daddy. It's not important…"

"Try again, and tell me the truth this time."

Tristan smiled. "We can talk about him later, it really isn't important now. We need to talk about your surgery."

Her father was shaking his head. "We're gonna talk about it right now, Tristan. This very minute."

"He's somebody works for Flying R. He's a hand, but I don't think anyone really considers him that. He's so much more than he gives himself credit for."

Ten minutes later, her father was smiling from ear-to-ear, and Tristan couldn't believe how long she'd gone on about Bullet. There were certain things she left out, like how he had a little girl with a woman he never married, and about them being together at Black Mountain Ranch.

"You say he trained with Buck Bishop?"

Tristan nodded. "He thinks Bullet has a real good shot at regionals, at least."

Her father's expression changed. "So tell me, Tristan, why isn't Lost Cowboy sponsoring him?"

Now she wished she would've told him about the Lost Cowboy story first. If she told him about it now, she'd have to explain why she believed he was lost in the first place. This was getting too complicated, and just like before, if she lied, he'd know it in an instant.

"He has Flying R's sponsorship."

Her father raised his eyebrow and crossed his arms.

"Knock, knock," said a man who Tristan could only guess was the cardiac surgeon based on his white jacket and the fact that he looked to be all of twenty-one years old. His timing was impeccable.

"I'm Dr. Fredericks," he said, confirming her assumption. He shook her hand and her father's and then pulled a stool over a stool just as Dr. Perry walked in. She motioned for him to remain seated and leaned against the wall.

Tristan listened as the surgeon explained the differences between the two types of valves, and gave the pros and cons.

"What would you recommend if he was your father?" she asked.

By his reaction, she guessed that wasn't an appropriate question.

"I can't answer that," he told her.

Her father asked a few more questions, and the surgeon excused himself from the room.

"If it were my father, in the shape your father is in," said Dr. Perry, "I'd go with the bovine valve."

She explained her reasoning, mainly because her father was so active, having a mechanical valve would significantly restrict the things he was able to do because he'd be on blood thinners the rest of his life.

She had taken a seat after Dr. Fredericks left, and now she stood.

"This cardiologist will be taking over your case." She handed both her and her father business cards. "I'll stop in and see you from time to time though."

Tristan could've sworn she saw the lady doctor wink at her father before she turned around to leave.

"By the way, that was the only way I could ethically answer your question. If I was your doctor of record, it would've been impossible for me to give you a personal opinion."

Tristan looked at the card. "I hope that isn't the reason your not my father's cardiologist any longer."

"No, no." She smiled. "I have other reasons."

When the doctor winked *again,* she knew she wasn't imagining it.

Tristan fell onto her bed almost too tired to consider taking off her clothes. How long had it been since she'd slept? It was after ten now, and other than the catnaps she took at her father's bedside, she hadn't slept since she was in Colorado.

Tomorrow morning her father was schedule for several tests in preparation for his surgery, and as long as nothing else presented itself, they'd replace his valve the following morning.

She looked at her phone and scrolled through the text messages she'd received. Other than when he called earlier, she'd only gotten one other message from Bullet.

I'm sure worried about you, his text read.

If she wasn't so far beyond exhausted, she'd call him tonight, but the way she felt, it would have to wait until morning.

"Liv said Tristan's father needs some kinda heart surgery," Lyric told Bullet.

"Yeah?" he scowled.

"What's your problem?"

"Nothin'," he said before he walked outside and slammed the door behind him. He still hadn't heard from her, even though he'd called and texted. It was a little after seven, which meant it was what…eight…nine in New York? He could next keep track of that kind of shit. He went inside to ask Lyric, but she was head-to-head with Gram about something.

He'd just taken a seat at the kitchen table when he heard a rap on the back door.

Bullet stood and opened it. "Hey, King. Sorry, but I've got some other things to take care of this morning. You can head to the barn and see if anyone else needs help."

"I already did. And Bill told me to take the day off. Said we'd be damn busy the next few weeks so I should enjoy today."

"Then why are you here?"

"I'm not here for you, Bullet, I'm here to see your sister."

Lyric pushed Bullet out of the way, and invited King inside. "Why didn't you call?"

King waved his cell phone. "Didn't get your number last night."

"Let's fix that right now."

Bullet walked outside and closed the door behind him. He didn't want to hear his sister's conversation with his soon-to-be traveling partner. And he didn't want to witness what was likely the start of a new relationship, not when he was so sure the one he wanted so badly didn't seem to be going anywhere.

Someone knocking on the bedroom door woke Tristan from a deep sleep. She propped herself up on her elbows wondering what time it was. Whoever it was knocked again.

"Sorry," she answered. "Come in."

Liv stuck her head in the door. "I'm sorry to wake you, but—"

Tristan waved her hand. "It's okay. What time is it?"

"A little after ten."

Tristan flew out of bed. "Oh my God. I can't believe how late I slept."

"You were exhausted, sweetheart."

She picked up her phone, but there were no messages. "My dad. He's supposed to have tests this morning."

Liv came in and sat on the edge of the bed, patting it for Tristan to sit back down. "Ben took your grandfather to the hospital a little after seven this morning. Your dad hasn't been alone, he's been with him the whole time."

Tristan laid back on the bed and covered her eyes with her arm. "I was just so tired."

"Your dad would've wanted you to sleep. You know that."

Tristan nodded. Liv was right. She still felt terrible that she'd slept as late as she had.

"Whenever you're ready, we'll drive over together. How's that?" Liv offered.

Tristan moved her arm and looked at Liv. "That would be great, but I feels so bad. Don't you need to get back?"

"We do, but we aren't going anywhere until after your father's surgery."

"Are you sure? I mean…if you need to go, I understand."

Liv smiled. "I guess you didn't hear me."

Tristan smiled back. "Thank you."

Liv stood. "You're welcome. When you're ready there's coffee and a couple out of this world homemade blueberry scones waiting for you."

"You're a gift from heaven," Tristan murmured.

After Liv closed the bedroom door, she looked up at the ceiling. "Did you send her to me, Mom? Cuz I'll tell you, I don't know what I'd do without her right now."

Liv stuck her head back in the door. "By the way, if you have a minute, you might want to give Bullet a call. I think he's close to a breakdown."

Tristan's eyes opened wide.

"I'm kidding, but he is very anxious to speak with you."

"Thank you," she said as Liv closed the door.

She hit the call back button, but Bullet's phone rang a couple times and then went straight to voice mail. Instead of leaving him a message, she'd just call back in after she got out of the shower.

Bullet grabbed his phone when he climbed out of the shower and saw he'd missed a call from Tristan. When he called back, she didn't answer. *"Shit!"*

With the towel slung around his waist, he went into his bedroom to get dressed. His parents and Gram had taken Pearl and Grey to the zoo today, since it was sunny and supposed to stay warm all day. He would've gone along, but he knew he'd be lousy company until he talked to her.

When his phone buzzed again, Bullet jumped on it before it rang twice. "Hello?"

"Bullet, it's Tristan."

"Hi," he sighed. "Damn, it's good to hear your voice."

"Yours too. I'm sorry I didn't call you back last night."

"I'd tell you it's okay, but I haven't gotten a whole lot of sleep the last two nights, hopin' you'd call."

"God, Bullet, I'm so sorry."

"Don't be. Just tell me how you are now."

Tristan told him what happened with her father, and about the surgery that was scheduled for the following day.

"What's the recovery like?" he asked.

"He'll be in the hospital for a few days. And then once he's home he'll have rehab. I'm not sure for how long."

Bullet didn't know what to say. He couldn't exactly ask her when she might be back in Colorado.

All he could come up with was, "I miss you."

"I miss you, too."

If Pearl wasn't here with him he'd hop on a plane and go be with her, but he hardly had any time with his little girl as it was. Soon he'd be on the road, and away from Grey too. And it wasn't like he could bring them to New York with him.

"I want you to know, if I could, I'd be there."

"I know, and I appreciate it. You have a lot on your plate right now, Bullet, and so do I."

"So no idea when we might see each other again?"

"I'm sorry, but no."

He wanted to keep talking to her, but he had no idea what else to say. Everything he wanted to say seemed wrong given her dad's health and his...life.

"Well, bye for now then, but you call me every chance you get. Okay?"

"I will. And you call me too. Okay?"

Bullet disconnected the call before he realized he'd been shaking his head and hadn't said goodbye.

* * *

1972

Dottie had been in the hospital ten long days. She had four broken ribs and a collapsed lung, but that wasn't as bad as what the doctors initially thought. The first thing they told him was they suspected her back was broken, and she may never walk again.

She could walk, but it was very painful for her to do so. There wasn't a lot they could for broken ribs, they told him. They'd heal on their own.

Clancy couldn't say what spooked the horse Dottie rode over to their house that morning, but he watched as she was thrown. He yelled for Jane to call the ambulance as he ran out of the house.

"You saved her life," Bill told him. He knew Clancy felt terrible that there wasn't more he could've done, but Dottie was alive, and that was all that mattered to Bill.

The nurse told him the doctors were planning to release Dottie from the hospital in the next couple of days, but there was something important they wanted to discuss with him before they did.

Bill sat in the private waiting area the next afternoon as a doctor he hadn't met before told him it was unlikely Dottie would be able to have children.

"Does she know?" Bill asked.

"We thought it best if we told you first."

"Do you want me to tell her?"

The doctor told him it was up to him. They could tell her, with him present, or he could wait until she was home, and more comfortable.

"She broke some ribs, and her lung was hurt. What would that have to do with her ability to have children?"

"Your wife was pregnant at the time of the accident Mr. Patterson."

The timing was right. The first time he and Dottie made love was over spring break. He'd convinced her that in just a few weeks, they'd be married anyway. He told her he didn't want to wait any longer.

If they had waited, if he hadn't pushed, Dottie wouldn't have been pregnant, and she'd still be able to have children.

Bill was devastated. He had no idea how to tell the most loving woman he'd ever known besides his own mama that she'd never be a mama herself. And it was all his fault.

19

Bullet was riding like crap. He hadn't covered the last seven bulls he'd gotten on. No one really said anything about it. Bulls prevailed over cowboys far more often than the other way around.

"You'll get after 'em next time," Bill would say at the end of a buck-off. But then when he'd find a place to practice, Bullet would be the one Bill was getting after.

Tonight they were in Colorado Springs, for the Pikes Peak or Bust Rodeo. It was the first time Bullet would get on a bull at what he considered his new "hometown rodeo."

His parents, Gram, Lyric, and most of the Flying R Rough Stock partners were here with their wives. In total they had four boxes reserved on the south side of the event center. Several of the Flying R team was competing including him, and King West, who was predicted to do well in the steer wrestling timed event. Unlike Bullet, he'd been in the money on several of his recent outs.

Regardless of whether he covered his bulls tonight, or through the weekend, he'd be home for the next week. He'd been on the road pretty near non-stop since

May, so the break was welcome—and unusual at this time of the year.

July was considered "Cowboy Christmas," because of the number of rodeos taking place. Competitors could potentially earn thousands of dollars traveling from one rodeo to the next, virtually non-stop. The higher they climbed in earnings, the better chance they had of being in the top fifteen invited to compete in the NFR in December. Bullet had lost hope seven bulls ago. He wasn't feelin' it tonight either.

"You give up before the bull's in the chute you might as well go home now."

Bullet looked up to see Buck Bishop sitting on the back of the bucking chute. No one told him Buck would be here, but it may have been no one expected him to be.

"Yes, sir."

"Where's your head, son?"

He shrugged his shoulders, but not because he didn't know the answer. He shrugged his shoulders because he didn't want anyone else to know.

"Brought you some good luck." Buck tossed a brown-paper wrapped bundle at him, and walked away.

"What's this?" Bullet shouted after him, but Buck didn't answer. He jumped down, and went around the corner to open the heavy package. Inside he found a pair of chaps. Buck gave him a new pair of chaps? What the hell? He didn't get it, but when he turned them over, he saw the tag. McCullough Cowboy. *Tristan.* He ran back over to the rail and looked at all four boxes Flying R had reserved. If she was here, she'd probably be sitting with Liv. He didn't see either one of them.

"Lookin' for somebody, cowboy?"

Bullet turned and looked in the prettiest eyes he'd seen in weeks. "Sure am, darlin'."

"How many times do I have tell you I'm not your darlin'?"

"How many times do I have to tell you that you are?"

"I shouldn't be back here."

"I don't give a shit." Bullet picked her up and spun her in a circle, right before he covered her mouth with his. "God damn, I missed you, girl."

"Better watch your language around my daughter, cowboy." When the man came around the corner, Bullet set Tristan back on the ground. "Hello, sir. I'm Bullet Simmons."

"Pleasure to meet you. I'm Hugh McCullough, and Tristan's daddy." The man shook Bullet's hand, and winked at him.

Bullet looked him up and down. "Dang, you're lookin' pretty good for a guy who just had heart surgery. I don't know how you looked before, but..."

"Thanks," Mr. McCullough answered. "But it wasn't exactly just. I've been on the mend for a couple of months. Thought it was about time I let this one out of her nursing duties."

Tristan smiled.

"What are you doin' here?" he asked Tristan, hoping her daddy wouldn't overhear him.

"I missed you too, Bullet. Ready, Daddy?" With that she put her arm through her father's and the two walked in the direction of the Flying R boxes.

"Do me proud since you're the first bull rider wearin' McCullough Cowboy chaps," she shouted over her shoulder.

Bullet had to bend over, put his hands on his knees and take a deep breath. *Was he dreaming?* He'd certainly dreamed about seeing Tristan again often enough. Buck Bishop? The chaps? Had to be a dream. Maybe he could keep it going and dream he covered his bull tonight too.

Tristan couldn't believe she was finally back in Colorado. It felt so good to be with her Flying R family. That's the way she thought of them—her family.

When Lyric called and invited her to their grandmother's ProRodeo Hall of Fame induction, Tristan said yes without giving herself time to think about it.

When Liv called back a few minutes later, and told her they were making a week of it by having all the partners meet opening night of the Pikes Peak or Bust Rodeo, she agreed to that too.

She also asked if she could bring her father and grandfather along, who, of course, were welcome. She hadn't asked them yet, but there wasn't any reason her father couldn't travel. He'd been cleared to do most anything since he'd successfully gotten through rehab.

Tristan had talked about little other than the Flying R partners, and the cast of characters that surrounded the rough stockers. Her father said at one point that the next time she got together with them, he wanted to go along and meet this infamous group in person. This would be the perfect opportunity.

When she asked him if he wanted to go, she dangled another carrot. "I heard the Mark Cochran, Nate Simmons, and Ben Rice are performing at the party following the PRCA Hall of Fame Induction Ceremony.

A few weeks ago she'd found him on the treadmill listening to blaring rock music. When she turned it down and asked him who the band was, he was dumbfounded. "You talk about these guys all the time. You don't recognize Cochran and Satin's music when you hear it?"

Tristan and her grandfather, who had come in behind her, raised their eyebrows.

"I used to listen to Cochran and Satin all the time."

"Wanna try again and tell me the truth this time," she teased.

"What? I did. Every time I could, I'd change the radio station from country music to rock. And then as soon as I'd see Gramps headin' toward the barn, I'd change it back."

Tristan had spent the last couple of months assisting her father with his recovery and working every chance she could on the first pieces of her new collection. She hoped it would be ready for a fall release.

It didn't matter how hard she worked or how much she tried to distract herself, Bullet had been on her mind all the time. Now, her she was and so was he. It was like a dream come true.

She watched him climb up the back of the chute. He was easy to find amidst the other cowboys. He was wearing the chaps she'd designed. He looked over, caught her watching, and tipped his hat in her direction.

"We both have cowboys ridin' for us tonight," said Lyric sliding into the seat next to Tristan left empty when her father went to talk to Nate Simmons. He was almost fan-boying it. "Good to see you here."

She smiled at Lyric. "Better to be here. I missed you." She turned her head and looked in the direction of the bucking chutes. "All of you."

"He's been ridin' like shit."

"I know."

"How?"

"RodeoChat."

"Right on, girlfriend," Lyric high-fived her.

"Which cowboy are you watching tonight?"

"You know me, Tristan, I watch 'em all, but the one whose time I care the most about is a bulldogger."

"Which one?"

Lyric rolled her eyes. "King West, but I bet you already knew that."

"Yeah, I kinda' figured. Although I have been a little out of the loop."

"Did you know he's been sittin' in when my dad, Ben, and Mark play?"

"No. You're kidding? Does he play the guitar?"

"Wait until later and we get a jam goin' wherever we end up celebratin'. That man has a voice as smooth as silk, and the songs he writes—damn, they're good." Lyric fanned her face and her cheeks turned pink.

Tristan liked seeing her this way, for two reasons. One, she'd liked seeing Lyric happy. Two, if Lyric was distracted by King, she wouldn't be paying as much attention to Bullet and her.

Bullet put on his protective vest, kissed the tips of two fingers, and touched them to the spot he saw on his chaps where Tristan embroidered her initials. It would have been easy to miss, but when he was removing the McCullough Cowboy tag, something in the detail caught his eye. It was a small heart, and the initials "TdM." He couldn't wait to ask her what the "d" stood for. When he did, she'd know he found her little love note.

"Where's your head now?" asked Buck, who Bullet hadn't seen sitting on the back of the chute.

He smiled. "This bull is mine."

Bullet didn't lie. After a near-perfect eight second ride, Bullet's score came in at eighty-eight.

"Eight for eighty-eight," he overheard Buck say to Bill. The two men were all smiles when Bullet walked back behind the chutes. When he glanced over to the box, Tristan blew him a kiss.

"Dottie used to do that," mused Bill. "Always made me feel like I was on top of the world."

"I know that feeling."

"Hell, Bullet, when you break a losing streak, you go all out, don't ya?" joked Bill.

"It's his career best," answered Buck, who seemed to be studying another bull rider. "Come on up here, Bullet, I want you to see this."

Buck and Bullet sat on the back of the chute and studied the final five bull riders. With each rider Buck asked Bullet to tell him what the cowboy did right, and what he did wrong.

"You should do this every time you enter a bull buckin', even when you're practicin'. Watch the guys who aren't riding well just as much as you watch the earnings' leaders."

Bullet was listening to every word Buck said, but he could feel his body leaning in the direction of the box where Tristan sat. It was almost as though there was a magnetic pull between their bodies.

What Buck had to say was more important though, so he refocused. He looked around the chutes and could see visible envy on the face of every other rider. Buck Bishop was in the house, and he was coaching Bullet.

"Are you Bullet Simmons?" one of the cowboys shouted over to him.

"Yep. Who's askin'?"

The cowboy walked over to the chute where Bullet and Buck were. "I'm Harris Jones," he reached up to shake Bullet's hand.

Huh. Harris Jones. The name didn't sound familiar to him. And if Buck knew him, he wasn't in the mood to say hello. He didn't even look the cowboy's way.

"We have a mutual friend," said Harris.

"That right? Well, I'll tell you. I've got a hell of a lot of friends here tonight."

"This one's pretty damn special, though."

"Yeah?" Clearly this Harris fella was talking about a lady. "What's her name?"

"Tristan McCullough."

Who was this asshole? Was he the one that turned her heart forever black toward bull riders? Given his smirk, Bullet would lay odds it was. What the hell did he want?

"We're goin' back out to Billy and Renie's tonight. Pretty quiet out there, not to mention the only neighbors are here with us anyway," Lyric told her.

Tristan wasn't sure her father and grandfather would be up for it.

"I'm Lyric and Bullet's grandmother. Everyone calls me Gram," Tristan overheard her say to her grandfather.

"Hugh McCullough Senior," he answered. "That one there belongs to me." He pointed at Tristan. "And you aren't gonna believe this, but everyone calls me Gramps."

"I don't know about you, Gramps, but I'd just as soon sit on the porch and listen to sounds of the prairie tonight."

Tristan's grandfather smiled. "Sounds perfect to me."

When everyone was ready to leave, Lyric volunteered to take them to Bullet's place, but Bill and Dottie insisted they ride with them. "It doesn't get much better than sittin' on our deck and enjoying such a beautiful summer night," said Dottie.

Tristan looked around, but hadn't seen Bullet since the rodeo ended. He would go to Billy's, wouldn't he?

"Where's Grey?" Tristan asked Lyric.

"Bullet took him to stay with Callie's parents for the week. They miss him like crazy, ya know? Wait. Do you know who Callie is?"

"Grey's mother. I know, Lyric."

"Oh, good. That would be a downer of a story to have to tell you tonight." Lyric pointed toward the barns. "Look there. You think there are any finer lookin' cowboys at this rodeo? I sure don't."

King and Bullet were walking toward them. Each had their own unique swagger, and Lyric was right, there wasn't anyone better looking than the two of them here tonight.

"Who's that?" Lyric pointed in a different direction. "I ain't lookin' right now, but if I was, that cowboy would be on my dance card tonight."

Tristan looked over and squinted. Who was that? He looked familiar...*oh no.* "Uh, Lyric, let me tell you, King West has everything goin' on, and that man has nothin.'"

"Really? From here he looks pretty hot."

"He may be hot, but it's because he spends all his time in hell."

"Huh?"

Tristan looked away. "That man is the devil, Lyric. Stay as far away from him as you can."

"I see."

"Yeah, you do." Tristan didn't need to explain further. Lyric got it. Fortunately she didn't ask his name, because she did not want to ever utter it again in her life. She opened up her program and looked at the bull riding page. His name wasn't on it. Odd. What was he doing here if he wasn't riding?

Bullet knew Tristan had seen Harris, but he wouldn't let on he'd spoken to him just yet. Best to pretend the guy didn't exist. He was pretty sure Tristan was thinking the same thing. The look of disdain she had on her face when she watched Harris Jones head toward the barn immediately turned to a smile when she looked in his direction.

"Now, that's what I like to see," he said.

"What?"

"That beautiful smile. Those eyes that draw me in and make me want to look at nothin' else for the rest of my life."

"Nothing else?"

Bullet put his arm around her shoulders and drew her in close. "Before I make a mess of this, tell me, is it okay to kiss you out here in front of God and everybody?"

Tristan leaned over, kissed Bullet's cheek, and gave him a sweet smile.

He'd be keeping the more heated stuff at bay until she gave him the all clear. He wasn't going to push her in any way.

"We've got some celebratin' to do, ol' Bullet." Billy Patterson slapped him on the back. Bullet was so happy tonight even Billy wouldn't get to him.

"Back to our place, right, darlin'?" Billy said to Renie.

"God, yes," she answered. "Mom is taking Willow and Sutter over to Bill and Dottie's tonight. I pumped breast milk every chance I got so I could have a *cocktail.*"

"Oh, I hoped to see the baby," sighed Tristan.

"You can see him all you want tomorrow. You can hold him all you want tomorrow." Renie smiled. "I say that now, but tonight is the first time I'll be away from him, so you probably won't be able to pry him out of my arms tomorrow."

"I swear Willow wasn't as big as him at a year old." Billy put his arm around Renie waist and kissed her neck. "Our two-month old is gonna eat us outta house and home before he can walk."

"Good thing we have more than one home," she smiled at him. "Come on, Tristan, need to catch up."

Bullet watched Renie lead Tristan over to talk with Blythe and to sister. She fit in with this bunch even better than he did. He wondered if she missed them when she was in New York. They sure as hell missed her.

"You up for this?" he asked her when she when she walked back over to him.

"Oh, yeah. Who would want to miss the chance to be in a room with three legends of rock?

"My gram, your gramps."

"How about that? It was sweet of her to recognize it wouldn't be his thing. Something tells me it's just the kind of night she'd enjoy."

"You're right, she would," Bullet laughed. "She's a firecracker, ain't she?"

Tristan had never seen so many guitars in one place, and all of them were acoustic. Mark, Nate, and Ben each had a stool, and right behind them, their own rack of instruments.

"Tonight will be the first time anyone but the three of us have heard these songs," Ben told them.

"And they're damn good," added Nate.

"These two jokers think we should go out on tour," added Mark. He'd been away from touring and the music business for two decades. He still wrote music, and made a hell of a lot of money at it, but he kept his involvement quiet by writing under a *nom de plume*.

"Liv should be here," Tristan whispered to Bullet.

"She is." He pointed toward the door Liv had just walked through.

While the guys were still tuning guitars and testing sound equipment. She came over and sat next to Tristan.

"I was just saying to Bullet that you should be here."

"Dottie agreed. She informed me Sutter was just as much her grandson as mine, and she'd be the first to get to watch him overnight since she was the oldest."

"Really?" Tristan laughed.

"She was teasing, of course. Although she is the oldest," smiled Liv. "Dottie is like a second mother to me, and has always been like a grandmother to Renie. And now here we are...in-laws."

The guys started to play their first song, "Mountain Harmony." Their sound was so different from what Tristan expected. Their voices blended beautifully. She supposed that most heavy metal rock songs started out this way. Simple voices, unplugged, melodic.

Lyric got up and went to the front door. King West walked in, guitar in hand.

"Did you know he played guitar?" whispered Bullet.

"Lyric mentioned something about it."

"I have a feeling he's gonna be way out of his league with these guys."

Before they started the next song, Ben invited King to join them. And proved Bullet wrong.

"Where're you stayin' tonight?" Bullet asked Tristan, but was looking over at her father.

"Lyric was gracious enough to offer to let us stay at her place tonight when she heard we had booked a hotel in Colorado Springs."

"I guess sneakin' in your window would be out of the question."

"My daddy and Gramps have concealed carry, so I wouldn't recommend you trying."

Bullet pulled her close and rested his chin on her shoulder. "Damn. I want to be alone with you, Tristan. I missed you so much."

"I know."

"Think we can make it happen one day this week?"

Tristan shook her head. "I don't see how, Bullet."

Shit. That was bad news.

"Bullet, please don't…"

Oh no. More bad news. "Let's go outside a minute." He pulled her with him toward the door leading to the outside deck.

"Please don't what?"

"I was going to say please don't worry about it. We'll find the time. What did you think I was going to say?"

He put his hands on her shoulders and pulled her close to him. "Something about please don't do this, or I don't know. Just whatever I was thinkin' sure as shit wasn't please don't worry about it."

"I'm sorry."

Bullet leaned down and covered her lips with his. "There you go, sayin' you're sorry all the time." He kissed her again and again. He could kiss her all night long, and through the next day too.

"Hey, the chaps. They're amazing. Before I forget to ask, hat's the 'd' stand for?"

"You saw it?" She smiled so sweetly. God, he loved this woman. It took every ounce of willpower he had not to tell her so.

"I did."

"Daughtry. It was my mama's maiden name."

"It's beautiful." Bullet pulled Tristan over to the Adirondack chairs. He sat, and pulled her onto his lap, wrapping his arms around her.

"Tell me about her."

Under the starlit sky, Tristan told Bullet everything she remembered about her mother. At first she wasn't sure she could. She never talked to anyone about the woman who loved her more than anything, and vice versa.

Tristan saw her mother everywhere she looked, in every beautiful thing God made. She could still hear her voice whisper to her, especially when she was feeling all alone. And if she closed her eyes real tight, and concentrated real hard, she could still imagine how it felt to have her mother's arms around her.

She told Bullet the first time Dottie hugged her, she cried. Dottie hugged the same way her mama did, all in. It wasn't just Dottie's arms wrapped around you, she wrapped you in her love too.

Her mother loved to draw, and taught Tristan. She still had some of the dresses her mother made for her when she was growing up.

"That's why you became a clothing designer."

Tristan nodded. "She never used a store-bought pattern." Tristan told him her mother would draw the dress, and then take it apart in her mind, drawing each piece on what would become her own hand-drawn pattern.

"I bet she'd be so proud of you."

"I like to think she is. Sometimes I feel as though it isn't my hand drawing. Or sometimes I look back through the pages, and I'll see a design I don't remember."

"That's awesome."

"I miss her so much, Bullet."

He gathered her closer still. "I know you do, darlin'."

Tristan was quiet for a while, but then said something Bullet didn't expect.

"The bull rider, you know, the one who broke my heart. He was at the rodeo tonight."

"I know."

Tristan sat up. "How did you know?"

"He approached me. Introduced himself."

"What else did he say?"

Bullet wasn't sure whether to tell Tristan the full extent of their conversation, but decided that with her, even white lies wouldn't fly. "He said he knew you, and that you were somebody very special."

Tristan looked up at the sky, but didn't speak. He could feel the tension in her shoulders.

"That was all he said. I'm not sure if it was meant as a warning, or what."

"I don't know why he's here. He didn't enter the competition."

After the cowboy walked away, Bullet had asked around. No one seemed to know who he was, or why he was behind the chutes. Except Buck.

"He's a dirty rider," Buck told him. "Glad to see he wasn't entered here."

"If he's not entered, what's he doin' here? Cowboy Christmas and all."

Buck told him he couldn't say for sure, but he'd heard talk that there had been thefts at several of the rodeos where Harris Jones had been seen. No one could prove it was him, but he was definitely a suspect. "He's down on his luck. Hasn't ridden well at all for the last couple of years."

"You think he's casin' this rodeo?"

"I can't say, but why would a fella who's been a contender in years past, not compete at every rodeo he could this time of year?"

Bullet agreed. It didn't make sense. But then again, Buck didn't know about Harris' past relationship with Tristan. Maybe that was the real reason the cowboy was in town.

"Buck knew him," Bullet finally said to Tristan. "Said he was dirty. Also said there're folks who think he's responsible for thefts at other rodeos he's been to."

Tristan shuddered. "How was I ever with him?"

Bullet could answer that, but wouldn't. If he had he would've said it was because he was charming, and women like Tristan were easy to read. She was an easy mark. Just enough spunk to be tough, but when it came to men, an innocent. Instead of the usual buckle bunnies,

Tristan was a nice girl, a real cowgirl. A challenge. Guys like Harris preyed on girls like Tristan. There'd been a time Bullet was one of them, but not anymore. Tristan wasn't his prey, she was his forever.

"Bullet?"

"Yeah, beautiful girl?"

"I'm sorry I ever compared you to Harris. You're nothing like him."

Bullet wished Tristan hadn't said that. There'd been a time he was, and he was ashamed of that part of his life. If it wasn't for his two precious babies, he go back and do it all differently.

Even though he couldn't change his past, he sure as hell could make sure his future was very different. He'd be a better man, not just for her, but for himself. He was committed to it. When Pearl and Grey were older, he wanted them to look at him with love and respect, and be proud of their daddy.

* * *

1980

"Where would you like to celebrate our anniversary this year?" Bill asked Dottie.

Bill had continued competing on the rodeo circuit and the two traveled often, especially around Colorado and the mid-west. Sometimes Clancy and his mama would travel with them. But he never entered a rodeo the week of their anniversary.

Every year for the last eight, Bill planned a trip for just the two of them. Being home only reminded him of Dottie's terrible accident two days after their wedding. He was sure Dottie thought about it too.

"I want to stay home this year, Bill," Dottie was looking out the window, toward the main house where Clancy and Jane still lived.

"Why don't we go to Gunnison? I'm sure some of your high school friends still live in town."

"Bill, I need you to sit down."

"Why?"

"Just sit. There's something I need to tell you."

Bill's heart went into his throat. "What is it, sweetheart?"

20

"Will you be at the rodeo tomorrow night?"

Tristan smiled. "Of course I will be. I'll be here all week."

"What do you say just the two of us go someplace quiet for dinner after? I promise I'll bring you home safe and sound before curfew."

She was a twenty-seven-year-old woman. She shouldn't need a *curfew*. It wasn't as though she had one, but since she was staying at Lyric's house with her father and grandfather, she had to show them respect, and that meant not staying out all night with Bullet.

"I'd like that very much, Bullet."

Buck Bishop couldn't be at the rodeo tonight, but he told Bullet he'd be back the following night, and he expected to see his name on the short go. To move on to the next round, Bullet had to cover his bull again tonight. He sure hoped he did, especially with Tristan watching.

"Hey, Simmons," Bullet heard someone shout. He turned his head to see Harris Jones approaching him. Bullet threw his rosin and leather straps down on the ground. "What the hell do you want?"

"Just wanted to give you a heads-up, I'm here to win her back."

"I'm afraid you're in for disappointment, son. The lady has a date with me later on tonight, and every night after."

"I'm sure she'll change her mind once she knows I'm here."

"She already knows, and I get the impression she doesn't give a shit."

"You never forget your first. Ain't that what they say? And I'll tell you, after the first time, she turned into a real wildcat in bed. Woohee, she was some kind of—"

Bullet had heard enough. He turned his back on Harris and watched as the next rider rosined his bull rope.

"She's a damn fine piece of ass, but my guess is you know that. She been makin' the rounds of the bull riders here? Is that her thing now? I got her started—"

Bullet jumped off the back of the chute and took a swing at Harris, then another. Stormy and some of the other guys from the Flying R team ran over and pulled Bullet off of him.

"You keep your dirty, lyin' mouth shut, you hear me, asshole?" he shouted at him. Bullet rubbed his knuckles. He hit him with his riding hand, and that was damn stupid.

The guys got between Bullet and Harris. "Get your head where it belongs, Bullet. And, you," Stormy pointed at Harris. "Get the hell out of here. You don't belong back here. If you don't leave, I'll have you thrown out."

Harris rubbed his jaw and smiled at Bullet. "Mark my words, that cowgirl will be leavin' with me tonight." He motioned in the direction of the Flying R reserved boxes.

Bullet spun around to finish what he started, but Stormy stopped him. "He's tryin' to get into your head. Don't play into his bullshit. Think, Bullet. Get ready for your ride, and forget this asshole."

Tristan watched the whole thing take place. She hated that Harris was able to get such a reaction out of Bullet, especially when he was about to ride. Why the hell was Harris back here again tonight? She was about to find out for herself.

"Where you goin'?" asked Lyric.

"I need to ask someone something."

"You're goin' to talk to that cowboy that Bullet just leveled, aren't ya? Isn't that the same guy I asked you about last night?"

"Yep. Same guy."

"You sure as hell aren't goin' to talk to him by yourself. Come on. I'll go with ya."

"Lyric, please. You don't have to."

"Sisters stickin' together," Lyric said as she put her arm through Tristan's and tugged her in Harris' direction.

"Well, hey there, Tristan, I was hopin' I'd run into you tonight. Who's this pretty young thing with ya? If you two are lookin' for some two-on-one action, I'll tell ya, I'm all for it."

"I hate you," Tristan spat at him. "I don't know why I even bothered to try to talk to you."

"Come on now, you know why you did. You miss me, admit it."

"I don't see much about you there'd be to miss," added Lyric. "What're you, some kinda wannabe cowboy? Hangin' out at the rodeo, hopin' to pick up a cowgirl too stupid to know you aren't the real thing?"

"Oh my, I like this one. Fiery as hell." Harris got closer to Lyric and was about to put his arm around her when she elbowed him in the stomach.

"You touch me and I'll finish what my brother started."

Harris dropped his arm. "Well, well, ain't this interestin'? Bullet's your brother? Is that what you said?"

"Yep, that's what I said. C'mon, Tristan. This scumbag isn't worth our time."

"Before you run off, there's somethin' important you need to know about your boyfriend."

"There isn't anything you tell me that I'd believe." Tristan turned to walk away. "Go to hell, Harris."

"One day soon you'll find out the truth about Bullet Simmons, and when you do, I'll be here waitin'. No denyin' it, Tristan, you and I will be together again one day very soon."

"Hell will freeze over first," Tristan said to Lyric. "I don't know what I ever saw in that man."

"Well…"

"What? After all the filth he just spewed? You can't seriously think he's anything but disgusting."

"It isn't that, it's just…"

"Say it, Lyric. It's just what?"

"Now that I've seen him up close, I never could've gone for him. I mean I know he's an asshole, but before he opened his mouth, I never could've."

"I hate to even ask, but why not?"

"You never noticed how much he looks like Bullet?"

Ew. Now that Lyric mentioned it, they did have several physical characteristics in common. They were about the same height, same color hair, same blue eyes. They probably weighed close to the same too. If she had to describe either of them to a sketch artist, the description would be the same.

"You don't think it has anything to do with your brother and me, do you?"

"Does it?"

"God, Lyric. Of course it doesn't."

"That's good to hear. I'm sure Bullet wouldn't notice. Guys never do."

"It's a coincidence."

"He's disgusting. No offense."

Tristan shuddered. "You got that right. And none taken."

Bullet's second ride was okay. Scored in the seventies, but with last night's eighty-eight, his average put him in the top three. Tomorrow night's ride would be the most important. Even if he covered his bull, he'd have to ride a score over eighty again to be in the top two that went on to the finals.

Given the mosh-up with Harris Jones earlier, it was surprising he rode as well as he had tonight. Bullet knew better than to let another rider get into his head right before he got on a bull. He wished he knew why the hell the guy was still in town.

Tristan was sitting in the stands alone when he came out from behind the chutes. He needed to stow his gear, but when he went to look for his rosin and tie-downs, they were gone. He wondered if that bastard Harris was the one who took them. They weren't worth a lot, but that wasn't the point. Among cowboys, a rider shouldn't have to worry about his gear going missing.

"Hey, pretty lady." Tristan sure was a sight to behold. Her long dark blonde hair shown through her straw drifter cowboy hat that sat low over her eyes. Her light pink tank top showed off her dark skin, tan from the sun, and her tight jeans were tucked into her Cinch Edge pink wave boots.

"You talkin' to me, cowboy?" Tristan looked over both shoulders. "Guess I'm the only one here, so you must be."

"Even with a crowd of thousands, you'd always stand out as the prettiest of 'em all."

"Aw shucks, guess you know how to win a girl's heart, don't ya?"

She was playing. Bullet knew that. But given what he wanted to talk to her over dinner tonight, their flirtation was turning his stomach.

"Bullet? What's wrong?"

He wrapped his arm around and pulled her close to him. "Not a thing now that you're in my arms."

"Did Harris get to you? I saw what happened."

"Nah. He's not worth even thinkin' about."

"Lyric and I went and talked to him. It was a waste of time."

He wished she hadn't. And as much as he wanted to know what they talked about, he didn't want it to monopolize their time together. "You ready, darlin'?"

"I am." He took her hand and she followed. "Bullet, are you sure everything's okay?"

"Yes, ma'am. Everything except I'm starvin'. How 'bout you?"

Every time he tried to bring up his past over dinner, Tristan said something that made him want to wait. They were seated in a corner booth at the new Cowboy Star restaurant, and she cuddled right up next to him. There were things he wanted her to know about his past, so nothing would ever pop up that would cause her not to trust him, but it never seemed like the right time to bring it up.

"I have an idea," she told him over dessert.

"Yeah? I have a lot of ideas," he nuzzled her neck, and trailed kisses back to her nape.

"We have the same idea. And I have a surprise for you."

"You do?"

Tristan had arranged for a room at the Broadmoor for the night. She told Bullet she hated lying to her father, but she told him she was going out with the girls, and instead of risking the drive home, they were adding on a sleepover at the posh hotel.

"Won't he find you out?"

"Your sister swore everyone to secrecy. He and my grandfather are having dinner with your gram at Bill and Dottie's again tonight. Everyone else is on their own."

"I sure hope nobody slips up and tells him."

"You scared of my daddy, cowboy?"

"You're damn right I am."

"Yeah, you're right to be."

"He ever meet Harris?"

"Ugh. I wish you hadn't brought him up."

"I'm sorry. Forget I asked."

"Just once, and he didn't like him much. Turns out he was right. He usually is."

"What's he think of me?"

"I overheard him talking to your daddy last night. He said he thought you were a fine young man."

Really? That was a surprise. Unless Hugh McCullough was starstruck enough by his daddy that he just said it to be nice.

Tristan watched Bullet as he slept. When they made love earlier, he was so tender. A couple of times he held still, her face in his hands, looking into her eyes. It was as though he had something to say, but couldn't bring himself to say it. If she didn't know better, she would've thought he was getting ready to say goodbye.

When Liv planned a real girls' get together the following night, Tristan was in a bit of a bind. Bullet didn't know whether her daddy knew she'd really been with him the night before, but when he told his daughter he understood and to go have a good time with her friends, Bullet breathed a sigh of relief.

He'd miss being with her tonight, but she deserved to have some fun on her own.

"You sure you don't mind?" she pulled him around the corner to ask.

"Of course I don't."

When she asked what he was going to do, he told her he'd probably just go back to the house and get some rest.

Things didn't exactly go the way he'd planned, though. The guys from Flying R Rough Stock, along with his daddy, hijacked him and King for a guy's night out.

"Hell," said Billy. "If they can do it, so can we."

Bullet wondered who was watching Billy's new baby, but that wasn't any of his business so he didn't ask.

At four the next morning, he stumbled into bed, glad that he didn't have to be back at the rodeo until four that afternoon. He hoped to hell he'd be sober by then.

"I wonder how the guys are feelin' this mornin'."

"Which guys?" asked Tristan asked Lyric.

"All of 'em. From what King told me, things got pretty wild last night."

"Did Bullet go out with them?"

"Oh yeah, and I guess he really tied one on. I think there might've even been some dancin', and something about a fight. That reminds me, he also said that Harris guy showed up."

"*Are you serious?*"

"What? That's what boys do when they go out to play Tristan. You oughta know that. It's Cowboy Christmas. Not only do the cowboys get to ride and win, they also get to play."

"What happened with Harris?"

"I'm not sure, but King said something about him confronting Bullet again."

"You don't think Bullet and King ended up…"

"Ended up what?"

"You know…with other women?"

"Of course not, where did that come from?"

From Harris. That's where. He was the type of man she couldn't trust to go out with the guys, because he'd end up with another woman. Why did Harris always have to taint her opinion of Bullet. It was completely unfair, and while she knew it in her head, her heart led her down a different path.

***

1980

"I think I'm pregnant."

Bill was glad she told him to sit down, because if he hadn't, he might've collapsed. "But I thought you couldn't."

"The doctor said he didn't *think* I could."

"Is it safe?" If Dottie put her health in jeopardy in order to have a child, Bill didn't know what he'd do.

"I have a doctor's appointment tomorrow to confirm that I am really pregnant. I want you to go with me. We can ask questions then."

What if the doctor told them it wasn't safe? What would they do? Would Dottie want to abort the baby? Or would she? Knowing his wife, she would never take the life of their child. Even if it meant her own life was at risk.

Neither got much sleep. When Bill saw faint light through the window curtains, he got up and fed the animals. Dottie's appointment was at nine. He had to keep himself busy until then or he'd go crazy.

"Your test came back positive," said the doctor. Dottie held Bill's hand so tight while they waited, she near cut off his circulation. "I'd like you to have an ultrasound so we can determine how far along you are."

When the technician called Dottie's name, Bill stayed in his chair in the waiting area.

"Come on, Bill Patterson, this child is as much your responsibility as mine," Dottie winked at him.

In the exam room, the technician rubbed gel all over Dottie's belly and then ran a wand over the gel. A black and white image appeared on a screen that was partially obstructed from Bill's view.

The woman studied it for a few minutes, hitting buttons on a keyboard near the screen, and then recording information on a chart.

"When was your last menstrual cycle?" she asked Dottie.

"I don't quite remember. I think it was two months ago. I didn't think about it until the other day."

Bill wished he hadn't been in the room for this part of the exam.

"Do you want to know the sex of your baby, or do you want to wait?"

Dottie looked at Bill. He couldn't tell whether she wanted to know, or didn't.

"I want to know. Don't you?"

He did. But he still didn't know if it was safe for her to be pregnant. He hated to get his hopes up, and hers, if something happened. "I think we should wait until after we talk to the doctor."

Dottie's eyes filled with tears, but she nodded her head. "I understand."

Bill's heart was breaking into a million pieces. She looked so full of joy just a few minutes ago, and now she looked crestfallen. Once again, he'd been the one to cause her hurt.

The technician got out another instrument. "This will let us hear the baby's heartbeat," she told them. She ran it back and forth over Dottie's belly and a minute later they heard a swishing sound.

"Is that it?" Dottie asked.

"Yes, it is," smiled the woman.

"Oh, Bill, that's our baby."

Tears spilled down Dottie's cheeks. Bill squeezed her hand, and prayed. He made a deal with God that day. If he'd watch over Dottie and their baby, Bill would give up rodeo for good.

21

"I'll be in Cheyenne in two weeks, and then Nashville mid-August," Tristan told him.

"I'll take it. And then come January, I want to fly someplace warm, and have non-stop, sun-drenched sex with you for two weeks straight."

Tristan raised her eyebrow. "Straight?"

"Eatin' and sleepin' will be the only allowable interruptions."

"You're on, Bullet. But don't forget there's a couple of other important rodeo weeks in between."

"That's if I qualify."

There were the Professional Bull Riders World Finals in Las Vegas in October, and then the Professional Rodeo Cowboy Association National Finals also in Las Vegas, in December. Tristan would be at both with Lost Cowboy and the new McCullough lines. Bullet would be at both too. Even if he didn't qualify as a rider, he'd be there with Flying R Rough Stock.

It was unlikely Tristan would be able to see him in September. She'd be showing at least two of the McCullough lines at the fall shows. Every minute between now and then, when she wasn't at one of the bigger rodeos, she'd be working twenty hour days to have the collections ready.

"I'm gonna miss you so damn much," he said for the hundredth time.

"I'm going to miss you too, but we'll both be so busy, the time will pass quickly."

"Do you really believe that?"

"Nope."

"That makes me feel a little better."

Tristan checked the time on her phone. Her father and grandfather would be getting anxious soon. They were at the gate waiting to board the flight that would take them back to New York. It was due to take off in twenty minutes, and she wasn't through security yet.

"Bullet, I *have* to go."

"Just one more kiss."

One more turned into ten, until Tristan finally pulled away and ran in the direction of security. As it was she was the last person to board the flight, and they held the door open because her father insisted she was on her way. He wasn't very happy with her the rest of the way home. Gramps just smiled and winked.

"Quite a series of shindigs you invited us to, Tristan," he said once she was in her seat.

"Did you enjoy yourself?"

He smiled and nodded. "I *sure* did."

Tristan really didn't have to ask. Gramps and Bullet's grandmother spent a lot of time together. He even served as he date for the PRCA Hall of Fame Induction Ceremony. He looked so proud that night anyone would've thought the two were a married couple.

The initial pieces in the McCullough Cowgirl collection sold out at the first show Tristan attended. Liv and Paige flew to New York to help Tristan find factories able to expand production. It would've been easier if they could outsource to China, or somewhere else overseas, but Tristan and her investors agreed that the brand would be made in America, or not made at all.

Bullet insisted that the only way to ensure his consecutive streak continued, was to talk to Tristan before and after each out. He'd ridden fourteen bulls consecutively. Two more and he'd tied J.B. Mauney and Silvano Alves, who had each ridden sixteen consecutive times.

As Buck Bishop predicted, Bullet would almost certainly qualify for the PBR finals this month. If he managed that, competing at the NFR would be a sure thing.

"Where did this guy come from? No one heard of him before this year." Tristan would hear the commentators ask when she watched the broadcasts. "Not until Buck Bishop started training him," they'd usually added.

She streamed every competition he entered on her computer. If he knew he was on camera, he'd blow a kiss.

"You see me blow you a kiss tonight, darlin'?" he'd ask. Her answer was always yes, because she never missed watching him ride.

Before she knew it, was October. In just a few days, she'd be in Las Vegas for a whole week, and so would Bullet. They'd both have a lot work to do, her presenting her line, and Bullet riding bulls and helping Flying R when he could, but they'd spend every night together.

Lyric offered to pick Tristan up at McCarran Airport since Bullet had a mandatory riders' meeting.

"You have an press conference at three," she told her.

"I do?"

"Yeah, you do, and you know why? Because you have the best damn PR person in the business. How else are you gonna let everyone know how the launch of McCullough Cowgirl and Cowboy have gone?"

Tristan smiled, but inside she wondered when she might have a change to see Bullet. Would it be this way the whole time they were in Las Vegas?

Lyric smiled. "You'll have time to see him in between."

"Thanks." Tristan smiled too. "I'd hoped I would."

"You two gettin' serious?"

"I think so." It was hard to say they were serious, they hardly saw one another. But once January rolled around, they could take some time to figure out where they wanted their relationship to go. It wouldn't be as though things would change much once the rodeo season kicked off again in the spring, but there were plenty of other couples who figured it out, including most of the Flying R partners.

"Speaking of which," said Lyric. "I heard a rumor that Bullet was going to be offered a buy-in."

"From who?"

"I got my sources."

Tristan guessed it had to be Billy that told Lyric. "Does Bullet know?"

"Nope. They're makin' him the offer at the end of the week, here in Las Vegas."

"Will he be able to do it?"

"You mean financially?"

"Basically. Is it bad of me to ask?"

Lyric laughed. "Who's gonna judge you, girl? Me?"

Tristan laughed too. Lyric asked whatever she wanted to ask, whenever she wanted to.

"He'll be able to do it. Bullet's loaded."

"Since when?"

"You haven't been keepin' track of his earnings so far this year, have you?"

She hadn't. He'd tell her where he ranked each week, but they hadn't talked about the money he'd won. Not to mention the additional sponsorships he was being offered as he climbed higher in ride earnings.

"Speak of the devil."

Tristan turned around thinking Lyric was talking about Bullet, but instead she saw Harris Jones near the luggage carousels.

"Why does he keep showin' up? He didn't come close to qualifyin' this year."

Tristan didn't know. She stopped paying attention a long time ago. She hoped he'd keep walking, and not notice she was there.

"Tristan, I thought that was you."

Something was different about him. He wasn't as cocky, and he didn't well.

"Harris, are you ill?"

He didn't answer right away, and Tristan thought he might just ignore her question and walk away.

"I been busy," he said finally. He glanced at Lyric. "You still with her brother?"

"Your damn right she is—"

"Look, uh, Lyric...that's your name, right?"

"Yeah, that's my name."

"Could you give me a minute with Tristan? It's important."

There was something about the tone of his voice, and the way he looked, that made Tristan feel sorry for him. She could take five minutes to talk to him. "It's okay, Lyric."

Lyric shook her head and glared at Harris. "I'll be right over here, *watchin'*."

"What's going on?" she asked him.

Harris reached out to touch her, but Tristan backed away. "I hate that you won't let me touch you," he sighed.

"It's your own fault."

"I know it is. But, Tristan, I'm not lyin' when I say I want you back. It's more than that. I need you."

"You don't need me, you don't need anyone. Permanently, that is. Rodeos are full of women willing to give you just about anything you want—"

"It isn't what I want. It's what I need. Ever since we broke up, I can't get a decent ride for anything. You were my good luck charm, Tristan. When we were together, I rode better than I have any other time in my life."

"You can't be serious."

"I am. I need you to give me another chance."

"Harris, I can't. And I don't want to. There was a time you had my heart, but you stomped on it, and threw it away. There's no going back for us."

"Tristan, I'm in trouble. I piled up some debt thinkin' I'd be able to make it up once rodeo season kicked in again. I haven't been able to…"

"I'm sorry you're in trouble, but that isn't my fault or my problem. If you're in debt, get a job. Most bull riders have a day job, Harris. You always thought you were above it, but clearly you're just as human as the rest of us."

When Tristan walked away, he grabbed her arm. "Wait."

She jerked it away from him. "Keep your hands off me." The hair on the back of her neck stood on end, and bile burned her throat.

"You heard her," Lyric stepped between Tristan and Harris. "Keep your filthy hands off her."

Harris leaned in as close to Lyric as he could get. "You and your brother can't keep me away from her forever. His world is about to come crashing down, and when it does, I'll be there for her."

Lyric backed away, but didn't turn or take her eyes off Harris until she was several feet from him.

"What was that about? What did he say to you?"

"If I'm not mistaken, he just threatened Bullet."

"What did he say?"

"That Bullet's world was about to come crashing down."

"Don't pay any attention to him. He's in some kind of trouble. He thinks I'm his good luck charm or some other ridiculous nonsense."

"Let's go find my brother."

Bullet waited by the front entrance to the hotel, hoping this was the way they'd come in. Every time a cab approached, he looked to see if Tristan and Lyric were in it. He wished he could've been the one to pick Tristan up at the airport, but he would've been disqualified if he'd missed the riders' meeting.

Another cab drove up to the valet. It looked to Bullet as though only one person was in it. That wouldn't be them. He was about to turn away, when the door opened and out stepped Harris Jones—the one guy he never wanted to see again in his life.

He expected a confrontation, but instead Harris acted as though he didn't see Bullet. Fine by him. A few minutes later, when the cab Tristan and Lyric were in pulled up, Bullet forgot all about seeing the guy who was fast becoming his nemesis.

Bullet opened the door and offered his hand to help Tristan out of the car. When she took it, electricity sizzled between them as it usually did.

Tristan dropped her bag on the ground next to the cab, and put her arms around his neck. Nothing felt as good as having her next to him, body to body. It had been almost six weeks since the last time he saw her, and his body reacted instinctively. He hoped Lyric wouldn't mind if they went straight to the room he'd reserved.

"Hi," he breathed her scent. It was soft, like baby powder. He looked into her deep, soft eyes. Felt her soft breasts pressed up against him. Her softness in contrast to his hardness drove him wild. One whiff of her scent and he wanted to take her straight to bed.

"Hi," she smiled.

"It's so damn good to see you. And feel you."

"You too."

"Think Lyric would mind if we…"

"Not at all. Look." Tristan pointed near the door. King West was walking toward Lyric with the same look on his face that Bullet had a few minutes before.

"We have a lot to talk about," he said in the crowded elevator.

"We do?"

"*Yes,* we do."

Bullet led the way to the room, but kept turning around to kiss her. The fourth time he stopped, she asked him how much further it was. He looked at the numbers on the door, and realized they'd passed the room. They both laughed, but the heat between them didn't dissipate.

Bullet opened the door and dropped her luggage. "You can unpack later."

"I'd like to take a quick shower. You know, the plane ride…"

"Uh. Sure. Okay." She was probably tired from traveling, and here all he could think about was her naked and him inside of her. She was here, with him, they had at least ten days ahead of them. He could be patient.

He stretched out on the bed, and took off his socks, shoving them into his worn cowboy boots he'd set by the side of the bed. He unbuttoned his shirt, but still felt uncomfortable. He wanted to unbutton the top button of his jeans, but then what would she think?

He stood and shoved his boots in the mirrored closet, where he couldn't miss his own arousal in the reflection. He stretched out on the bed again, and turned on the television, hoping the din of a mindless infomercial would distract him from the sound of running water in the bathroom.

When the water stopped, Bullet stopped breathing, waiting for the door to open Would she wrap herself in the hotel robe he'd seen behind the door? Would she step out of the steamy room already dressed?

When she finally opened the door and rounded the corner, her sweet body was wrapped only in a towel. Bullet groaned, and Tristan let the towel drop to the floor.

She hadn't taken the time to dry the dewy wetness that beaded on her skin. Bullet stared at her, unsure whether he dare move, and break the spell of her standing naked before him.

"Stay where you are," she told him as she strolled toward the bed, seating herself on the mattress with her hip next to his.

"Are you, uh, hungry or anything?"

Tristan rested her hand on his bare chest. "No. Not hungry. Why don't you take the rest of your clothes off?"

Bullet leaned forward and shrugged his arms out of the shirt he'd left unbuttoned.

Both her hands came forward, resting on his shoulders, easing him back. They trailed slowly over his abdomen, to the waistband of his jeans. When she leaned against him, and brushed her cheek against the line of hair that ran from his navel to where her hand crept, he groaned again. "Tristan…"

Without a reply, she unsnapped his jeans. Bullet shuddered as her touch skimmed over his boxer briefs. "Time to take these off too."

Bullet wrapped his hand in her hair. "Wait."

"I don't want to wait, Bullet." She lifted her head to look at him, her eyes soft, but heavily lidded.

"Let me get these off." Bullet pulled his jeans and briefs down in one swoop, and tossed them aside.

He caught her around the waist, and turned her until she rested against the mattress where he'd been moments before. "God damn, woman. What you do to me." He moved over her until he could feel her naked skin against his.

"Bullet."

Moments ago all he could see in his mind was a frenzy, getting inside her as quickly as he could. Now, he wanted to take his time, make her feel as desperate for him as he felt for her.

He took her mouth with his, slow and deep. When she moaned, he scattered soft kisses on her ribs, moved down and dipped his tongue in her navel. He breathed deeply loving that her natural scent was overpowering the smell of soap from her shower.

Tristan tangled her fingers in the sheets, and pulled at them, as though she was pulling at him to hurry. He looked to the side, and saw the reflection of their bodies in the mirrored closet door. "Look," he told her.

When she did, she spotted the condom he left on the bedside table. She ripped it open with her teeth, and handed it to him. She came up on her elbows, but fell back when he moved over her.

Her broken cry echoed through the spacious hotel room when he slid inside her. Her hands flew to his shoulders, the nails digging in as she tried to urge him closer, faster.

"I take what I want, remember that." Bullet kept his pace slow, and even. Her body arched, and she turned her head to the side. "Look at me, Tristan. I need to see your face." Her eyes met his, and her body shivered. "That's it, darlin'. Come for me."

Teeth clenched, muscles straining, Bullet held off as long as he could, but seeing that look on her face, the one he was addicted to, did him in.

He rolled onto his back and brought her up next to him.

"You're such a cuddler," she teased.

"Tristan, I…"

"Shh. It's okay. We don't have to talk right now."

But he wanted to. When her eyes met his, right there, he knew he'd never loved anyone the way he loved Tristan. Heart and soul. Forever and ever. But she still wasn't ready to hear it.

He had a few hours before he had to head over to Thomas and Mack Center for the first round of bull riding. Maybe he'd close his eyes for a few minutes.

He was snoring. She couldn't believe it. Bullet never snored. He sounded so cute. The more time she spent with him, the more she realized she'd actually fallen in love with him. The time they were apart, the distance between them, sometimes made her think she just missed him. But being with him now, watching him as he slept so soundly, strengthened the feelings she questioned.

Thinking about leaving in just a few days, and being apart until December, she wasn't sure how she'd stand it. Maybe she should invite him to her family's Thanksgiving dinner. But he probably wouldn't want to be away from his family. And what about his kids? Surely he'd want to be with them too. Tristan couldn't ask that he take his children away from their grandparents for such a special holiday.

Tristan rested her head back on his chest, and listened to his heart beating. Soon it lulled her to sleep too.

"Beep, beep, beep." Bullet woke and looked around for his phone. *"Beep, beep, beep."* The sound would get louder the longer it took him to figure out where the hell he'd left it.

Tristan rolled over. "What is that?"

"The alarm on my phone."

She sat up in bed. "What time is it?"

"Two." He had an hour to shower, shave, and get to the arena for check-in. Oh, and he was also supposed to meet Buck Bishop fifteen minutes early.

He leaned over and kissed her hard on the mouth. "In case you haven't figured it out, I love you Tristan."

He turned around, went into the bathroom, and left her there. Mulling over his words.

What reaction had he been expecting? Was he waiting for her to join him in the shower and tell him she loved him too? He could wait until the water ran cold. Unlike him, Tristan wasn't a chicken shit. When she told him she loved him, it would be when they were in bed together. Maybe she'd tell him while they were making love. Maybe she'd tell him right after they finished making love. Whenever it was she decided to tell him, she wouldn't blurt it out and then get away from him as fast as she could.

Her phone was ringing. Bullet was still in the shower, or shaving, or doing something. Whatever it was, he hadn't come out of the bathroom.

She found her bag where they dropped it by the hotel room door, and pulled out her phone.

"Hi," she answered quickly before it went to voice mail.

"Tristan, it's Liv."

"Hi Liv, how are you?"

"I'm good. Uh, by any chance are you with Bullet?"

"Why?"

"Well, there's someone down here looking for him, and it seems kind of important."

"Where are you?"

"I'm in the lobby of the Thomas and Mack Center."

Tristan told Liv they'd meet her there in a half hour. She was headed there too for the press conference Lyric had arranged.

When Bullet came out of the bathroom, Tristan was dressed.

"What's goin' on darlin'?" He put his arm around her waist.

"Liv called. She said omebody's at the arena looking for you. And that it was important."

"Ain't nobody as important as you right now, darlin'."

Clearly Bullet was feeling very amorous after his declaration of love, but the tone in Liv's voice worried her.

"I think it's serious, Bullet."

"I doubt it, but if it's botherin' you, let's get over there and see who it is."

Liv was alone when Bullet and Tristan walked in the front door of the arena.

"Well," he said. "I thought somebody was looking for me."

Liv pointed in the direction of the hallway. "Do you know that man?"

"Never seen him before in my life."

"I don't think he knows you either, but he's been asking everyone if they've seen you."

"Huh. Well, only one way to find out." Bullet walked over to the man who was on his cell phone. "Hey, mister." He tapped the man on the shoulder. "I hear you been lookin' for me."

The man pressed a button on his phone and dropped it in the pocket of his jacket. "Are you Bullet Simmons?"

"The one and only."

"Mr. Simmons, you've been served." The man handed Bullet a folded piece of paper.

"What the hell?"

At the same time the man went out the door to the parking lot, Billy, Lyric, and King walked over to where Tristan and Liv waited.

"What's with him?" Billy asked.

"Someone just served him papers."

Bullet stood completely still, with a stunned look on his face. Billy walked over and took the paper out of Bullet's hand.

"What the hell?" Billy repeated what Bullet had said moments earlier, when he finished reading through the document.

"What is it?" asked Lyric.

"A subpoena," Bullet answered.

"For what?"

Bullet turned and looked at Tristan, who hadn't moved from where she stood when they walked in. His eyes met hers, as though he was trying to tell her something.

"My DNA."

"For what?" she murmured.

"A paternity test."

"*Wait,*" she heard Bullet yell, but she was already through the door. She raised her hand to hail a cab. When it pulled up, she recognized the person getting out of it.

"Tristan? Are you okay?" asked Harris.

"I'm not." She was too stunned to explain, too stunned to ignore him.

"Where are you going?"

"The hotel."

When Tristan climbed in the back seat Harris followed. "I'll make sure she gets there okay," he explained to the driver, who looked as though he really didn't care.

"Let me see that." Lyric pulled the subpoena out of Billy's hand and started reading. "Do you know anything about this?"

"It's gotta be wrong," he told her.

"Why? I mean, how can you be sure?"

"Look at the date." Bullet pointed to the section that said, "On or about..."

"Why do those dates sound familiar?"

"Pike Peak or Bust," said King, who hadn't spoken to that point.

"Then he's right!" Lyric shouted. "He couldn't have been with someone else. He was with us every night. And by us, I mean Tristan."

"Not every night," said Liv. "There was one night he wasn't."

Lyric first looked puzzled, then her expression changed. Instead of looking at Bullet, she looked at King. "You wanna tell me what the hell went on that night?"

"Lyric—"

"Stay out of this, Bullet," she snarled at him, and then turned back to King. "You find some buckle bunnies to polish your spurs that night?"

The fact that King didn't answer wasn't helping Bullet's cause. He had a hell of a lot to drink that night, and there were bits and pieces of it that he didn't remember. He was damn sure he didn't have sex with anyone, though. Not Tristan, and not anyone else.

* * *

1981

"It's a boy," said the doctor, who handed the baby to a nurse who wrapped him in a blanket and took him to the other side of the room. "I'll just get him cleaned up a little," she told them.

Bill had witnessed heifers and horses giving birth, even a goat, but watching his own dear wife suffer through labor was almost more than he could bear. He'd held her hand, rubbed her back, and fetched her ice chips and a cool damp cloth to soothe her brow.

"We have a boy," Dottie beamed at him.

How could anyone look this beautiful, this happy, after what she'd just endured? Bill didn't know. She'd been his hero since the day he met her, but today, Dottie was superwoman.

The nurse brought the little blanketed bundle back over and handed him to Dottie. "Look, Bill, isn't he beautiful?"

Bill was looking at the two most beautiful people he'd ever seen in his life, his wife and his son.

"What should we name him?"

Tears ran down Bill's cheeks, and he couldn't speak. Dottie held the bundle with one hand, and with the other, reached for Bill.

"It's okay, honey. I'm okay. And the baby is perfect."

Bill looked up at the nurse who nodded her head. "He's perfect," she concurred.

Bill closed his eyes and said a prayer. God had kept watch over his wife and his baby. They were both okay.

Better than okay, they were perfect. He opened his eyes and looked up. "Thank you," he whispered.

"I think we should name him William Flynn Patterson, Junior," said Dottie.

"That's a right beautiful name, sweetheart," Bill answered.

He looked up again and closed his eyes. He'd never, ever forget his promise. And he'd never, ever compete in another rodeo.

22

"I understand, sweetheart," her father said. "But you simply don't have a choice."

"If I was sick I'd have a choice."

Her father folded his arms. "You're not sick."

"Daddy, please. I can't go."

"I've said it once, twice, three times, and I won't say it again after right now. You have commitments, Tristan. And you will honor them. I don't care if there's one or twenty cowboys you don't want to see at the NFR. There are people counting on you to be there. And you will not let them down."

They'd had this argument at least once a day for the last week. Tristan tried everything she could think of to get out of going to Las Vegas for the PRCA National Finals Rodeo. Her father wouldn't hear of any of it.

It had been almost two months since she'd talked to anyone from Flying R Rough Stock other than Liv, who promised she'd let everyone know how hard Tristan was working to have more of the line ready to present in Las Vegas.

If Lyric or Bullet called, and they did often, she ignored the call. If it wasn't from a number she knew, she ignored that call too.

She'd apologized to Liv twenty times or more about missing the press conference as well as her other commitments at the PBR Finals.

"We covered it," she told her each time Tristan brought it up, and then told her to let it go and quit worrying about it. It was done and there was nothing they could do to go back and change it.

Liv didn't realize it, but those words were like a knife in her belly. They couldn't go back and change what Bullet had done either.

After Liv first explained what was in the subpoena, she never mentioned the paternity test, or anything else about Bullet again. The only thing she said was, "if you want to talk about it, I'm here."

Every time the scene at the Thomas and Mack Center played over in her memory, her humiliation grew. What a fool she'd been. To think she'd been figuring out when to tell the lying, cheating bastard that she loved him.

Harris had ridden in the cab with her back to the hotel that day, but she hadn't let him walk in with her. She'd told him she was picking up her bags and catching the next flight home.

"I told you there was something important about him you needed to know," he'd said as she was getting out of the cab.

Those words stuck in her head. When had Harris said that to her the first time? Wasn't it at Pikes Peak or Bust? From what Liv told her, the woman said she had sex with Bullet that week. But didn't all the guys go out the day *after* Bullet fought with Harris behind the chutes?

It continued to nag at her, and no matter how hard she tried, she couldn't let go of it. Something wasn't adding up. The problem was, in order to get to the bottom of it, she'd have to talk to Bullet, and that was something she wasn't ready to do.

Need a ride from the airport? the text from Lyric said.
Catching a cab.
Need to talk.
I know.
Drink at 5. Hotel bar.
That worked. None of this was Lyric's fault, and Tristan felt bad that she'd avoided her friend for the last two months. She needed to apologize, and hoped that Lyric understood why she'd been so distant.

Lyric was already at the bar and had a drink in front of her when Tristan walked up.

"Hi."

Lyric jumped off the stool and threw her arms around her. "God, girl, I've been so damn worried about you. You look like shit, by the way."

Tristan smiled. Only Lyric could get away with telling her she looked like shit, and not mean it in an insulting way.

"What're you drinkin'?"

"I think I could use one of your five-ingredient cocktails, but that probably isn't a good idea right now."

Lyric motioned to the bartender. "Two shots of Makers," she told him. He nodded and went to get the shot glasses. "Wait," she added. "Better make that four."

Tristan smiled. "What the hell, I don't have any meetings tonight. Might as well get lit up."

"It isn't his," Lyric said after they both downed their second shot.

"That really isn't the point."

"Why the hell not?"

"I can't do this, Lyric. I can't be with a man who randomly fathers children."

"But it isn't his."

"Again, that isn't the point. It could've been."

"No, it couldn't."

How could Lyric be so sure? Was it because Bullet swore he didn't have sex with anyone else that week?

Or did King come to his defense and swear Bullet didn't hook up with any women the night they all went out and got drunk? What about the rest of the Flying R partners, were they willing to vouch for Bullet too?

It didn't matter if they all swore on a stack of Bibles. Tristan was done with Bullet. She couldn't trust him, and she couldn't be with someone she didn't trust.

"Oh God, not him again."

Tristan looked over to where Lyric motioned. There stood Harris Jones, and to her shock, he looked even worse than the last time she saw him.

"You keep turnin' up, like a bad penny. Or shit on the bottom of my shoe," Lyric said to him.

"I'm not here to see you." Then he looked at Tristan. "Can we talk?"

"I'm sorry, Harris, but I don't have anything to say to you."

"*You're back with him?* How could you be? You swore over and over again that you couldn't forgive my infidelities, but he gets some whore pregnant and you just look the other way?"

Tristan didn't know where Harris got the idea she was back with Bullet. Maybe because she was sitting at the bar with his sister. "This isn't any of your business," she told him.

"I can't believe this. I never dreamed you'd forgive him." He turned and walked away.

"Didn't that strike you as odd?" Tristan asked Lyric who looked over at Harris walking away.

"Yep."

"No, not him. What he said. He never dreamed I'd forgive him. Isn't that a weird?"

"To be honest with you, I think the guy is as dirty as they come. I wouldn't be surprised to find out someday that he set this whole thing up to get you away from Bullet. Problem is, there's no proof."

"What about the girl, Lyric? Why would a woman claim someone is the father of her child, if she knows he isn't?"

"I don't know, but I'm gonna make you a promise right here and now. By the time the last gold buckle is awarded this week, I'm going to get to the bottom of this."

"He's ridin' great," Bill told Buck. "But otherwise, it's as though the light went out."

"Damn mess." Buck shook his head. "Has he found out anything yet?"

"Nope, but he said somethin' about gettin' the results in January."

They thought he couldn't hear them, but Bullet could. Their voices carried to where he sat on the back of the chute waiting for his turn to get on the back of a bull. He rode by rote. No emotion. No excitement. His nerves were icy steel. Part of him hoped he'd buck off, because then maybe he'd feel something.

He was loading broncs to bring them to Las Vegas a couple of weeks ago, and cut his hand good on a sharp piece of metal on the trailer. He watched the blood pour from the wound, but couldn't feel it.

Billy, Jace, even Ben tried to talk to him about the paternity test, but he didn't have anything to say on the subject. He may have been drunk that night, but there's no way he had sex with the woman accusing him.

It had been months since he had sex with anyone other than Tristan McCullough. A fella may be able to forget having sex when he was doing it with randoms every night of the week, but once you committed yourself to one woman, it wasn't something you'd forget.

He rode. He didn't buck off. He waited for his score. Robotically. Eighty-two points. He walked through the back of the arena to gather his gear and heard someone talking on a cell phone.

"It didn't matter to her." He recognized the voice, and the man speaking. *Harris Jones.* He went back around the corner, out of sight, to listen to more of the conversation.

"You have to make sure the test comes back with him as the verified father." Silence. "What's it gonna cost me?" More silence. "You better make damn sure your cousin gets the samples switched." Another long pause. "Yeah, well, as long as she don't show up here, we're all good."

He had to find Lyric. If anyone could find out who this woman was, and get her here, Lyric could. If she didn't, Bullet was going to get slapped with a paternity suit that would seal the fate on the rest of his life. Tristan would never believe it was rigged and he wasn't the child's daddy.

Tristan rode the elevator alone from the twenty-second floor to the nineteenth, where it stopped. She closed her eyes and leaned back against the wall. She opened them again, when she didn't hear anyone get on. She looked up, and Bullet stood in front of her.

"I don't know what to do," he said. The elevator doors started to close, and both reached out to stop them.

"Get on the elevator, Bullet," she told him, and then folded her arms.

"How are you?" he asked once the doors closed.

"I'm okay. How are you?"

"Okay. I guess." Bullet reached over and hit the emergency stop button. "That isn't true, I'm not okay."

"Bullet—"

"No, Tristan, I need to say this. You may not believe me, but I swear on Pearl and Grey's lives that what I am about to tell you is the God's honest truth."

When he told her what he overheard in Harris' conversation, she believed him. She might not have if she didn't have her own suspicions. She didn't admit it out loud though.

"I couldn't have done it, Tristan. I know I didn't handle it very well, but when I told you I love you, I meant it."

"I know." She sighed and looked at the floor.

Here she was, at her own crossroad. Bullet's reputation was such that no one was surprised when he was served with the paternity subpoena. That reputation was borne from the way he'd lived his life.

Even with her, sex was the way their relationship had begun. From the first time she saw him in Liv and Ben's hot tub, she wanted him. Somewhere along the way, it had turned into more.

"Can we talk? I mean really talk?" Bullet pleaded.

Tristan reached forward and hit the emergency button again, and the elevator continued its descent. When it came to a stop in the lobby, she didn't disembark, instead she pressed the number twenty-two.

"We can talk in my room."

"But we need to talk, Tristan. Nothing else."

She rolled her eyes and smirked at him. "Yes, Bullet, I'll try my hardest to keep my hands off you."

"I don't know about tryin' your hardest," he smiled.

He smiled. It had been so long since he had, and God, it felt good. Once he started smiling, he couldn't stop himself.

"What's so funny, cowboy?" The smirk hadn't left Tristan's face.

He *had* to touch her. He put one hand on her waist, and hesitated. When she didn't back away from him, he put his other arm around her shoulder and pulled her close to him.

Her body was taut, but she didn't resist. She even rested her head on his shoulder.

"I missed this so damn much. Just holdin' you against me feels so good."

"I missed you too, Bullet."

No buts. She didn't say "but." He had no idea where her head was, but he was about to find out.

Tristan's suite was much bigger than his room. The furniture in the outer room was draped in McCullough

Cowgirl and McCullough Cowboy clothing. There was a garment rack that held more. "You got a fashion show you're doin' or something?"

"Yes. It's this afternoon."

"How come you didn't ask me to model for you?"

He was joking, but Tristan looked serious. "I wasn't sure it was a good idea for us to be together."

"Really? I mean you actually considered it? I thought you'd have professional models."

"No, the clothes are going to be worn by NFR competitors. The show is a fundraiser for the Justin Cowboy Crisis Fund."

Bullet was familiar with the organization that provided need-based financial assistance to athletes injured through their participation in professional rodeo. He looked around the room.

"No chaps?"

"I only made one pair of those, Bullet. They were custom."

"You gonna do more custom work? I mean can fellas order custom chaps from your company?"

"I guess so. It isn't something I've thought much about, but you're right. Professional cowboys would want something custom, not something off the rack. It's a good idea, Bullet."

"Then I guess I need to be in your show after all."

"Oh yeah? Do you have yours with you?"

"C'mon, Tristan, they're my good luck charm. Why do you think I'm ridin' so good?"

Tristan bristled. "We need to talk, Bullet."

"Wait a minute. What just happened? What did I say?"

"It's what Harris says. He needs me back because I'm his good luck charm."

Whenever the comparisons between the two men came too close, she couldn't help the irritation she felt.

"There's a difference. I said the chaps were my good luck, not you."

She smiled again, and punched his arm.

"You're right though. Let's talk." Bullet motioned to the two chairs by the window, and helped Tristan move the clothing out of the way.

"Since we saw each other at Pikes Peak or Bust, I've been wantin' to have this conversation with you. I put it off then, and I can't put it off any longer. I don't know if it woulda helped or hurt what happened in October with the subpoena, but I know this, Tristan." He leaned forward and looked into her eyes. "I'm not ever gonna lie to you about anything ever again. Even if the truth is hard to tell, or even if I'm gonna hurt your feelings, I'm not gonna tell you any lies."

"You sound like, Lyric."

Bullet laughed. "That's the thing with her. We may not like what she says, but we always know Lyric is tellin' the truth. I wanna be more like that."

As uncomfortable as it was for them both, Bullet told Tristan everything he could think of about his past. All of it. That he'd never been faithful to Callie; the dares he took from his buddies when they'd go out drinkin'; even how one night he'd had sex with three different women.

"I'm not proud of any of it," he told her. "But if the day comes that we're together and someone from my past decides to tell a story of what we did one night when we were out drinkin', I don't want to feel as though I have to hide it from you."

Tristan closed her eyes and took a deep breath.

"Tell me what you're thinkin' right now."

"This is not a conversation I ever imagined myself a part of."

"How much are you hatin' me right now?"

"I don't hate you, Bullet." She took a deep breath. "You have lived the life I imagined you had. Not just you, most of the guys that compete in rodeo live that life. A lot of the girls too. Or some anyway."

"But not you."

"No, not me. I've had sex with two men in my life. You and Harris Jones. Do you want to know what I worry about?"

"Yes, I do." He was solemn. He dreaded the words she was about to say.

He knew without her saying it that she was worried he'd never be able break out of that life. That she'd never be able to trust him not to sleep with women who offered. He couldn't blame her, and there wasn't any way for him to prove her wrong.

"What if I'm not enough?"

"You think I'm gonna get bored?"

She lowered her eyes. "Yes."

Bullet reached over and touched her chin. "Look at me, darlin'." When she did, he took his own deep breath. "I love you, Tristan. Up until I met you, I didn't know what it was to truly love a woman. Now I do. It's the same way I feel about my kids. When I'm not with 'em, I think about 'em all the time. I can't imagine a world without them in it. If they're hurt, I wanna take their pain and carry it for them. If they're sad, I wanna make 'em smile. Whatever isn't workin' in their life, I wanna be the one who fixes it. And with you? I want to be the only man who ever touches you. The only man who ever makes love to you again, until the day I die.

The idea of touchin' a woman other than you makes me sick to my stomach."

He couldn't tell by the look on her face whether she believed him, or thought he was full of shit.

"Ask anybody. I've been a monk the last few weeks. And it wasn't because I had the idea that bein' that way would win you back. There wasn't anybody other than you I wanted to be with. Nobody."

"Maybe I shouldn't, maybe I'm playing the naive fool again, but I believe you."

His eyes opened wide. "You do?"

"Yes, I do," she told him. "I also believe you aren't the father of the child in the subpoena."

"And what if it comes back that I am? Will you believe it's a setup?"

"That's harder, but...I will."

"There are ways to prove I'm not, you know, but no until after the baby is born. At some point I'm gonna have to know who this woman is, and once I do, I can ask for my own test. It's the time in between that will be hardest."

"Maybe we can find out who she is now."

"That's what I was thinkin', but I haven't come up with any ideas how to yet."

"Lyric is working on it."

"She is? I was gonna ask her what she thought, but then I ran into you in the elevator…"

Tristan told him about the conversation they'd had earlier at the bar.

"I don't have any ideas myself, but you know Lyric. God knows what she'll come up with."

Bullet didn't have any ideas either. At least short term. As he'd just said, once the baby was born, he could ask for another test, and have it performed by someone neither of them knew. He'd get a court order to make it happen if he had to.

"Bullet, there's something I need to tell you."

Here it came. His shoulders tensed as he waited for her to speak.

"No matter what happens, you need to know this. I love you too, Bullet."

"You do?"

Tristan smiled and shook her head. "You're all I've thought about, Bullet. I've wished with everything in me that we would somehow find out this was a mistake. It never occurred to me that it was a setup, but it should've. I owe you an apology, Bullet. A big one. I should've trusted you. Jesus, I should've just talked to you."

"So what's next for us, Miss McCullough?"

"Right now we need to get you into those chaps."

* * *

1994

"No, Dottie. This is not up for discussion."

"But you saw him as well as I did. Billy is a natural born bronc rider."

"We saw him one time, tryin' to break a spirited horse. That doesn't make him a bronc rider."

"You may have seen him one time, but I've seen him a lot more."

"What are you talkin' about, woman?"

Dottie told Bill that their son had been getting on broncs for over six months. He'd been going to practice pens without Bill knowing it.

"Who's been takin' him?"

Dottie stood from where she sat at the kitchen table, and walked over to where Bill stood near the sink, looking out the window.

"I have. Clancy too."

Bill was furious. Beyond furious. He couldn't yell at Dottie, but he sure could yell at Clancy. He walked toward the back door, and put his hat on.

"Where are you going?"

"To give Clancy a piece of my mind."

"Clancy? Did you hear me? I've been taking him too."

Bill opened the door.

"Don't you walk away from me, Bill Patterson."

"Dottie, please don't push this."

"I'm gonna. You turn right back around and say what's on your mind. *To me*. Not to Clancy."

He couldn't. Spitting in the face of God was something he couldn't do, and telling his wife about the deal he'd made was something he couldn't do either.

"If you walk out that door, I'll never forgive you for it."

"Dottie…please."

"Say whatever you need to say to me."

He walked over and took her by the shoulders. "Do you know why I quit rodeo? Do you?" he shouted.

"Of course I do."

"No. You don't. I quit because I had to. I quit in order to keep you and Billy safe."

"Yes, Bill, I know."

"How could you?"

"Do you think you could just tell me one day that you didn't want to compete anymore without me knowing what was behind it?"

"I told you then it was because you were pregnant."

"And then you sold all your gear, threw away anything that came in the mail about rodeo, changed the subject if anyone, including me, brought it up."

Bill nodded his head, but didn't answer.

"You quit because you promised God that you would as long as he let me survive the pregnancy and have a healthy baby."

"How do you know that?"

"Because I know you."

"Then why in the dickens have you been letting Billy get on broncs?"

"Because that's his decision. He hasn't made any deals with God. And sayin' you don't want anything to do with rodeo ever again isn't the deal you made either."

"But it is." Bill slunk down in the kitchen chair and put his hands in his face.

"No, it isn't. My darling, sweet, wonderful husband, it isn't."

"If somethin' happens to him…"

"I agree. If something happens to Billy, I don't know how I'll go on, but I will. And even if you forbid him to ride another bronc, something still might happen to him. He could be in a car accident tomorrow and get hurt much worse than if he bucks off of a horse."

"I know that, but…"

"Bill, look at me." He looked into Dottie's eyes. "It brings him such joy. Don't take it away from him. God gave him to us, but that doesn't mean we own him. He's our son, to raise up to be the best man he can be. Let him to do this, Bill. Let him for me."

23

It took Lyric until the last day of the NFR, but she did it. She was on her way to the airport to bring the woman who accused Bullet of fathering her child to the competition tonight. In the end it was King who came up with the idea. It took going back to Colorado Springs, but he'd figured it out. Lyric would be picking him up at the airport too; he was the one bringing her here.

She called Tristan earlier to tell her. She hadn't told Bullet yet, and asked Tristan not to either. Tristan did have a job to do, though. She had to get Harris Jones to the Thomas and Mack Center tonight, at the same time Lyric arrived.

"This is Ashleigh," King introduced Lyric. "She's the one we met at the bar, you know, that night."

Ashleigh was quiet, but Lyric didn't expect her to be any other way. "Let's go see him, then. If Bullet is your baby's daddy, you two are gonna need to spend some time gettin' to know each other."

The girl's cheeks turned pink, as Lyric expected them to. It must be awful to be getting ready to "meet" a man you already had sex with.

"I tried to call him…"

"Yeah? He gave you his number that night?" That surprised Lyric. Bullet would be more apt to take her number, and never call, rather than give his number out.

"Not the right one."

That didn't sound like Bullet either. He may have slept around, but he was usually upfront about not wanting to see someone again. It wouldn't be like him to give a girl a wrong phone number intentionally either. But Harris Jones wouldn't know that.

"Almost there," Lyric patted Ashleigh's hand. They sat in the back seat of the cab, King sat in the front with the driver.

As was prearranged, Bullet was out front, waiting for Tristan to arrive. Tristan wasn't there yet, but she wasn't supposed to be.

"Here we are," said Lyric, climbing out of the cab. Ashleigh followed behind, got out, and stood on the sidewalk waiting as King paid the driver. Thankfully Bullet was looking at his phone, and hadn't noticed them pull up.

He raised his head and looked at Lyric, who shook her head and put her finger in front of her mouth.

"Okay, you ready to go find my brother?" she asked Ashleigh.

"Yes," she answered softly and walked right past where Bullet stood. When Ashleigh looked at him, Lyric watched. No recognition. As they passed, King motioned for Bullet to follow.

It took a minute for Lyric's eyes to adjust from the bright outdoors to the more subdued lighting in the convention center. When they did, she spotted Tristan talking with Harris, near the box office.

"We'll have to pick up your pass at will call," Lyric told Ashleigh. "And you'll have to show your identification."

Lyric walked slowly, so Ashleigh was beside her. She watched the girl as she looked around. When she spotted Harris, she stopped, and put her hand on Lyric's arm.

"There he is," she said.

"There who is?"

Ashleigh's expression was puzzled. She looked at Lyric. "Your brother."

"Where?" Lyric asked.

"Right there, don't you see him?" Ashleigh was pointing at Harris, who at that moment, turned away from Tristan, and looked at Ashleigh.

The expression on his face confirmed what they already knew. Harris knew Ashleigh, and Ashleigh knew him. She just didn't know his real name.

"That isn't my brother," said Lyric. "He is." She pointed at Bullet.

Ashleigh turned around to look. "I don't know that man," she said. "Is this some kind of trick?"

Harris tried to deny he knew the woman with Lyric, which resulted in Ashleigh breaking down in tears.

"I don't understand what's going on," she said to Lyric.

"You've been tricked, but not by my brother."

"But he told me his name was Bullet Simmons. It isn't a name I'd ever get confused with Harris."

"He lied to you." Lyric motioned for Tristan to come closer.

"Harris and Tristan used to date. She can tell you all about the kind of man he is."

"That's okay," Ashleigh said through more tears. "You all must hate me. I'm so sorry. I had no idea I was bein' played."

Tristan wanted to tell the girl she could've avoided all this by not having sex with someone she didn't know, but lecturing a total stranger wasn't her business. Bullet was though. She looked for him behind Lyric and King, but he wasn't there.

"Did you see where Bullet went?" she asked King.

"No. Not with all the commotion goin' on. I wasn't payin' attention."

"Excuse me," she said to the group, and went in search of him. She ran into Billy and Jace first. "Have you seen Bullet?"

"Yep, he's behind the chutes gettin' ready to ride."

Tristan looked up at the big scoreboard over the arena. The clock was ticking down to the official start of tonight's competition, the final of the week.

She ran to the stands and found Liv with Dottie, Renie, Blythe, and Bree. Most of the gold buckles were awarded previous nights, but bull riding was the last competition each evening, and the last event to be awarded.

Scores were close between the six riders slated to ride tonight, including some of the best riders in the world. After four buck-offs, and a disappointing ride from the fifth contestant, Bullet was up next.

When the chute boss told Bullet he'd be the last rider of the night, barring any re-ride options, he was relieved. Mentally he could prepare himself better. As long as he didn't buck-off, he was in a damn good position to finish in the top two or three. A good ride, a really good ride, and he might be able to win this thing.

Bullet grabbed his bull rope and handed it to Buck, who'd be pulling for him. He climbed over, grabbed the opposite side of the chute, and rested his boot on the bull's back.

He crawled over and slid his legs down the sides of the bull, making sure his toes were pointed forward and in, so his spurs didn't touch the animal. He sat right down, keeping a tight hold on each side of the chute, until his spotter, Jace, was in position.

He reached over and ran his gloved hand down the resin on the rope, warming it up, getting it hot and sticky. He tapped it with the back of his hand, letting Buck know he could slack it off. Buck may be his trainer, but when Bullet was in the chute, he was the boss. He couldn't afford to let the bull think Bullet was anything but the aggressor.

Next he warmed up the handle on the bull rope. He set it on his knee and pulled, allowing him to keep the rope off the bull's back, and let him get up under his handle. He turned the rope over to shake his bells further down, and then rolled it back over to put it in position in the pockets of the bull's side. He never pushed the rope forward, to him that was a waste of time.

He grabbed the handle and positioned his hand so his pinky rested against the middle of the bull's back, and then moved it just to the right. With his long arms, it's where he felt most comfortable. Then he rolled his hand in the handle until it felt secure. Buck pulled the rope, tighter while Bullet kept his free hand on the rope near the bull's body, so it didn't move with Buck's pull.

Bullet shook his head, and Buck tightened the rope once more. Using his opposite hand, Bullet took the rope from Buck, and laid it across his riding hand. He made sure the rosin started right at his pointer finger, and took the wrap behind, making sure there wasn't any slack in the bubble, and then forward again to lay it back across his hand. He took the tail of his rope and threw it behind him. He'd ridden too many hooky bulls. If the bull felt the rope, it might throw its head back to get rid of the nuisance.

He got up on his rope with his knees bent slightly. His feet were in front so his center of balance was ready to ride the buck. His calves were tight, his toes out, so every part of his leg was right against the bull's body. His riding arm was slightly bent, his back was straight, and his chin was tucked so he was looking right in front of his riding hand, at the bull's shoulders. He put his free arm in front of him, kept his toes forward, and nodded his head for the gate to be opened.

As soon as he felt the bull move out of the chute, he turned his toes out and squeezed his legs, going with the bull's buck.

When the bull went right and reared, Bullet kept his back straight, and got up on the inside of his legs. He kept his chin tucked and rode into the kick. He transitioned from being up on his legs to shoving his hips and lifting on his rope.

The bull spun away from his hand, to him that was an easier ride. He got over the bull's shoulder and drove his body down with his own riding shoulder. He kept the line tight, and when the bull kicked again, Bullet shoved his hips forward. The bull went back into a spin, kicked again, but Bullet stayed right with him.

He heard the whistle blow, and positioned himself to get off into his hand. With the bull still moving, he rocked over his shoulder, and kicked his leg at the same time. He let go, and landed on his hands and knees on the ground. He crawled out, and watched as the bullfighters distracted the bull, and got him through the gate.

He jumped up, threw his fist in the air, and then spun around until he found the section of the arena where he knew Tristan was sitting. He looked straight at her and stood perfectly still, until the announcer gave the score.

Bullet won the round with an eight-five-five point ride on K-Bar's Rusty Rags, which pushed his season earnings to $431,230, and beat his next closest contender, who sat at $407,475.

Bullet Simmons was the first rookie ProRodeo cowboy to win a world title in his first year since Hall of Famer Joe Beaver won the tie-down roping in 1985 at the first finals held in Las Vegas.

The crowd went wild, but Bullet didn't take his eyes off Tristan. When PRCA's Clown of the Year, Timmy Islip, approached him in the arena, the crowd went silent.

"Damn, son," Timmy said to him through the mic. "I ain't never even heard of you before."

Bullet laughed, and then thanked Bill Patterson, Buck Bishop, and the guys from Flying R Rough Stock. He put his hand over his eyes to shield the glare from the bright lights. "And I've got a question for a very special lady who's here watchin' tonight."

Catcalls and hollers sounded from around the audience. When everything quieted down, Timmy handed the microphone to Bullet. He walked forward a couple of steps to where Tristan, who had run down the aisle, was standing at the rail.

Bullet knelt down on one knee, but kept his eyes riveted on her. "Tristan," he began. "I wore these chaps tonight, believing they'd bring me good luck."

Tristan smiled and nodded through her tears.

"And tonight, I won the world title for bull riding."

She nodded again.

"So I'm just wonderin'…you think Lost Cowboy might consider sponsorin' me now?"

The crowd was on its feet, roaring and cheering for him again. Bullet couldn't hear anything above the beat of his own heart. Timmy put his hand on Bullet's shoulder and guided him toward the chutes.

He looked over his shoulder in time to see Tristan wave and blow him a kiss.

* * *

2014

"*Look at him,*" Dottie nudged Bill. "Just look at him. That's our boy. Billy's the World Champion Saddle Bronc Rider."

Bill closed his eyes just briefly, and said a silent prayer of thanks to God, for keeping his boy safe.

Epilogue

Tristan put the finishing touches on the story of the Lost Cowboy who found his way.

It was Bullet's story, but it was so much more than that. She had two more drawings to do, and when she finished, she'd send them off, along with the manuscript, to the designer who would turn it into a book ready to be published.

It would be the first book in the Lost Cowboy series, picture books for little cowboys and cowgirls, who could read about their heroes and dream of one day becoming rodeo champions.

She already had the idea for the second book. It would be about Bill Patterson and his wife, Dottie, and how even though he gave up his own chance to be a rodeo champion, his son, Billy, grew up to win a world title instead.

About the Author

USA Today and Amazon Top 15 Bestselling Author Heather Slade writes shamelessly sexy, edge-of-your seat romantic suspense.

She gave herself the gift of writing a book for her own birthday one year. Forty-plus books later (and counting), she's having the time of her life.

The women Slade writes are self-confident, strong, with wills of their own, and hearts as big as the Colorado sky. The men are sublimely sexy, seductive alphas who rise to the challenge of capturing the sweet soul of a woman whose heart they'll hold in the palm of their hand forever. Add in a couple of neck-snapping twists and turns, a page-turning mystery, and a swoon-worthy HEA, and you'll be holding one of her books in your hands.

She loves to hear from my readers. You can contact her at heather@heatherslade.com

To keep up with her latest news and releases, please visit her website at www.heatherslade.com to sign up for her newsletter.

MORE FROM AUTHOR HEATHER SLADE

BUTLER RANCH
Kade's Worth
Brodie's Promise
Maddox's Truce
Naughton's Secret
Mercer's Vow
Kade's Return
Butler Ranch Christmas

WICKED WINEMAKERS
FIRST LABEL
Brix's Bid
Ridge's Release
Press' Passion
Zin's Sins
Tryst's Temptation

WICKED WINEMAKERS
SECOND LABEL
Beau's Beloved
Coming Soon:
Cru's Crush
Bones' Bliss
Snapper's Seduction
Kick's Kiss

ROARING FORK RANCH
Coming Soon:
Roaring Fork Wrangler
Roaring Fork Roughstock
Roaring Fork Rockstar
Roaring Fork Rooker
Roaring Fork Bridger

THE ROYAL AGENTS
OF MI6
Make Me Shiver
Drive Me Wilder
Feel My Pinch
Chase My Shadow
Find My Angel

K19 SECURITY
SOLUTIONS TEAM ONE
Razor's Edge
Gunner's Redemption
Mistletoe's Magic
Mantis' Desire
Dutch's Salvation

K19 SECURITY
SOLUTIONS TEAM TWO
Striker's Choice
Monk's Fire
Halo's Oath
Tackle's Honor
Onyx's Awakening

K19 SHADOW OPERATIONS
TEAM ONE
Code Name: Ranger
Code Name: Diesel
Code Name: Wasp
Code Name: Cowboy
Code Name: Mayhem

K19 ALLIED INTELLIGENCE
TEAM ONE
Code Name: Ares
Code Name: Cayman
Code Name: Poseidon
Code Name: Zeppelin
Code Name: Magnet

K19 ALLIED INTELLIGENCE
TEAM TWO
Coming Soon:
Code Name: Puck
Code Name: Michelangelo
Code Name: Typhon
Code Name: Hornet
Code Name: Reaper

PROTECTORS
UNDERCOVER
Undercover Agent
Undercover Emissary
Coming Soon:
Undercover Savior
Undercover Infidel
Undercover Assassin

THE INVINCIBLES
TEAM ONE
Decked
Edged
Grinded
Riled
Smoked

THE INVINCIBLES
TEAM TWO
Bucked
Irished
Sainted
Hammered
Ripped

THE UNSTOPPABLES
TEAM ONE
Furied
Merried

COWBOYS OF
CRESTED BUTTE
A Cowboy Falls
A Cowboy's Dance
A Cowboy's Kiss
A Cowboy Stays
A Cowboy Wins

www.ingramcontent.com/pod-product-compliance
Lightning Source LLC
Chambersburg PA
CBHW060613300726

48975CB00005B/1555